MW00586106

ONE LAST BULLET

JAMES P. SUMNER

BOTH
barrels
PUBLISHING

ONE LAST BULLET

Third Edition published in 2021 by Both Barrels Publishing Ltd.

Copyright © James P. Sumner 2015

The right of James P. Sumner to be identified as the Author of the Work has been asserted by him in accordance with the Copyright, Designs, and Patents Act 1988.

All rights reserved. No part of this publication may be reproduced or transmitted in any form or by any means without prior permission of the copyright owner. Any person who does any unauthorized act in relation to this publication may be liable to criminal prosecution and civil claims for damages.

Editing and Cover Design by: bothbarrelsauthorservices.com

ISBNs:

978-1-914191-11-4 (Paperback)

This novel is a work of fiction. All characters, locations, situations, and events are either products of the author's imagination or used fictitiously. Any resemblance to any person, place, or event is purely coincidental.

Visit the author's website: jamespsumner.com

Writing this was emotional...

ONE LAST BULLET

ADRIAN HELL: BOOK 3

1

ADRIAN HELL

September 30, 2014 — 08:37 CDT

We left San Francisco a couple of days ago, deciding to take Josh's Winnebago all the way to Pittsburgh. It's a long journey, but we're not in any great rush to get there. I've decided it's finally time to go after Wilson Trent. Now that the wheels are in motion, I figure it's best to take our time, get our heads straight, and make sure we do this right.

Josh is driving, whistling along occasionally to the radio. I'm sitting next to him with my feet resting up on the dash. Outside, the gray clouds overhead start to spit down on us. I gaze out the window, my mind racing in every direction as it tries to process what lies ahead.

"You all right?"

His trademark British enthusiasm sounds subdued, laced with concern.

I nod absently, transfixed by the view outside. "I'm good. You?"

"Honestly? I'm a little nervous. But also a little excited, I guess."

I smile but remain silent.

He clears his throat. "So, I've taken the liberty of arranging a job for you along the way."

I turn to look at him. "I dunno about that... I wanna stay focused on Trent, not get distracted by some small-time hit that anyone could do."

"I wasn't asking for your opinion, Boss. You're *doing* the job. You absolutely need to stay focused on Trent—you're right. But you also need to stay sharp and keep on top of your game. Pellaggio took it outta you, and practice doesn't do anyone any harm."

I smile as I watch him driving. His shoulder-length blond hair gives him the look of an aging surfer. Josh Winters has been by my side almost half my life. Over the years, we've come to know each other better than brothers. We can have an entire conversation without saying a word. He knows what's best for me even when I don't. I know it goes without saying he's got my back, right to the bloody end of this crusade we're embarking on.

I sigh loudly, mostly for effect, acknowledging one of the rare occasions when he has me beat in an argument. "All right, fine. What's the job?"

"That's the spirit! The job's in Vermillion, South Dakota. A rich investment banker has put the word out that his sister's being violently abused by her husband. It's been going on for years, apparently, and she's too scared to do anything about it. Our client has taken matters into his own hands and wants to hire us to take out the husband."

My jaw muscles clench as a wave of white-hot anger sweeps over me. I might be a highly skilled, highly paid assassin, but that doesn't make me a monster. I can't abide any kind of violence toward women. There's the occasional exception—namely, if the woman's trying to kill me. In those rare situations, it's perfectly acceptable to impose violence. But something like this thing in Vermillion—there's nothing anyone could say to me that would convince me it's justified.

I take a deep breath to subdue the growing rage I feel inside. "Tell the guy I'll do it for free."

"Really?"

I shrug. "I need the practice, not the money. And from the sounds of it, I'd be doing the world a favor. So, yeah, set it up."

He nods. "All right, then."

I turn back and resume staring out the window, watching the world pass by at eighty miles per hour. Since we hit the road, I've found myself in a reflective mood. Understandable, I guess. I'm heading into a war I inadvertently started eight years ago. A war that's already cost my wife and daughter their lives. A war I've been running from ever since. I know I'm a vastly different person than I was back then. I'm far more capable than I used to be, and mentally I'm in a much better place, but that doesn't mean I'm not still a little apprehensive.

I quickly massage my temples and rub my eyes, eager to get out of my own head. I try to think about something else. *Anything* else. After a moment, my curiosity gets piqued. I look back over at Josh. "How do you find these jobs?"

Josh laughs. "All these years, and that's the first time you've *ever* asked me that."

"Is this going to be one of those things, like when you first find out where milk comes from? Is it going to ruin the magic for me?"

He laughs again. "Not quite. There's a network of people

out there who collaborate with each other to find work. They look at who's best suited to take the job, then pass the details on to guys like me, who then send guys like you to carry out the hit. We get paid by the client, and my contact gets a percentage, like a finder's fee."

I raise my eyebrows. I'm genuinely surprised by how organized it all is. "Huh. It actually sounds like a pretty slick business. I can't believe I never knew that! So do we have, like, a union or something, then?"

Josh laughs so much that he almost swerves the Winnebago off the road and has to quickly fight to keep control. I smile to myself and resume my observations through the window.

We drive on in silence for a few more miles.

Josh glances over at me. "It's not too late, y'know... if you wanna change your mind?"

I shake my head. "No going back now. One way or the other, when all this is over and the dust has settled, I'll have put both my girls to rest."

Josh nods slowly. "Amen, brother." He reaches into his pocket and pulls out a small device, which he connects to the vehicle's radio.

I frown. "What's that?"

"It's my music player..." His tone suggests I just asked one of the stupidest questions he's ever heard. "It's stocked full of MP3s."

I roll my eyes. "I stopped paying attention when CDs hit the shelves."

He smiles. "You're such an old fart sometimes, d'you know that?"

"Is that a British insult?"

He shakes his head with mock disbelief and selects a

song, which starts blasting through the Winnebago. The opening guitar riff is brilliant, but I don't recognize it.

I nod along to it. "What's this? It's good."

"Sure is! A bit of British rock and road music. *The Road to Hell*—one of Chris Rea's all-time classics."

I shrug. "Never heard of him."

He sighs. "You Yanks don't know you're born!"

"You Brits don't speak proper English!"

We laugh again, relaxing and enjoying the light mood during such heavy times.

2

ADRIAN HELL

The weather's grown increasingly dull and miserable since arriving in Vermillion, South Dakota. We headed straight for the first place we could find that offered food and drink. Josh pulls up in the parking lot out front and we both get out, stretching appreciatively. My back and neck crack—a small cry of relief after a few hours on the road.

It's not particularly cold, despite the clouds and the light rain, but I quickly duck in the back of the Winnebago and grab my jacket anyway. I put it on but leave it unfastened. I step back out onto the parking lot as Josh appears beside me. He's wearing a black T-shirt with a silver skull on the front of it, knee-length denim shorts, work boots, and a backpack over his left shoulder. I haven't the heart to tell him that he looks like he refuses to accept he's no longer in his twenties. I doubt he'd care, even if I *did* say anything.

I'm wearing a more conservative, plain white T-shirt underneath my leather jacket, with simple jeans and boots.

My custom holster is attached, holding both my Berettas in place at the small of my back. I never leave home without them.

We walk into the diner—a long, low building with simple décor and a family-run look. We sit down in a booth at the back, giving us a full view of the interior, the main entrance, and the doors to the kitchen area and restrooms. We take a quick look at the menu. After a few moments, a waitress walks over to us—a young, pretty girl with dark, shoulder-length hair and a practiced smile. We both order coffee and stack of pancakes.

The place looks nice enough. It's not too big, and it's half-full with what I presume is a local crowd who probably sit in the same seats at the same time every day. The morning rush has long since died down, and the lunchtime crowds are likely still an hour away.

The counter runs along almost the full width of the back wall, facing the entrance. Two career waitresses approaching retirement age are standing behind it. I suspect they have the younger, better-looking waitresses working the floor, bringing in the tips.

A few minutes pass, and our waitress reappears with the coffee and explains our pancakes will be along in a few moments.

Josh opens his bag and takes out his laptop. He sets it up on the table in front of him, boots up, and starts typing away. "I'm just contacting our client, letting him know we've arrived in town. How do you wanna do this?"

I haven't thought about the specifics of the job yet, but it's a simple hit. I know complacency can get me killed, but this won't take much planning or time to execute.

I shrug. "Just get me the guy's address and find out when he'll be home. I don't want to spend too long on this. We've got a long drive ahead of us. Should have it done in the next few hours, hopefully."

He nods as he types.

Our pancakes arrive, and we both eat with gusto, swilling them down with another mug of coffee.

Josh is working away in silence on God-knows-what, so I sit back and let my mind drift again. I run through the past eight years in my head, like viewing a thirty-second movie. From finding my wife and daughter dead on my kitchen floor to dealing with my demons to working the hundreds of contracts I've done—Heaven's Valley, San Francisco—all the way up to that last mouthful of pancakes and the journey ahead. I'm under no illusions how hard this is going to be. Even setting foot in Pennsylvania again after all these years isn't going to be easy.

I shake my head to clear my mind and re-focus on the task at hand. Wilson Trent is still close to a thousand miles away, and right now I've got a job to do here.

"Tell me about my target..."

Josh closes the lid on his laptop and looks up. "The guy's name is Jonathon Faber. He's been married to his wife, Tania, for five years, but they've been together almost twice that. According to Tania's brother, the beatings started a couple of years into the marriage. She'd have a fresh bruise or a black eye every other week and explain it away with a weak excuse of having fallen or walked into something—the usual sad tale, I'm afraid."

I stare blankly at the table, momentarily distracted by disbelief. A part of me simply can't understand why any woman would allow herself to be treated that way. The first sign of domestic abuse and they should get out without looking back. But at the same time, I fully understand that fear can do strange things to you. Thanks to her husband's abuse—which I imagine would be mental, as well as physical—poor Tania probably blames herself or feels she deserves it. You hear about it all the time—too scared to walk away, too ashamed to ask for help. Still in love with their other half, in spite of everything.

My jaw muscles tighten. I force myself to stop thinking about it, to stay detached. Emotions will get you killed.

"So, why wait three years to make the call?"

"Well, about a month ago, he happened to call round to see his sister and was standing on the front porch when he heard a beating taking place inside. He said he was too afraid to react but stood listening as Faber hit her. That particular one was nasty—put her in hospital for almost a fortnight."

"Jesus..."

"He asked around locally and finally got in touch with a contact whom I deal with from time to time. The request was pretty simple: money was no object, and he wanted this Faber guy dead."

I nod, absorbing the information and formulating the plan in my head.

One of the many reasons I'm so successful at what I do is because I harness the rage and violence that circles around inside me and use it to my advantage. Josh is always on hand to rein me in and make sure it doesn't consume me completely. But I use that unbridled fury to walk into any situation and pull the trigger with zero hesitation. It's one of my rules. Don't think too much about it; just do it—like an instinct.

I can feel my Inner Satan cracking his knuckles, limbering up, ready to rush out from behind his door and claim another soul.

"Where do I find him?"

As if on cue, the laptop dings. Josh opens it up to check the incoming message. After a few moments, he spins it around to show me the screen. "I just heard back from my contact. "Here's the address, along with confirmation that Jonathon Faber is at home right now."

I nod and take a final gulp of my coffee. "Drink up. We've got a job to do."

11:23 CDT

The Fabers live in a small suburb just outside the center of town. It's a nice, quiet neighborhood. All the houses on the street have a good-sized front lawn, driveway, and a garage.

It didn't take long to find the place. We're parked across the street now, a few doors down. We've been here five minutes or so, looking for any sign of life, but we can't see any movement.

Josh looks over at me. "How do you wanna play this?"

I absently stroke the stubble on my chin. "I figure I'll knock on the door, wait for him to answer, then shoot him between the eyes."

"Huh. It's not the most subtle approach, but it's undeniably effective. Can I suggest that you at least talk your way inside the house first, so the entire street doesn't see you *off* the guy?"

I shrug. "Fine, but I'm not saying anything to that piece of shit I don't have to."

"I can live with that."

"Okay, wait here."

I get out of the Winnebago and adjust my jacket to make sure it's covering my Berettas. I quickly cross the street, walk up the driveway, and knock on the front door. There's no answer. I knock again. This time, I hear movement inside. After a few moments, a key turns, a lock clicks, and then the door swings open.

In front of me is an average-looking man, just a shade below six feet in height, with a thick head of black hair and a handlebar mustache. He has brown eyes that seem to permanently frown and a thickset jaw. He has an average build—not fat or slim, not well built or lean, just... average. He's wearing a pair of black suit pants and a light-blue shirt with no tie, as if he's about to head out to the office. Or maybe he just got back from it.

I stare at him for a moment, looking into his eyes. I'm somewhat of an expert on hidden demons, and I can see the angry, drunken bastard that lies just beneath the surface.

His eyes narrow. "What?"

"Jonathon Faber?"

"Yeah... who's asking?"

I throw a lightning-fast right hook, which connects flush with his nose. I feel the cartilage break underneath my fist. He staggers back into the hallway, his eyes wide with shock.

I quickly look over my shoulder, glancing up and down the street. I see Josh sitting behind the wheel of the Winnebago. Our eyes meet and he shakes his head. I just shrug.

What?

Happy none of the neighbors are watching, I step into the house and push the door shut with my foot.

Faber's struggling to his feet, his eyes watering from the impact to his nose. Blood's dripping steadily down his chin and onto his shirt.

"What the fuck?" he shouts.

Before he can stand up straight, I punch him again, this

time on the side of his face. Not hard enough to knock him out, but it sends him sprawling to the floor again. I know from experience he'll have a serious headache. Albeit for a few minutes.

"Shut your mouth, Jonathon."

I take one of my Berettas out and reach inside my jacket to retrieve the suppressor. I screw it into place with practiced efficiency and take aim at Faber's head. He looks first at the barrel of my gun, then at me. A look of sheer terror spreads across his face and his bladder weakens. The stench of urine is instantly strong on his clothes.

I screw my face up in disgust. "Oh my God, *really*? You pathetic piece of shit!"

"I... I don't understand... P-please, take whatever you want!"

"Amazing how cowardly you are *now*, yet you're the big, scary man when Tania's at home."

I don't think his eyes could get any wider. Honestly, they look like they're going to pop right out of his head.

"Wh-what's this about?"

"What's this... This is about *you*, you overwhelming waste of sperm, and the fact you've been beating on your poor wife for so long that somebody has felt it necessary to hire a professional assassin—that's me, by the way—to kill you. And for the record, I'm incredibly good. So, any last words?"

Pure terror is etched on every inch of his bloodstained face. He repeatedly opens his mouth to speak, but every time he does, words seem to fail him. He's the epitome of a beaten man, and he's about to reap everything he's spent the last few years sowing.

"I'll take that as a *no*..."

Without any further warnings, I squeeze the trigger

three times, putting one bullet in his balls, one in his stomach, and one between his eyes. In that order.

I'm a killer. There's no escaping that. I made peace with what I am a long time ago. But I don't see myself as a bad person, and I take no pleasure in doing what I do for a living. I certainly don't intentionally make people suffer unless I absolutely have to. I look at what I do as being similar to working in a slaughterhouse. It's a dirty, messy business, but it needs to be done, and you should do it as humanely as possible. But as a rare exception to my rules, I felt compelled to make sure that in the last few seconds of his life, Jonathon Faber felt pain he couldn't have imagined. It might not seem like much, but I did it for his wife, and I'm sure she'd agree it made all the difference.

I look around the hallway. Blood has sprayed across the walls and the expensive-looking beige carpet. I make sure not to step in any as I walk around his body and into the lounge. I ignore the room completely. I'm looking for a pen. I move carefully around the room, ensuring I don't touch anything and leave any forensic evidence.

Oh, there's one, on the table next to the TV. I pick it up, then reach into my back pocket and pull out a blank check. Like many people in my line of work, I have a legitimate business in place to hide the large, regular payments I receive for work. Josh set it all up with an accountant who specializes in this sort of thing for people like me, so it's as above board as it gets.

I lean on the table and make out the check to Tania Faber for fifty thousand dollars—the exact amount her brother intended to pay me for the job.

I keep the pen and retrace my steps back into the hallway, knocking a few ornaments over, opening drawers, that kind of thing. Not too little, not too much—enough to make it appear like a break-in without much thought behind it.

I place the check on Jonathon Faber's dead body. I unscrew the suppressor and put it back in my pocket, then re-holster my Beretta. I take one last look around, then open the front door, covering my hand with my jacket so that I don't leave any prints on the handle. I walk casually across the street, for the sake of appearances to anyone who might be looking, then climb in the Winnebago.

Josh looks at me. "You good?"

I stare at the house for a moment, then nod. "Yeah, I'm good. Whole thing looks like a robbery. Tell our client to tell his sister she should make a fresh start. I've left her a little something to help her on her way."

I shift in my seat, getting comfortable, and put my feet up on the dash. I gaze out of window at nothing in particular. My mind instantly wanders back to the larger task ahead of us. I feel Josh watching me, but I ignore him. He worries too much. I'm fine, just a little pre-occupied, which I think is understandable.

Without another word, he pulls away from the curb and we set off, back on the road and heading for Pittsburgh.

3

WILSON TRENT

Wilson Trent looked over the balcony as Tommy Blunt dangled precariously, held by his ankles by Trent's two enforcers, Duncan and Bennett. Blunt was only a small man, around five-eight, and he weighed just under one-seventy. A stark contrast to the men holding him. They could've been twins. Both were over six feet tall and weighed around two-forty—which was solid muscle. They looked like their bodies were chiseled from granite. They had loyally served Trent as his personal bodyguards for several years.

"Holy shit!" yelled Blunt. "Please, God, let me go!"

Blunt lived on the fourteenth floor of a high-rise in downtown Pittsburgh, overlooking the Ohio River. It was expensive to live there, but he could easily afford it on what he made. He was in charge of the day-to-day running of one of the larger-scale cocaine distribution operations that

Wilson Trent owned in the city. They also made a healthy profit from crystal meth and ecstasy, but cocaine was the primary source of income. Blunt managed the finances and logistics for the entire northwest area, from Brighton Heights all the way down to the North Shore. So, when Trent reviewed the books and saw that every month for the past six months, he was exactly fifteen thousand dollars down, Blunt was the first person he queried.

All the blood was rushing to Blunt's head, making his temples and ears throb. Understandably panicked and afraid, it took him a moment to realize he'd just said completely the wrong thing.

He waved his arms wildly. "Okay, no—wait! Don't let me go! Pull me up! Please!"

He heard laughter above him. Straining his stomach muscles, he looked up at the two men who had a hold of him to see big smiles on their faces. Clearly, they enjoyed their jobs.

Next to them, Trent looked on impassively. After a moment of watching the man squirm, he shouted down to him, his deep voice and East Coast accent bellowing all around. "So, Tommy... I think you and I need to talk. You got anything important you wanna say to me?"

"Oh my God. Please, Mr. Trent. I don't know anything about any missing money, I swear to you!"

Trent shook his head. "Why don't I believe you?"

"I swear! I've never stolen from you in my life. I make good money for you, Mr. Trent. I've always done right by you. Fuck! You have to believe me! Please!"

Trent didn't say anything. He regarded him from the balcony, clenching his jaw muscles, trying to decide if he was telling the truth. After a moment, he tapped both his enforcers on their shoulders and nodded, signaling them to pull Blunt up. They did so with ease, heaving him up and over the edge of the balcony. They stood him straight between them, facing Trent. Bennett was on his right, holding him in place with one large hand wrapped around his neck.

Trent folded his arms across his barrel chest with a look of impatience on his face. He was wearing a three-thousand-dollar, tailored, navy blue Valentino suit with a white shirt, blood-red silk tie, and shiny black shoes.

He sighed. "Tommy, either you're lying to me, or you're just plain fucking stupid. Which is it?"

Blunt knew there was no correct answer. He stammered a couple of times before giving up trying to say the right thing.

Trent leaned forward, his face inches from Blunt. "It ain't a difficult question, Tommy. Have you been stealing from me yourself, or has someone on your payroll been stealing from the both of us, and you were just too fucking dumb to notice?"

"I swear, it wasn't me," said Blunt, who was almost in tears.

Trent raised his eyebrow. "So, you're a fucking idiot. Is that what you're telling me?"

Blunt hung his head in shame. "I guess so, Mr. Trent."

"I guess so? I fucking *guess so*? Tommy, do you have any fucking idea how much goes on in this city that I don't know about?"

Blunt shook his head.

"Nothing. *Nothing* goes on in this city that I don't know about, Tommy. I'm behind nearly every drug deal. I own nearly every hooker, and the ones that aren't mine pay me a percentage out of respect. I've got cops and politicians who will do whatever I say, and do you know what that means, Tommy?"

He shook his head again.

"It means that if someone steals from me or lies to me, not only will I find out, but I can do whatever the fuck I want to them afterward."

Trent paced away and sighed heavily. He stared for a moment at the skyline of the city laid out before him. The sun was hidden behind low, gray clouds that threatened a downpour. It wasn't particularly cold, but there was a breeze coming in over the river that occasionally picked up and caused a slight shiver.

Without any warning, he turned around and lunged at Blunt with a speed not befitting a man of his size and build. Duncan and Bennett sidestepped as he grabbed Blunt by the throat with a strong right hand and forced him backward until he reached the balcony edge. Then, with little effort, he lifted him over and watched as Tommy Blunt plunged fourteen stories down to the ground, screaming until he hit the parking lot below. The sound of the dull, wet thud was barely audible. He saw the bloodstain from where Blunt's head exploded on impact, like a pinprick on the ground.

Trent turned to face his bodyguards. He looked at Duncan. "Search this asshole's apartment, top to bottom. See if he was hiding anything." Then he looked to Bennett. "You—go pay a visit to his office and look through the books. Find out which greedy little bastard has been skimming from me and bring me their fucking head in a gift-wrapped box. Understood?"

Both men nodded, without fear but with complete respect.

Trent looked back down over the balcony at the remains of Blunt's broken body, which had attracted a small crowd of people. He spat over the edge, more as a gesture of disgust than a genuine attempt to hit him.

"Fucker..."

4

ADRIAN HELL

After leaving South Dakota, we continued east and made it to Illinois in good time. The weather had brightened briefly along the way, but the sky has darkened now as we're passing through Chicago. We decided to stay here for the night and get some food and drink. It's been a long day on the road, and we could both do with the break.

Josh fiddled with his GPS to find us a motel for the night. We made our way there, dropped our stuff off in our rooms, and came straight back out. The first order of business was food. We were both starving, having not stopped for anything since leaving Vermillion. We soon found a place that served steak, so we treated ourselves to a nice sirloin before looking for a bar. We've been walking for fifteen minutes and haven't found a place we like.

The night sky's rumbling with menace as we make our way through the city. I glance up at the clouds. There's a storm coming, no doubt about it. Josh nudges my arm and

20

points to a place up ahead on the right. There are some motorcycles parked out front. A couple of bikers, dressed in their leathers, are standing beside them having a cigarette. As we approach, the low bass from inside becomes clearer, and I recognize the song.

I look at Josh and grin. "I think this place will do nicely."

He laughs. "Yeah, this'll do the trick."

We walk in and push our way through the small crowd toward the bar. We lean forward and rest on it while we wait for the bartender. It's busy and loud. The whole place has a hazy neon blue glow to it, and the patrons are a mixed blend of bikers, like the ones outside, and young people.

We both look around, getting a feel for the place. Aside from the main area, there are two big rooms at the back as well. There's a large screen in one of them, with a small group of people sitting in front of it, cheering loudly at the football game that's on. I can't tell which teams are playing, but given sports don't interest me, it wouldn't mean much to me even if I *did* know.

I hear Josh scoff beside me. I turn to look at him and raise an eyebrow.

He points at the screen. "I don't know why you people insist on calling *that* football. You hardly touch it with your feet. And it's not a ball—it's not even round!"

I shake my head. "Josh, while I completely understand your one-dimensional, British point of view, I honestly couldn't give any less of a shit right now if I tried."

He laughs. "Fair enough."

The bartender comes our way and Josh orders two beers. He hands one to me and we head over to the main area. We grab a couple of empty seats by the pool table. There are old movie posters framed on the walls around us. We both relax and savor the taste of a refreshing beer. I watch a large group of men and women who are surrounding the table, all laughing and having a good time. Well, I say men and women—I'd be surprised if any of them are over twenty-one.

I turn to Josh. "How long until we reach Pennsylvania?"

He shrugs. "Not sure. We've made good time so far, so in theory, we could make it by this time tomorrow. But personally, I'd rather we take our time and get there the day after, mid-morning. That way, we'll have time to find our feet and get a plan together. We've waited eight years. Another couple of days isn't gonna make any difference, right?"

I raise my bottle of beer slightly in the air, tipping the neck toward him in silent cheers. "Sounds like a plan."

We fall silent, sipping our drinks gratefully and allowing our bodies and minds to switch off and take a well-deserved rest. We've known each other long enough that silence is never awkward. I watch him as he looks around absently, relaxing. It's good to have the company for a change. Before San Francisco, I saw Josh maybe once every couple of months, if that. And even then, it was usually just for an hour or two. Then I was back out on the road, alone. We've not been in the field together for a long time.

"How are *you* feeling about all this, Josh?"

He frowns. "Me? How d'you mean?"

"Well, you're usually tucked safely behind all your computers and gadgets. It's a big change being out in the line of fire with me."

He smiles. He knows I'm not trying to antagonize him. "It's certainly different, but it reminds me of the buzz we'd get back in the day, on the old unit. You never forget it, and while I don't necessarily miss it—*especially* seeing as I got shot on my first mission alongside you in God knows how long—it's nice to change things up every now and again. There's no place I'd rather be, under the circumstances."

I notice him subconsciously scratch his leg where he caught a bullet, but I don't say anything. It might be nothing. I mean, he didn't scratch his chest, and he was shot there too. Maybe I'm reading too much into it.

I extend my hand across the table and we bump fists. "Amen to that."

We laugh together. It's nice to—

Uh-oh...

The music's changed, and *Don't Fear The Reaper* by Blue Oyster Cult has just come on.

I look over at Josh. I move to grab his arm. I hope I'm not—

"Oh, get in!" He slams his half-empty beer down, jumps to his feet, and breaks out into a small air guitar solo.

Too late.

I shake my head and smile. If ever there was a man who truly didn't give a shit what people thought, it was him.

While he's completely oblivious, lost in the moment of pretending he's on stage in front of thousands of people, I notice some of the crowd over by the pool table start to chatter and laugh, pointing at him. A couple of the guys are being derogatory, and some of the girls are giggling along with them. One girl leans over to her friend. I read her lips, and I'm pretty sure she said she thinks he's cute. Man, he'd love that! Oh, now a guy that's standing nearby has gone over to her. I'm guessing it's her boyfriend. Huh, he looks pissed. I can't tell what he's saying to her, but judging by his body language, he's not happy. He keeps looking over at me as he's shouting at the poor girl.

I really hope he doesn't do something stupid... I'm trying to have a night off.

The boyfriend turns, taps another guy on the arm, and gestures him to follow. They both start walking toward our table. The boyfriend's throwing me his best evil look all the way across the floor.

Great.

I pat Josh on his arm, and he spins around to look at me with his eyebrow raised. Normally, I wouldn't dream of interrupting his air guitar solos, but I subtly nod toward the pool table and he sees what I've seen. He rolls his eyes and sits back down next to me. He picks up his beer and takes a sip, waiting.

The two young guys ignore me as they approach the table and stand directly in front of Josh. The boyfriend points his finger at him. "What the fuck are you doing?"

He immediately looks behind him, which prompts all his friends to laugh and signal to him how cool they all think he is.

Jackass.

Josh completely ignores him and looks at me, questioningly. I simply hold my hands up, gesturing it's nothing to do with me. I smile at him. "I'm not the only one who needs practice."

He takes a deep breath and winks at me, acknowledging I've made a good point. I can spot a bar fight a mile away—a skill I've honed over years of inadvertently finding myself involved in a number of them. I figure he's maybe a little rusty when it comes to being on the front line. I'll let him handle it. It'll do him good.

"Hey, I'm talking to you, you old fag!" continues the boyfriend.

Josh looks at him with fake confusion. "Am I missing something? Since when is calling someone a cigarette classed as an insult?"

I love it when he over-accentuates his English accent!

He looks at his friend, stunned, then back at Josh. "Are you fucking retarded?"

Josh looks at me and gestures to the pair of them. "Can you believe this guy?"

I smile, knowing when it's time to play my part. "Oh, yeah, over here, *fag* is a derogatory term used to insinuate you're homosexual."

Josh looks offended in light of this new revelation. Seriously, he should be an actor. He turns back to the boyfriend. "I apologize for my ignorance, but who are you, and why should I care that you're even breathing?"

We're both pretty useful in a fight, but where I fail spectacularly at diffusing a situation by talking, Josh excels at it. He's the diplomatic one in the relationship.

The boyfriend shakes his head. "You look ridiculous, and it's offending me and my friends. So, why don't you take your old, faggy friend over here and piss off?"

Did he just call me faggy?

I make a move to stand, but Josh signals for me to stay seated. I do, holding up my hands in resignation. He looks at the boyfriend. "Okay, you're like, what, eleven years old? When I was your age, I respected my elders. And if I stepped outta line, my old man would clip me 'round the ear."

The guy frowns. "He'd what?"

Josh slaps the guy on the side of his head. Not hard enough to knock him over but with enough force that he knows about it. He quickly does the same to the guy's friend standing next to him.

"I was fighting for Queen and country before you were a glint in the mailman's eye, you pointless sack of shit. Now come back when your balls have dropped, and I might take you seriously."

The guy's raging, but as Josh stands and squares up to him, he quickly backs down, as does his friend. They slowly walk back to their group of friends, tails between their legs. Josh sits back down and looks over at the group. The remaining guys are still trying to look intimidating in front of the girls, who seem divided. Some look disgusted, either at their friends' behavior or ours. Others are smiling at us both and giggling.

Josh gestures to the crowd. "And as for the rest of you... there's a valuable lesson to be learned here. *Never* interrupt a man when he's playing his air guitar!"

One of the girls catches his eye and smiles, which he returns—more out of politeness than anything, I think. But one of the other guys sees it and rushes over to her, grabbing her arm and dragging her back around the pool table.

That's it.

"Hey!"

I get out of my seat, feeling myself go from zero to pissed in a heartbeat. I vaguely hear Josh say something behind me, but it's too late. The flash of anger has taken control. I walk over, right into the middle of the group and up to the guy with his hand on the girl.

"Let go of her arm."

The girl's an attractive young blonde with naïve brown eyes and a red dress her father probably doesn't know she wears in public. She yanks her arm free, rubbing where the guy had gripped it, and looks at me. "Thanks." Her voice sounds sweet and full of innocence. "But it's all right. He meant nothin' by it, I swear."

She has an oddly soothing effect on me, causing the sudden explosion of rage I just felt to quickly subside. I back down a little and look at him, pointing a finger close to his face in a silent warning. I turn and walk back to my seat.

I take three steps and hear someone shout out behind me. I turn around in time to see a pool cue coming at my head. Instinctively, I raise my left hand and catch it in mid-air. The impact stings my palm, but I grit my teeth and ignore it. The guy who swung it stands still in complete shock, his eyes wide as fear creeps slowly across his face. I stare at him, allowing the entire scene to freeze.

With a sudden movement, I yank the cue out of his hand, take it in both of mine, and break it across my knee. Again, the impact stings my leg, but I don't acknowledge it. I throw both pieces of the broken cue to the floor. Without any warning, I whip my right leg up and kick him hard in the stomach. The impact takes him by surprise, and both his legs fly out from under him. He drops like a stone and groans as he face-plants the sticky floor. I take my time as I look around the rest of the group, eyeballing every one of them around the pool table in turn. Then I walk away and sit back down next to Josh.

He looks at me and raises an eyebrow.

I shrug. "What?"

5

JIMMY MANHATTAN

Jimmy Manhattan spent the past week recovering in San Francisco General Hospital, after Adrian Hell had thwarted the attempt on his life. Despite his wounds and his advancing years, he was making an impressive recovery, and he hoped to be discharged in the next couple of days. The surgery to remove the two bullets was successful, and any internal damage was minimal.

He had seen on the news that the FBI had averted Danny Pellaggio's attempted attack, although he knew it was due to Adrian Hell's intervention. He thought about everything that had happened leading up to the events surrounding Pellaggio's demise.

Manhattan had struggled to deal with his deception and, understandably, with being shot. He had spent the last year of his life working with him, funding him, training him, putting him in touch with the right people to make his plan happen... He felt used and betrayed, although he knew it

28

was probably never his intention for things to end the way they did. Pellaggio was weak and lacked vision. Adrian Hell's intervention made him decide to sever his ties with Manhattan. His mental illness was his downfall, often clouding his better judgment. He knew that Adrian could exploit that to stop him.

That was no way to do business.

He thought about Adrian Hell too. That man was capable of immense things. Now that the opportunity had presented itself to wipe the slate clean and start afresh, Manhattan was smart enough to know that, despite his instinct to seek revenge, it would be far more beneficial not to have Adrian as an enemy. Some things were simply best forgotten about, even if they were never forgiven.

Outside, the sun was high and warm, and the sky was clear. The light was beaming in through the slits in the blinds. He sat in bed reading the morning's newspaper. There were still articles detailing the attempted attack on the S.S. Jeremiah O'Brien.

He realized he was also a little disappointed. He'd expected great things from his partnership with Roberto's son, but sadly, it wasn't meant to be. Still, he had plenty of money saved and invested, as well as his own reputation to work with. He'd be back on his feet in no time.

There was a knock on his door, which disturbed him from his thoughts. It opened and a nurse walked in. She was a large, dark-skinned woman in her forties with long, braided dark hair tied in a ponytail.

She grinned. "Hey, sugar. How you feelin' today?"

Manhattan nodded courteously. "Very well, thank you."

She moved to the end of his bed and flipped through his chart, intermittently nodding at the information. "Yeah, you doin' all right. You in any pain, sugar?"

He shook his head. "There's a dull ache in my shoulder but nothing of any concern. I feel fine, honestly."

"Good. In that case, I think we can look at getting you outta here. How does *right now* suit you?"

She beamed at him and started laughing.

He smiled back politely. "That's excellent news. Thank you."

The nurse replaced his chart and left to make the preparations.

In no particular hurry, he returned to his newspaper, to finish reading a particularly interesting article in the business section. But he found his mind wandering to thoughts of what would happen once he left the hospital...

11:35 PDT

Manhattan stood in front of the mirror in his room, fastening his tie. His bloodstained suit and shirt had holes in them from where he'd been shot. He looked at the poor condition of his clothes with frustration as he straightened his tie and stepped into his shoes.

He regarded his reflection for a moment. He was fifty-four, and the years had been less than kind to him. He conceded that it was mainly self-inflicted, due to the life he'd chosen to lead from a young age, and he had no issue with his looks. He was old enough to not care about such trivialities. He used his hands to smooth down his thinning gray hair. His dark, deep-set eyes looked back at him impassively.

He had a second chance now. Any ties he once had to the Pellaggio name were dead and buried, simply because every member of that family was now dead. What was left of the organization was in limbo, and the opportunity to seize control was his for the taking. He had people who were loyal to him, and it wouldn't take him long to establish himself as the next man in charge. He could run the business single-handedly, having had previous exposure to most areas of it while working for Pellaggio Sr.

He turned and walked out of the room, heading to the front desk, where he was given all the obligatory paperwork to complete before being discharged. It was the same nurse from before, and she seemed genuinely happy to see him up and about.

"That's everythin', sugar," she said, taking the last of the completed forms off him and shuffling them on the desk to make a neat pile. "You need anything else before you go?"

"Actually, it'd be a big help if I could borrow your telephone to make a call before I leave," he replied.

"No problem, honey. It's just over there." She pointed to the far side of the semi-circular reception desk, where a phone was standing on its own at the end.

He smiled faintly. "Thank you."

He walked over and dialed a number from memory. It picked up after a couple of rings, and he said, "It's me."

"Mr. Manhattan?" The surprised voice belonged to his trusted associate, Paulie Tarantina, who had assisted Manhattan for many years during their mutual service to the Pellaggios. "Sir, we heard what happened to you, but we had no idea how to come and get you without drawing more attention to ourselves. Under the circumstances, we—"

"Paulie, it's fine. There's no need for apologies. What's done is done, and we can all chalk the last twelve months up to experience and move on. Now listen to me very carefully. Danny's dead. He went behind our backs and it blew up in his face. I want to head home, regroup, and look to rebuild the family."

"Just tell me what you need, Mr. Manhattan."

"I'm just about to leave the hospital in San Francisco. But I think it's time to relocate the business to somewhere new, so it can flourish without any ties to the past. I need you to arrange a flight and connecting travel for me. There's an old business over on the East Coast that Roberto kept legitimate. I'll head there. Once I'm settled, I'll call you with further instructions."

"No problem," said Tarantina. "So, where exactly are you goin' to, Boss?"

Manhattan paused for a moment, thinking things over one last time before committing to the path he was about to go down.

"Allentown, Pennsylvania."

6

WILSON TRENT

Wilson Trent rode in the back of his car with Bennett next to him. Duncan was riding shotgun as the driver navigated the busy streets. The previous day, he'd instructed his two enforcers to look into Tommy Blunt's life—search his home, look through the financial records, everything—to find out where the fifteen grand a month had been disappearing to.

He knew he could rely on his men to resolve the issue. They had proven themselves his most capable and most loyal employees. That was why they'd been by his side as his personal protection detail for so long. And while it was a trivial amount of money compared to what he had and what he earned, that wasn't the point. No one stole from Wilson Trent and got away with it.

And sure enough, after a few hours of investigation, they came up with the answer. It turned out Blunt *had* been stealing the money but not for himself. Duncan had found bank statements in the apartment documenting the fifteen grand going in on the same day each month. Strangely, it was transferred back out a day later. He had spoken to Bennett, who was searching the premises where Blunt worked at the time, and they began trying to figure out why Blunt would've been stealing money off Trent for someone else.

They concluded that he wouldn't, based on his loyal service over the years. Instead, they looked into whose bank account he had been transferring the money. An hour or so later, and they had both come up with a name.

Caroline Dawson.

She had a seat on the Pittsburgh City Council, and she had been on Trent's payroll since taking the position three years earlier. The money was transferred to her bank account every month like clockwork.

Duncan and Bennett took this information to Trent, who immediately arranged an appointment to see her at her office. They explained to him that Caroline Dawson was, in some way, blackmailing or extorting Tommy Blunt. There was no other contact, either historically or recently, between the two of them that could offer an alternative explanation.

The driver pulled up outside the Council Chambers on Grant Street. Trent looked out his window at the building for a moment before speaking.

"Wait here," he said to the driver before looking at each of his enforcers in turn. "You two, come with me."

He stepped out of the car with a grace not befitting a man of his stature. He walked purposefully up the steps, past the commemorative statue of Richard Caligiuri, and entered the building.

The entrance lacked the extravagance of the building's exterior. A standard front desk with a wooden counter and paneling sat just inside the doors on the right. The area was simply a wide corridor with elevators at the far end and offices along both sides. A single corridor about halfway along led off to right, accessing other parts of the building.

Trent completely ignored the receptionist, striding intently past the desk and across the tiled floor to the elevators. The heels of his polished black shoes echoed around the large entrance area. The receptionist stood, about to say something as they walked by, but Bennett shot her a glance that made her reconsider.

Trent knew everything about everyone he had on his payroll. For example, he knew that Caroline would be in the building that afternoon because of a monthly Council meeting scheduled at four p.m. She would be working out of one of the temporary offices the City Council members used when on the premises.

They took the elevator to the second floor and turned right once the doors had dinged open. They walked along a narrow corridor, illuminated by the gray light shining through the large windows along the left wall. After a few moments, Trent and his men came to the office. Without knocking, he thrust open the door and stepped inside.

Caroline was a slightly overweight woman in her late forties. She had light brown hair with gray streaks running through it, cut into a bob that rested on her slight shoulders. She was sitting on one side of a large table in the middle of the room, wearing a purple dress suit and matching shoes. Opposite her were two men, both in suits, whom Trent didn't recognize. He presumed they were other members of the City Council, but they didn't concern him in the slightest.

"You two..." he said to them as he entered.

Both men turned to look at him.

He gestured to the door with his hand. "Fuck off."

They opened their mouths to protest, but it only took one step forward from Duncan to convince them to leave. Both men looked at Caroline, gathered their papers off the desk, and left in a hurry.

Caroline remained in her seat, trembling slightly. She opened and closed her mouth, debating whether she should say anything. She glanced at the two men flanking Trent before resting her gaze on him. Her bottom lip was trembling slightly with fear.

Trent remained silent, staring long and hard at Caroline, watching her fight to maintain composure. He glanced at Duncan and Bennett, who immediately moved over to the left of the room, standing behind her and leaning against the wall.

Trent took a seat at the table opposite her. He leaned forward and rested his arms on the desk, clasping his hands in front of him. When he spoke, he sounded professional but with an icy calm to his voice. "Caroline... is there something you want to tell me?"

She glanced at the table for a second, frowning with thought, and then shook her head. "No," she replied, a faint quiver in her voice. "I was going to report anything of interest to you later in the week, once we'd had our Council meeting this afternoon. Looking at the agenda, I don't think there will be anything noteworthy."

Trent smiled, both impressed and frustrated at her convincing response. "Let me rephrase my question. You have something to tell me, don't you?"

He glared at her with his cold eyes, the professionalism giving way to anger. She looked over her shoulder at his two enforcers, who were both looking on with disinterest. She looked back at Trent. "Is... is this about Tommy?"

"It's more about the money he was stealing from me to give to you. I want to know why."

She put a hand over her mouth, looking down and sobbing uncontrollably. Trent rolled his eyes and sighed heavily, expressing his impatience.

"I'm sorry," she said. "I'm so sorry, Mr. Trent. You have to believe me!"

"Oh, I believe you feel apologetic now that you've been caught. But I want to know what you and Tommy Blunt were up to. You can either tell me now of your own accord, or my associates are going to make you tell me. And that... wouldn't be pleasant."

"Oh, God!" Caroline shrieked before bursting into tears again.

Trent got to his feet and sighed, then walked around the table to stand next to her. He placed his right hand on her shoulder, like a concerned friend, and looked down. "Caroline, you've been a big help to me over the last couple of years, and I've paid you well for it. Haven't I?"

She nodded eagerly but remained silent.

"And you know that if you ever have a problem, you can come to me with it, and we'll sort it together, correct?"

She nodded again.

Without warning, Trent stepped to her side and turned to face her. He grabbed her throat with his left hand and squeezed firmly, forcing her head back. When he spoke, his demeanor had changed dramatically. He was no longer calm or collected. He was furious. He yelled, "Then why the fuck was Tommy Blunt stealing fifteen thousand dollars a month from me and giving it to you?"

Her eyes were wide. She gasped for breath, clutching his wrist with both hands, struggling against his grip. "P-please..." she rasped, closing her eyes tightly, forcing tears to roll slowly down her cheek.

Trent released her. She leaned forward, panicking and sucking in deep breaths as she massaged her throat. "I'm... I'm sorry. I... I should've come to you. I know that now."

Trent said nothing. He just glared at her again.

"It's my son..." she continued. "He has leukemia, and I'm... I'm struggling to pay for the medical treatment he needs. I scraped together every cent I could for so long, but I was running out of options." She pulled a tissue from her pocket and wiped her eyes. "Then, about six months ago, I came across T-Tommy's name in a police report sent to us for assessment. It seemed he was being... being careless, attracting attention to what *really* makes the money at that strip club he works out of."

Caroline blew her nose and took a deep, jittery breath. Trent coughed impatiently and made a *get on with it* gesture with his hand.

She nodded, panicking. "There were plans to make an arrest and bring him in for questioning. I knew it was your club, so I took it upon myself to go and see him, give him a heads up. I told him everything, and he started to panic because he was so afraid of you. I... I told him I could make it all go away and save him, but he'd have to give me the money each month as repayment." She hung her head ashamedly. "He said no initially, but I threatened to come to you about how careless he'd been, and he gave in. I saw an opportunity to make some extra money for my son and I took it."

She broke down in tears again, holding her head in her hands.

Trent looked briefly around the room, thinking. He glanced at Duncan and Bennett, who were keeping a respectful distance from the conversation. They looked at him before turning away, offering no opinion on the matter.

He moved behind her again and placed both his hands on her shoulders, which made her jump. "If you'd only come to me first, Caroline... I would've helped you with the money. I'm not a monster."

"I know," she sobbed. "I'm so, so sorry..."

He patted her shoulders. "So am I. I'm sorry that your son is going to have to fight on through that terrible disease without the support of his mother."

She looked up and gasped as his words sunk in, but she could do nothing. He gripped the back of her head and her chin in his hands. She struggled, but it was no use. Trent took a deep breath and twisted her head around violently, snapping her neck. The crack was deafening in the quiet room. He let go and she slumped lifelessly down on the desk with a thud, her face contorted in shock and agony. Her head almost faced backward from the force of the snap.

Without another thought, Trent walked over to the door. "Get one of our guys in the PPD to clear this up," he said to his enforcers, who had moved to follow him out. "And get my ninety grand back."

They left the office, took the elevator down to the first floor, and walked back out the main door. Standing for a moment on the sidewalk of Grant Street, Bennett took out a cell phone and made a call, arranging for Caroline Dawson's body to be removed and explained away. The sky was dull with low, menacing cloud, and Trent sensed a storm on the horizon. They all climbed into the car and drove away in silence. Trent looked out the window, his mind clear, watching the world pass by.

7

ADRIAN HELL

18:14 EDT

We left Chicago early this morning, heading back to the I-80 before continuing on our expedition to Pittsburgh. We made good time, and by late afternoon, we'd hit the I-76 and entered the state of Pennsylvania.

Josh, to his credit, has insisted on doing all the driving, but despite his willingness to do so, I still feel bad about not doing my share. He is quite protective of his assets—like his Winnebago, his equipment, his contacts, et cetera. They're his, and he enjoys being the one I go to for all the answers without ever telling me how he gets them. Being out in the world and pulling the trigger—that's my thing. The magic behind *how* I can do what I do... that's his.

We pass a sign that says *Welcome to Pennsylvania*. My stomach knots up. This is it. The big one. After eight years and a couple thousand miles, I've finally returned to the East Coast, ready, willing, and able to avenge my family's death. But this is still one of the most intimidating things I've ever attempted.

Wilson Trent is a kingpin—top of the food chain. Even thinking about taking him on will incur the wrath of more people than I can imagine. Politicians, local authorities, gangsters—everyone's on his payroll, and a threat to him is a threat to them. They're well paid and well protected by Trent, and I'm about to walk in and change everything.

"We're about sixty miles out," announces Josh, breaking my concentration. "What do you wanna do, Boss?"

I shrug. "May as well keep going. Once we're there, we can find a place to stay, start digging around, and find out what Trent's weaknesses are and how we can exploit them."

"I'm all over that. Already started asking around, so we'll see what comes back."

"Really? How? You've been driving for three days…"

He looks at me and winks with a big grin on his face. "Magic!"

I laugh and let the matter drop, content to let him have his moment of mystery. All that matters is the information, not where it comes from.

We fall silent again, both distracted by everything and nothing until we enter Pittsburgh. The day's light is fading as we slowly make our way into the city. I think being here has finally hit home, because I'm suddenly full of ideas about to go about this.

Now if I were a hitman—which I am—and I'd gone to a city to kill someone—which I have—then the obvious thing to do would be to keep a low profile, base myself on the outskirts, and under no circumstances make my presence felt until my target was staring down the barrel of my Beretta.

That's the obvious thing to do.

And if someone like Wilson Trent were to get wind of my arrival in the city, that's exactly what he'd expect me to do, and that's exactly what he'd prepare for.

That's why I intend to do the complete opposite.

We take exit twenty-eight to the expressway along the Allegheny River, all the way into the center of the city. I lived in Pittsburgh back in the day, but it's been a long time since I was here, so I'm on unfamiliar ground. Thankfully, Josh has GPS and has found a Hilton hotel in the Business district, which isn't far. We're going to stay there, in the spotlight. It's the last place Trent would think to look for me once he knows I'm back.

And he'll know soon enough.

Josh navigates the traffic and heads around the back of the hotel, coming to a stop in the far corner of the parking lot. We get out and complete our stretching ritual after another prolonged period on the road, then get our bags from the back and walk toward the hotel entrance.

Josh looks up to the sky, at the top of the hotel looming ominously above. He whistles his approval and turns to me. "It's about time you started living a little. I mean, you've got, what, like, a *billion dollars* stashed away?"

I smile. "Not quite."

In truth, it's more like thirty million dollars, but I see his point.

He shakes his head. "Whatever. You should start enjoying yourself a bit. This whole wandering around on your own, staying in crappy motels, and living to a budget thing you've had going for yourself all these years... it's getting old, man. And no offence, but so are you."

"Gee, thanks!"

He steps in front of me and turns to face me. "My point is, Adrian, you should start appreciating the finer things in life. There are guys in this business that take private jets everywhere and live the five-star lifestyle everywhere they go. It's one of the perks of making so much money."

I nod and shrug. I know he has my best interests at heart, and that means a lot to me. "I know, Josh. But this job, this... lifestyle—it cost my family their lives. I think it'd be in poor taste to take advantage of it and enjoy it. Don't you?"

He sighs. "Honestly? No. I think if you felt that strongly about it, you wouldn't still be doing it. I understand completely how you feel, Adrian. You know I do. But I think you hold some things accountable for your guilt that really aren't to blame. You could've been a courier, or a pilot, or a goddamn milkman, and tragedy still could've befallen your family. Don't blame yourself or your job. Blame Trent. Cut yourself some slack."

I regard him silently for a moment, and I see in his eyes he's worrying that he's just overstepped the mark. Not many people can openly voice their opinion about my life without fear of reprimand, but he can, and we both know it. He probably knows the only reason I feel angry right now is because I know he's right, and I don't want to admit it. Over the years, I've found a certain level of comfort in the way I live my life and the reasoning behind it.

I scowl a little, frowning through the misplaced anger I'm feeling. "Finished?"

He sighs again, gesturing with his arms in frustration. "It would appear so..."

We approach the revolving door and walk through, into the lobby. We head over to the front desk in silence. We check in under our real names—something I would never normally condone in my line of work. We book two premium suites on the eighteenth floor for five nights. We walk across the lobby toward the elevator and, a few minutes later, come out on our floor. We find our rooms and agree to meet downstairs again in half an hour. I use the keycard to enter my room and close the door behind me.

Inside, the room is exquisite. It has a four-poster bed with patterned sheets on it that probably cost four figures, easily. The flat screen TV on the wall facing it must be at least fifty inches. A floor-to-ceiling window opposite the door offers a breathtaking view of the city. I look around, fascinated, as I walk over to the bed and drop my bags. I check out the bathroom, which is equally impressive. The shower stall on the left could fit three people in it, and it has showerheads on the sides and above. I think they're for some fancy muscle massage I vaguely remember reading about once.

I walk back out and lie on the bed, my arms behind my head. I clench my jaw muscles and take some deep breaths to calm down. I close my eyes. "What the fuck am I doing here?"

18:50 EDT

I grabbed a quick shower and changed into a fresh pair of black jeans and a thin matching sweater. I reattached my back holster and both my Berettas and set off for the lobby to meet Josh.

I'm sitting just to the left of the main entrance, in a comfortable light-brown leather chair. Across from me is the front desk, which is an L-shaped counter with four people permanently bustling around behind it. Beyond that, around the corner by the elevators, is a restaurant and bar.

The decor is subtle and expensive. The floor is gray marble, and there are beige marble pillars dotted around for effect.

I glance out through the entrance at the city outside. The street's busy, full of people rushing back and forth. It's dark now and looks cold, though the rain's holding off for the time being.

After five minutes, the elevator dings, and Josh appears. He strides purposefully toward me. I feel bad about before, and while I'm not normally one to proactively apologize, I figure I should make a bit of an effort.

I stand as he approaches. "Hey. Listen, about before... I—"

He waves his hand dismissively, cutting me off. "Water under the bridge, Boss," He holds out a scrap of paper. "More important things..."

I take it from him and look at it. There's an address scribbled hastily on it. I frown. "What's this?"

"It's the address of one Billy McCoy. He's a local scumbag and known coke addict, and he currently resides in the Shadyside district of the city."

"He sounds like a charmer. And I should care about him because..."

"Because his dealer is a guy named Jonas Pike, whom I've found out worked for the recently deceased Tommy Blunt."

I raise an eyebrow. "You're making these names up, aren't you? Is there a point to this?"

"Tommy Blunt was thrown off the fourteenth-floor balcony of his apartment block yesterday. Word is by Trent himself. Apparently, he was skimming from the money his operation brought in. If we can get McCoy to tell us where he meets Pike for his fix, we can use Pike to learn more about Trent's business."

My eyes light up. "Sounds like a good place to start. You know how to get there?"

"Yeah, it's not far. I figure we can set off early in the morning, try to catch—"

"We're going now, Josh."

"Oh, right." He's taken aback, maybe not expecting me to be so eager. "I just thought that maybe you'd wanna... y'know, get a feel for the place again?"

I shake my head and smile patiently. "It's fine. We're going now."

I turn and head for the door. I hear Josh follow a few steps behind. A rush of excitement comes over me, eradicating all previous doubts and fears.

The game has begun.

19:13 EDT

Shadyside is a mostly residential district close to the city center. The three-mile journey took a little over twenty minutes in the traffic. We found Billy McCoy's street easily enough. We're parked across from his house. There are no streetlights on nearby, and a low, menacing cloud is obscuring the faint half-moon of dusk, so everywhere is in almost total darkness.

"How do you wanna do this?" asks Josh.

I look over at the house. A light is on downstairs. I gesture at it with a nod. "Well, there's definitely someone at home. You go around the back and I'll knock on the front door."

"Am I not better taking the front? I mean, you're not exactly well known for your people skills, Boss."

I turn to him. "You're right. I'm well known for being an effective assassin. I don't need people skills."

He rolls his eyes. "Fine."

He gets out and crosses the street. I watch him crouch low and run around the side of the house. I wait a few minutes, then get out and cross over. I walk casually up to the front door.

It's a modest place in desperate need of some TLC. The wood is rotten in places and the windows are dirty, but other than that, it looks like any other house in any other neighborhood.

I knock on the door. I hear movement inside, but no one answers. I knock again.

"Who is it?" shouts a voice. It's high-pitched and sounds weak and whiney.

Showtime.

"I work with Jonas. We need to have a talk, Billy."

"What about?"

"You really want me to start shouting about how we know each other on your street, outside your house?"

There's silence for a moment. "Fine, gimme a minute..."

It falls quiet again. I roll my eyes and shake my head. I bet that piece of shit is making a run for it out the back door...

I wait patiently for a few more minutes, then I hear the locks click and the front door opens. Josh is standing there holding Billy McCoy by the throat in his left hand.

He smiles. "Hey, Boss."

McCoy struggles in his grip, so Josh jabs him in the ribs. He coughs and bends over in pain.

I smile and step inside, shutting the door behind me.

McCoy's a thin, sickly-looking little prick. His eyes are deep-set into his pale face. He has thick, dark hair and looks probably in his late twenties. He's wearing a thin gray T-shirt and matching jogging pants with nothing on his feet.

I look at Josh, then at McCoy. "Right, shall we go and sit down?"

I move past them and into the sitting room. Josh drags him in behind me and throws him on a battered, stained old couch. He moves around it to stand behind him and pins him to his seat by the shoulders.

I stand in front of him, glaring down at him for a moment. He looks very uneasy. "Billy McCoy, I need your help."

His face contorts as he tries to frown with confusion and widen his eyes with understandable fear at the same time. "Wha-what the fuck, man? Who the hell are you?"

I smile. "Probably best you don't ask questions you don't wanna know the answer to. Let's just say I'm new in town and looking for some information. If you can help me out, you might get real lucky and never see me again."

He glances behind him at Josh, who's doing a great job of glaring at him menacingly, playing the strong and mysterious part with ease.

I click my fingers. "Hey, douchebag, don't mind him. Worry about me."

He looks back at me. "Wha-what do you want from me?"

"Jonas Pike. Where can I find him?"

He shifts nervously in his seat. I can see his internal dilemma of potentially cutting off his supply of drugs versus self-preservation. After a few moments, he heavily sighs. "I've only got the number for his cell. I call him and he comes to me with the stuff."

I look at Josh and give him an almost imperceptible nod. He whacks McCoy around the side of the head. "Don't be fucking lying to us, Billy!"

I suppress a smile. I love it when he shouts. His British accent sounds even more *London* than usual, and it's hilarious.

McCoy screams and cowers on the couch with his hands up, protecting his head. "I swear! I don't know where he is. He comes to *me*!"

Josh looks at me and raises an eyebrow, silently asking if I believe him. I nod again to say that I do.

I crouch in front of him. "Okay, Billy, here's what you're gonna do. Call Pike and arrange a delivery for tonight."

His face changes from fear to concern. He frowns at me. "B-but I only got some a couple days ago. I don't need any more and he knows that. He'll suspect something if I call him again so soon."

I stand and draw a Beretta from my back. I regard it in my hand for a moment, taking my time, putting on a show for McCoy's benefit. Then I aim it at him. I smile an evil smile I've spent years perfecting. "I'm sure you'll think of something."

His already pale face turns ghost-white, and his gaze flicks back and forth between me and Josh. He sighs again and reaches into his pocket. He takes out his phone and starts dialing a number.

I hold a hand up to him. "Oh, and please don't get any silly ideas about saying something to him to warn him. I will absolutely shoot you in the face. We clear?"

He nods enthusiastically and continues dialing. The call is answered after a moment.

"Hey, Jonas. It's Billy. I need another kilo tonight... I know, but I'm throwin' a party, man. Some girls wanna have a good time... Uh-huh... I know, I've got the cash on me... You're a life-saver, Jonas... See you in an hour."

He hangs up, throws the phone down next to him on the couch, and looks at me. "There. You happy now?"

I nod and smile humorlessly. "I sure am. Tell me, does he make deliveries on his own?"

He shrugs. "Usually, yeah."

"Good." I look at Josh and nod. On cue, he drags McCoy to his feet by his neck. "Your part's nearly over, Billy. Don't worry. You just gotta get Jonas through your door when he gets here, then you're done."

He nods feverishly. "O-okay."

"Until then..."

Josh punches him in the stomach, then again on the side of the head, which sends McCoy crashing to the floor, out cold. He taps him with his foot to make sure he's out, then looks at me. "You have a plan, I'm guessing?"

I shrug. "Not really. Just gonna see what happens when Pike turns up."

"Oh, excellent. There's nothing like being prepared..."

I smile as I re-holster my gun. "And this is nothing like being prepared!"

8

ADRIAN HELL

20:22 EDT

The hour passed quickly enough. McCoy has regained consciousness and has started whining again. Sadly, I can't knock him out a second time because I need him to greet Jonas and get him in the house.

For this next part, Josh is the man inside. The plan is that once McCoy has let Pike in, Josh will close the door behind them, and I'll walk in through the back. Then we'll have ourselves a nice little chat...

I've gone out of the front door and walked around the side of the house. I'm crouched behind some bushes that separate McCoy's house from his neighbor's. I take a Beretta out and wait. I'm completely calm, focused and highly motivated. God help anyone who gets in my way. I already have a clear vision of how I intend to get to Trent, and I know that I'm on the right track going through Jonas Pike to get to him. All those years of guilt and worry, and when it all comes down to it, getting Trent is going to be a piece of cake. I can feel it.

A few minutes pass, then a car pulls up outside McCoy's house. It's an old black sedan with tinted windows and brand-new rims, which have no business being on a car that ancient. The passenger door opens and a man steps out. I can't make out too many features in the dark from this distance, but he's my height—just over six feet—with a slim build and awful fashion sense. He has ridiculously baggy jeans on with boots and a huge coat that could've fit three people in it. To round off the look of a complete asshole, he has a baseball cap worn with the peak raised high, to the point where it's almost falling off the back of his head.

This poses a problem. Not only am I going to have to talk to that idiot, but he's not alone. There's clearly someone else in the car, behind the wheel. I take the silencer out of my pocket and screw it into place. I'm going to have to improvise and be quick about it.

I watch as the man I figure for Jonas Pike makes his way to the front door and knocks. After a moment, McCoy sticks his head out and looks around. Not seeing me, he gestures Pike into the house and the door closes again.

Showtime.

Staying in a low crouch, I make my way slowly out from behind the bushes and to the street, pausing for a second in the driver's blind spot. Happy he's not seen me, I rush up to the driver's door, quickly yank it open, and fire two rounds into the driver—both chest shots to minimize any mess in the car. I close the door again as quietly as possible and stand still to see if I've attracted any attention. After thirty seconds, confident no one's heard anything, I make my way back down the side of the house and around to the back door. I quietly open it and step inside to the kitchen, closing it gently behind me.

I walk straight through and into the hallway, facing the front door. Josh comes walking out of the living room to meet me, frowning with concern.

"What's up?" I ask, sensing his mood.

"We have a... situation," he says, beckoning me to follow him.

We enter the room, and I see two unconscious bodies on the floor.

"Seems to me the situation has already been handled," I say with a smile.

"That guy there," says Josh, pointing to the man who just entered the house. "That's not Pike."

Oh, shit...

"What?" I say with heavy sigh.

"As soon as he came in, McCoy was on edge. I made my presence known and soon discovered that Pike's sitting out front. We've gotta get *this* guy outta here and Pike inside without him realizing and taking off to tell Trent."

I fall silent, running everything through my mind. Things have all just gone terribly wrong...

"I think we might have another situation..." I say finally.

Josh raises an eyebrow. "Why? What've you done?"

I sigh again, rubbing my temples and forehead with my hand as I grimace at my rookie mistake. "I shot the driver before I came in the house."

"Oh, bollocks."

"I never thought that Pike wouldn't be the one to come inside..."

"So, you've just killed our only solid lead into Trent's organization?" he says.

"Looks that way," I say with a slight shrug. I nod toward

the body on the floor. "Reckon we can get anything out of this guy?"

"Let's hope so. Otherwise, we're up shit creek without a paddle."

"Nicely put."

McCoy starts to stir. He emits a low groan as he slowly moves on the floor, consciousness drifting over him once again. Josh walks over and drags him over to the couch, slapping his face to wake him up.

"Hey! Billy!" he shouts.

He waves his arms around lazily, trying to defend himself.

"Leave me alone," he says half-heartedly.

"Billy," I say. "Who's this guy?" I point to the other body on the floor.

McCoy sighs.

"I dunno, I've never seen him before. I was expecting Pike to come to the door like he always does. Strange he's not here."

"He is," I say. "He was driving the car. He's dead now."

McCoy's eyes go wide.

"H-he's dead?" he asks, like he's struggling to comprehend the notion.

"Yeah," I reply with a smile, gesturing with my gun. "Whoops!"

"Oh, shit!"

He's having something that resembles a panic attack— sweating, hyperventilating... the whole nine yards. Josh and I look at each other, confused.

"You all right, mate?" asks Josh.

"Trent's gonna fucking kill me!"

"Why?" I ask. "*I'm* the one who shot him."

"You think that matters to him? One of his guys—sorry,

two of his guys are dead in my house! He's gonna slay me, and my family and my friends, just to prove a point! Oh, fuck!"

"Jesus, calm down, will you? *That* guy's not dead," I say, pointing to the guy on the floor. "Not yet, anyway."

"You clearly haven't ever dealt with Wilson Trent!" says McCoy, exasperated.

I don't say anything. I stare at him, clenching my jaw muscles to suppress my anger. He looks at me. He looks into my eyes. He goes quiet, shifting uncomfortably on the sofa and fidgeting with his hands. I stay silent a moment longer to let him squirm a little.

"Oh, Trent and I go way back," I say eventually. "And I can promise you, he should be more worried about me than you should be about him."

I hear another low groan as the new arrival slowly stirs.

"Josh, take Billy here into the other room and keep him occupied, would you?" I ask. He does, and I walk over to the guy and drag him onto the couch. "I'm gonna have a little talk with our guest."

The man slowly opens his eyes. It takes him a few moments to gather his senses and figure out where he is. In his peripheral vision, he can probably make out walls and a floor and minimal furniture. But he doesn't pay too much attention to them, choosing instead to focus on the barrel of my gun, which I'm aiming right between his eyes.

"Hi," I say, watching as he gradually focuses on me.

He frowns, more confused than afraid. But that'll soon change. He goes to say something, but I raise my hand to cut him off.

"Before you speak, let me fill you in on what you've missed," I say. "First, Jonas Pike is in the car outside with two bullet holes in his chest. Your customer, Billy McCoy, is in the other room being tortured by a colleague of mine, and I have a gun to your head and absolutely no issue with pulling the trigger. With some effort on your part, you'll be able to walk away from this, but you have to answer my questions honestly. You understand?"

His frown disappears and his eyes go wide, confusion giving way to fear. He nods vigorously but remains silent.

"Excellent. First question: Jonas Pike works for a drug operation owned by Wilson Trent. Is that correct?"

He hesitates momentarily, then nods.

"You *can* talk, you know?"

"O-okay," he says, breaking his silence. "Yeah, Pike worked for Tommy Blunt."

"And Tommy's the one who ran the operation for Trent, right?"

"Yeah..."

"I believe Mr. Blunt is no longer with us?"

"He died yesterday, so the story goes," says the guy, somewhat dismissively.

Now I can see him properly in the light, I study him for a moment. He's an average guy—short, styled hair hidden under that ridiculous cap, brown eyes, some stubble on his chin, over-sized but ultimately generic clothes. There's nothing remarkable about him. He's probably a mid-level guy—not big enough to be hired muscle and not intelligent enough to be the brains. He most likely handles the distribution side of things. That makes the most sense as he came here with Pike. A people person. Yet there's something about him—a calm-ness behind the fear that's beginning to seep through, despite his situation. He's definitely well informed. I feel a glimmer of hope that there's still a chance we can salvage something useful from this otherwise totally fucked up situation.

"I heard it was Trent that killed him. That right?"

He shrugs. "Dunno. But Blunt had it coming. Word on the street was he was stealin' from Mr. Trent. That was never gonna stand."

"Interesting. Okay, next question: where are you and Pike based? Where's your operation run from?"

He shifts uncomfortably again in his seat, not wanting to divulge such things to me.

"What's it to you?" he says after a moment. "What do you want?"

"Like I was saying to our friend, Billy—Trent and I go way back. I just want to understand how he works nowadays. See if anything's changed since the last time our paths crossed."

"Look, man, I don't know anything, all right? I just deliver the goods to fucked up addicts like Billy. I don't ask questions. I don't get trusted with the money. I'm just a middleman. You after answers? You're lookin' in the wrong place."

"I appreciate what you're saying, but given Pike—your boss—and Blunt—*his* boss—are both dead, that leaves you. If you can't help me, you need to tell me where your operation runs out of, and I'll go there and see what I can find out for myself."

"I tell you that, I'm dead."

"You *don't* tell me that, you're dead," I reply, gesturing to my Beretta. "Quite a dilemma."

He sighs. His gaze darts around the room, presumably looking for a way out. But he knows there isn't one. My gun's too close to his head. I can see him working out his best move, but logic would dictate he only has one. If he doesn't talk, I'll shoot him.

"All right, fine. We work out the back of a strip joint in Hazelwood, called Shakes."

"Let me guess—you supply to the customers and deliver out of the back, then launder the money through the club's legitimate business accounts?"

His eyes widen and he goes to speak, but he stops himself.

"Relax," I say. "This is hardly the first illegal operation I've come across."

He frowns. "Seriously, man, who *are* you? What do you want with Trent?"

"Eight years ago, I killed his son by accident. Then a few days later, he killed my wife and daughter—very much on purpose. As I say, we go way back, and I'm here to bury the sonofabitch."

"Fuck me. You're Adrian Hughes, aren't you?"

It's more of a statement than a question.

"I used to be," I reply after a moment, happy my reputation still precedes me.

"Jesus, you're a fucking dead man walking," he says with a laugh that's half-nerves and half-relief. "As soon as Trent finds out you're in town, he'll come after you with everything he has. Everyone knows that story. He's never been the same since you disappeared."

"Trent will find out I'm here when I want him to. And by that time, it'll be too late to come after me. What's the address of this Shakes place?"

His eyes narrow. "What are you gonna do? You won't find Trent there."

"I know. The address..."

"It's on Murray Avenue, toward the end, facing the cemetery. Look, man, I get that you got issues with Trent, but leave me outta this, please."

I raise an eyebrow.

"So, if I let you walk outta here, you solemnly swear not to call Trent the moment you're out the front door and tell him I'm back?"

"Cross my heart."

I nod, thinking it over. The obvious assumption is that he's going to call Trent as soon as the front door closes behind him. But have I got everything I need from this guy?

"Who's runnin' things from the club now that Tommy Blunt's dead?" I ask.

"It *was* Jonas," he replies with a shrug. "After tonight, I've no idea."

"Who's gonna be there tonight?"

"Probably just the bouncers, the girls, and the bar staff."

I nod again.

"Thanks," I say. I squeeze the trigger once, putting a bullet in the center of his forehead.

I turn and walk back into the kitchen. Josh is over by the counter on the left-hand side, leaning against it, looking bored. Billy's sitting at the table, resting on his elbows and intermittently twitching in his seat and looking in random directions, like he keeps seeing a fly in front of him and he's trying to see where it's gone.

Without saying a word and before he even had chance to look up, I aim and fire, shooting Billy in the side of the head. The spray of crimson hits the back door and window above the sink, and his body falls off the chair, crumpling to the floor.

"We're leaving," I say to Josh.

I turn and head for the front door, leaving Josh standing, wide-eyed and speechless, looking at Billy's dead body.

9

JIMMY MANHATTAN

October 2, 2014 — 10:08 EDT

It was a cool, gray day as Jimmy Manhattan walked down North Thirteenth Street in Allentown. He had a new, charcoal-gray three-piece suit on under a long overcoat, with new, shiny black shoes. Since arriving in the city the previous day, he'd immediately checked himself into a suite at The Carrington, an expensive hotel near the center of the city. From there, he'd contacted Paulie Tarantina, advising him that he was in the city. Manhattan asked him to gather as many people still loyal to him as he could find and arrange a meeting at a local bar. It was a modest establishment previously owned by Roberto Pellaggio, and Manhattan was on good terms with the current manager.

He walked with his hands buried deep in his pockets and his collar turned up against the wind. While it wasn't too cold, he was feeling the effects a little more after sustaining his injuries and the subsequent stint in hospital.

He felt the Walther PPK against his arm. He had it in a

holster under his suit jacket. He was no stranger to violence and was comfortable using a gun if he needed to. In the past, he had simply relied on his reputation to avoid any confrontations, but now things were different. At least for the time being, he would be wise to protect himself.

Manhattan took a left on Liberty Street and walked along until he came to Walkers Sports Bar. Out of habit, he glanced around before opening the door and walking inside.

It took a moment for his aging eyes to adjust to the poorly lit interior. It was quiet, as places like that tended to be at that time in the morning. The bar ran along the right-hand side; one guy stood behind it, cleaning glasses. He looked up, nodded once at Manhattan, and then resumed his duties.

Manhattan walked through the bar area toward a huge TV mounted on the far wall. The whole area was full of tables and chairs for when big sporting events were being shown there. Approaching it, he saw stairs off to the left, leading to another large, open plan bar area above. He went up and saw another bar facing him, although there was no one behind this one. To the right were some tables and a door leading to the restrooms. On the left, at the back of the room, was a group of fifteen men, all of varying heights and widths and ages. The low, idle chatter among them stopped when Manhattan appeared.

He walked over and stood in front of them, eyeing each one individually for a moment, seeing who was present.

"Gentlemen," he began as he took off his overcoat and threw it over the back of a nearby chair. "Thank you for coming."

Tarantina stepped forward and extended his hand to Manhattan. He was short and slightly overweight but still a well-built man. In his late forties, his weathered face had seen some difficult days, and his dark eyes had a stern glint in them that hid something but betrayed nothing. He had thick, dark hair that was flecked with gray, and a moustache that was the same.

Manhattan shook his hand firmly.

"Paulie," he said, "I appreciate you arranging this meeting on such short notice."

"Anythin' for you, Boss," he replied in a strong accent.

"Here's where we stand, gentlemen," said Manhattan, now addressing the crowd. "When Roberto Pellaggio died, his son Danny took over the family business. I acted as his advisor. We put things into motion that didn't pan out. As a result, Danny was killed and I was shot and hospitalized."

He paused and surveyed the crowd. There was no emotion, no concern, just understanding of the facts. Also, no sign of any loyalty to the Pellaggios, just as he'd hoped.

"I've called you all here today," he continued, "because I believe you are all like me—looking for an opportunity to start over and create something that will become great. I'm looking to build a new business on the East Coast, where I started out many years ago, and I want you all to be a part of it. Thanks to our friend Paulie, I'm aware of a number of small-time operations and businesses in this city, which I believe would benefit from new management. I'm eternally grateful to all of you for your support, and I can promise you, quite honestly, that you'll be rewarded handsomely for it. In the meantime, if you have any contacts of your own that you trust, you're welcome to introduce them to our new family."

There was a murmur of agreement and approval. Manhattan took a deep breath and allowed himself a small smile. Everything was working out exactly as he'd planned.

"So, how do we do this?" asked one man toward the back of the room.

Manhattan paused to make sure he used the most effective wording possible. "We will coordinate our efforts and reconnaissance and, looking at the locations of these businesses, aim to approach them simultaneously."

There was another murmur among the crowd, this time of shock and excitement.

"That's a pretty gutsy move," said another man admiringly.

"Yes, it is," Manhattan agreed. "When you're starting out, you need to make a bold statement. In one swift and uncompromising strike, we will establish ourselves as the driving force in this city. Anyone who doesn't join us will be removed. Is that clear?"

A final rumble of agreement rose in the room.

"Thank you for your time, gentlemen. Keep your phones close by. Instructions will follow later today." He looked at Tarantina. "Paulie?"

As the crowd slowly dispersed, Tarantina shook a couple of hands as he made his way over to Manhattan.

"Boss?" he said.

"You've done the legwork on all the people operating in Allentown. Is there anyone you're concerned about?"

He shook his head. "Not really. There's one guy who probably accounts for a third of all activity in the city—much bigger than the rest. He might be less willing to cut us in, but that still shouldn't be a problem. Especially when we'll have everyone else behind us."

"Good. I'll let you work out the logistics. You'll be able to reach me at my suite at The Carrington. Keep me updated."

"Will do, Boss."

Tarantina turned and walked back to the thinning crowd

of men. Manhattan put his overcoat back on and headed downstairs.

He left the bar, made the short walk back to his hotel, took the elevator up to his floor, and entered his room. He laid his coat and suit jacket on the bed, then walked over to the large window that ran floor to ceiling. He un-strapped his holster and placed it on the table next to him. He put his hands in his pockets and stared out at the city below him. He took a deep breath and let it out slowly.

All that lay before him would soon be his.

10

ADRIAN HELL

10:31 EDT

Josh hasn't spoken much since last night at Billy McCoy's house. There's no disputing that I had to take those guys out. I can't risk Trent getting word that I'm back in town just yet. I have to keep the element of surprise. That's the only advantage I've got.

After leaving McCoy's place, we went back to the hotel and got some sleep. We set off early this morning to get a quick breakfast before visiting Shakes.

We found a nice little café just a short walk from where we're staying. It looked clean and the menu looked appetizing, so we found a table and placed our order.

The tables have a standard marble effect with a wooden trim, and the booths are an aged red color. A row of seating runs in front of the counter, with a smaller stretch of booths down each side. The large window looks out at the parking lot out front.

"Adrian," says Josh as a waitress brings our coffee over, "about last night..."

"It was necessary," I say, cutting him off before he has the chance to say anything else. "We couldn't risk them talking to Trent before we've had the chance to plan our attack."

"Yeah, I get that," he counters. "But you've always, *always* pulled the trigger for a price, and even then, most of the time it was after I'd convinced you the target was deserving of a bullet. That's how we work, man. Last night..." He trails off momentarily, as if he's searching for the right words. "Last night you executed them, Adrian. I saw it in your eyes —there was nothing. No remorse or hesitation. I know I'm hardly in a position to argue the finer points of morality, given what we do for a living, but to me there's a difference between being an assassin and being a murderer. I saw you cross that line last night, Adrian, and it scared the shit outta me."

I take a sip of my coffee. I hadn't thought about it like that. I just see myself as being on a job and doing what I need to do, so I can get to the target—who, in this case, is Wilson Trent. I've done much worse for the sake of a contract than kill a drug addict and his dealer. I'm genuinely struggling to see his point, but at the same time, I know he wouldn't have said anything if there was nothing to it.

I take a deep breath and sigh heavily.

"Look," I begin. "This isn't just another contract. This is Wilson Trent. I'd tear this world apart if it meant I could put a bullet in his head. You said yourself this has been a long time coming. You must've known that once we got here, there would be no holding back? That I'd show zero restraint in going after him?"

Josh nods slowly, reluctantly conceding my point.

"Yeah, I know," he replies. "I guess, even after all these

years, it's just strange seeing you act in a way that I can't justify."

"What do you mean?"

"Well, like I've said, when we get a contract, we do our research and take them out. There's no emotion there. It's just a job. And I think knowing that makes it easy for me to justify doing it. But there was no job last night, no contract or moral justification. You simply murdered two people in cold blood—albeit really horrible people, but nevertheless, the lack of... *anything* on your part just looked borderline psychopathic."

"I understand what you're saying, Josh. I do. But I'm not apologizing. I fully intend to kill a lot more people before this ends, and every one of them will likely deserve it. Every now and then, my demons need to come out, so they don't consume me. I'm not a mindless psychopath or a calculated serial killer. I'm a professional assassin. I rely on my darkness to keep me alive. And I rely on you to keep me in check —which you do a spectacular job of, by the way."

He smiles. "Ah, shucks!"

We both laugh, and any tension quickly disperses.

"I appreciate you speaking up," I add. "But I need you to be okay with whatever I decide is necessary here."

He shrugs. "I remember watching you take out Roberto Pellaggio and his small army in the space of about ten minutes. That guy had pushed you farther than I thought possible, and he deserved everything he got. It was insanely beautiful to watch. But last night, Billy McCoy hadn't done anything to you, and you still unleashed that tiny Satan of yours. I guess I'm just used to seeing more... provocation. But I know why we're here and the bottom line is: whatever it takes. Right?"

"Amen, brother."

I lean over the table and we bump fists just as the waitress brings us our breakfasts. We eat heartily, pay the check, and head back to the hotel to collect our things. We're in the Winnebago and on the road within twenty minutes.

"Okay, so where is this place?" I ask as we stop at a red light.

"It's in Hazelwood," Josh replies. "Not far from here. We're gonna have to be discreet with this, though, Boss. If this *is* one of Trent's businesses, he'll have security cameras, hired muscle on site—you name it. You're about to make yourself very visible, and we need to minimize that as much as possible."

I smile. "It will be as if I'm a gentle breeze, disturbing no one."

He quickly throws me a skeptical glance. "Bullshit. Not only does that not even make sense, we all know you're about as subtle as a tank."

I shrug. "Guilty. But I'll do my best."

"Just give me five minutes when before you go in. Let me see what I can do with my toys to help you out."

"Like what?"

"Maybe get the blueprints of the building, disable the security feed, use satellite imagery to see who's inside..."

"Christ, you can *do* all that?"

Josh simply smiles and focuses on the road.

"Damn," I say quietly, shaking my head and laughing. "I'm glad you're on my side..."

11:22 EDT

.   .   .

Twenty minutes later, we pull up opposite the club. I get up and move into the back of the Winnebago, retrieve my guns from my travel bag, and attach the holster to the base of my back. I pull my jacket on and adjust it so that it covers them. Josh appears next to me, sits down at the workbench, and turns on his laptop.

"Right, gimme a minute," he says. His fingers move over the keys like a pianist in the middle of a concerto. I watch the screen as he works his magic, different windows opening and closing in a blur. "Okay, here are the schematics for the building," he says, pointing to the screen. "At the back of the main club area, you have two doors—one straight ahead and one off to the right. The one that will be facing you leads to a corridor at the back of the building. Turn left to the office and right to the changing rooms."

"Okay, so I'll head for the office and see who's there. You got a head count yet?"

"One second, and... yes! Thermal satellite imagery of the area is up and running. You know, I even impress myself sometimes!"

I pat him on the shoulder and smile. "Well, at least you impress *someone*."

"Piss off. Right, the place actually looks open for business."

"Really? It's not even noon! Who goes to a strip club before lunch?"

"I imagine it's not a diverse group of people," he offers, smiling. "This does pose a small problem, though."

"Yeah, witnesses. Not counting the customers, how many targets am I looking at?"

He taps away at the laptop and enhances one section of the feed.

"Well, ignoring everyone in the main area, you've got

two in the office, four in the changing rooms, and one behind the bar. And I can't see any security cameras, so I can't jam the signal, I'm afraid."

"It doesn't matter. What's out the back?"

"As you approach the office, there's a fire exit on the right-hand wall. That leads to a sheltered area, then the parking lot."

"Okay, let's go."

I pick up Josh's baseball cap from the counter and put it on, pulling it low over my forehead. Without another word, I open the back door and jump down to the sidewalk. The cool wind hits me, and the gray skies still threaten a downpour. I turn the collar of my jacket up, dig my hands in my pockets, and set off across the street.

I casually walk through the doors, entering a short corridor. There's a ticket booth on the left, for people to pay their entrance fee at night. Posters advertising special events in the club cover the walls. I carry on and, at the end, I descend a small staircase. At the bottom is an un-manned hole-in-the-wall counter on the right for coats. I walk past it to another set of doors and go through to the main club and bar area. I stand just inside the doors, looking out at the club. There's a faint smell of stale sweat—presumably, the remnants of the previous nights' activities. There are a couple of steps down, then the club floor spreads out in front of me and away to both sides.

I haven't had much experience with strip clubs, but inside it looks exactly like I imagined it would. It's dark, with a pale red glow coming from lights fitted around the walls, enhanced in places by a bright spotlight in the ceiling. I rub my eyes a little to focus. It's so gloomy compared to the light outside that it's taking a moment for them to adjust. To the left is a semi-circular bar, with one tired-looking waiter behind it.

Several low, square tables are scattered all around, each with a number of cheap-looking armchairs around them. On the right is a stage with a pole in the center. There's a young woman, dressed in quite possibly the smallest bikini I've ever seen, spinning herself around, much to the general indifference of the four or five men who are sitting and watching. They look miserable, all approaching sixty and each nursing a glass of spirits. Another woman, also wearing next-to-nothing, is strolling around, trying to attract attention. Our eyes meet briefly and she immediately heads straight for me.

"Hey there, handsome," she says as she approaches, her New York accent being made to sound as seductive as possible. "I'm Tammy. Are you looking for some company?"

She flashes me a practiced smile and steps in close, stroking my left arm. She has white-blonde hair—I'm guessing it's from a bottle since her roots are dark—and light blue eyes accentuated by far too much dark eyeliner. Her lips are glowing red, and her toned body is tanned. In addition to her bikini, she has black heels on, which make her a good three or four inches taller than she actually is. Even so, she barely comes up to my shoulder, so I figure her for five-two or five-three.

I raise an eyebrow slightly at her. There's no denying she's attractive. I doubt she's over twenty-one, which makes her less appealing to me, given I'm forty-three in a few months.

"I'm here to see your boss," I say. "His name's Tommy Blunt, I believe."

I know he isn't here because I know Trent killed him a couple of days ago, but it's interesting to see her reaction. To her credit, she never misses a beat, but I see the momentary flash of alarm in her eyes.

"Mr. Blunt isn't here today, sugar," she says. Her hand moves from my arm to my chest. "Maybe... I can help you?"

Again with the practiced smile. I'm starting to feel a little uncomfortable.

"What about his right-hand man, Jonas Pike? Is he here?"

She takes a step away from me, her entire demeanor suddenly changing. Her charms give way to a defensiveness only seen in the perpetually afraid.

"Okay, who the fuck are you?" she asks, her seductive accent replaced by a broad, New Jersey drawl.

"I wouldn't worry about minor details like that," I reply. "I just wanna have a word with the man in charge."

Out of the corner of my eye, I notice that our little exchange has caught the attention of the bartender. I also notice his right hand disappearing briefly underneath the counter. A few moments later, the door Josh mentioned at the far end opens. Two guys enter, heading straight for me with a purposeful stride.

The bartender must've hit a panic button.

"Tammy, right?" I say to the woman. "You might wanna take yourself someplace else for a minute."

She looks over her shoulder at the two brutes approaching, then looks back at me.

"Whatever," she says with a casual shrug. "It's your funeral."

She struts off with an over-emphasized shake of her hips as the two men stop in front of me. Both are dressed the same—a fitted black T-shirt over a steroid-induced muscular torso, with arms covered in bad tattoos. They're wearing light blue jeans and black boots, completing the look of a career bouncer.

The one on the left is standing with his arms folded across his chest. He's about my height and has a long beard, like a biker. He has a shaved head with a flame tattoo along the right-hand side.

His friend on the right is shorter and more relaxed. I figure he's the brains; the other guy was the brawn. He isn't as well built as the first guy, but he's still not small. He's clean-shaven and looks the younger of the two. He has a baseball cap on, which he's wearing backward, so I immediately assume he's a massive prick. He's the one who speaks first.

"Are you harassing one of our girls?" he asks, more professional than confrontational.

"Technically, she was harassing me," I reply, shrugging casually. "Although, I wasn't about to complain about it." I look over at her and wink to give them the impression I'm naïve and more mouth than anything else.

"Looked to us like you were causing problems," he says.

"I was just asking to speak to the boss, that's all. I was given the names of either Tommy Blunt or Jonas Pike. They around?"

Both men exchange a concerned glance. Everyone obviously knows about Blunt, but they're not about to say anything.

"Mr. Blunt's not here," he says after a moment.

"I know. Tammy's already said that. You know when he'll be back?"

He shakes his head.

"What about Jonas? Is *he* here?"

"Not seen him since last night, actually," he replies, sounding surprisingly helpful.

"So, who's in charge right this second?"

The guy on my right shrugs. "Me. Who's asking?"

"It's not important who I am. I'm just after some information. You help me out, I'll leave you all in peace."

"And if I don't?" he asks, smirking.

"Then I'll leave you all in pieces."

He smiles and looks around. His friend on the left starts laughing.

"Listen, asshole. I've no idea who you are, or what you're after, but you're in the wrong fuckin' place. Do you have any idea who owns this joint?"

I smile. Bingo.

"Yes. Does *he* have any idea you're dealing drugs out the back of this place?" Both men's eyes go wide. "What am I saying?" I continue, feigning stupidity. "Of *course,* he does. Because he's the worst kind of piece of shit there is, isn't he?"

In the blink of an eye, I whip one of my Berettas out from behind me with my right hand and place the barrel against the forehead of the man now in charge. The music stops, the girl on the stage stands still, and everyone's eyes are now on me. Luckily, I'm not the self-conscious type.

"What's your name?" I ask calmly.

"J-Justin," he replies. Any confidence he once had has now departed.

His friend shifts anxiously back and forth next to him. In another swift movement, I produce the other Beretta in my left hand and place it right between his eyes.

"And you," I say to him. "Name?"

"Eight Ball," he replies quietly.

"Eight Ball? Really?"

He nods silently, almost ashamed.

"Fine, whatever. Listen, I'm an old acquaintance of your

boss, and I'd like to get a message to him. Anyone gonna tell me where I can find him?"

Tammy, who's standing off to the side, watching on more with curiosity than fear, steps toward us.

"Hey, Mister, you want some advice?"

I look at her, somewhat bemused.

"Sure," I say.

"These guys won't tell you shit. They're more scared of Mr. Trent than they are of you. You're wastin' your time here."

"Tammy, shut your goddamn mouth!" shouts Justin, who then addresses me. "You've got no idea how much shit you're in right now."

Out of the corner of my eye, I see the bartender suddenly duck down behind the counter.

Well, he's getting his gun...

He quickly re-appears holding a shotgun, which he levels in our direction. Time slows down as I look on, assessing every possible outcome and planning my response.

He's holding an Ithaca, which is a versatile pump-action model designed to fire many different caliber rounds. The shotgun is a close-range weapon, and when it fires, it sprays the buckshot in a conical arc toward its target. The farther away you are from the gun, the less accurate the shot is. A wider target area means you're more likely to get hit but less likely to receive heavy damage. However, if it's fired in close quarters, it'll blow you in half.

I've got maybe three seconds before that guy fires.

I quickly flick my wrists toward Justin and Eight Ball, slamming the butt of each pistol into their noses. They stagger back a few steps but stay standing. Having made some space for myself, I rush to my right. I wrap my right arm around Tammy's waist as I move, scoop her up with ease, and drag her with me.

"Hey!" she shouts in protest.

The anticipated blast from the shotgun sounds out, thundering around the near-deserted club, drowning out her voice. She screams as the buckshot peppers a nearby wall, narrowly missing us. I throw her onto the stage and spin around, returning fire with both guns at the bar.

The guy ducks for cover, and I quickly sprint toward him. He springs back up again to fire off a round, but this time I'm directly in front of him with just the bar counter between us. We're practically nose to nose. For a split-second, he completely freezes, and the color leaves his face. I level one of my pistols and put a bullet in his head, causing a thick spray of blood and brains to explode across the back of the bar.

As his lifeless body slumps to the floor, I turn around to see the bouncers running away in opposite directions. Justin's heading toward the back, but Eight Ball's making his way over to the entrance, so I aim at him quickly and fire. I hit him in his right leg, just below the knee. He stumbles and sprawls over near the steps, his face contorted with pain as he lets out a scream.

Happy he's down for the count, I turn to see the door to the back office closing. I run over, navigating past the half-drunk, half-depressed patrons who are all rooted to their chairs, probably in a cross between fear and curiosity.

I pause at the door, listening for any movement behind it. I doubt he'll be lying in wait for me. I push the door open but pause before going through. Just like Josh had said, I'm in a corridor facing to my left. Ahead of me is the door I know leads to the office, with the fire exit just before it on the right. Behind me are the changing rooms. I figure he'll be heading to the office to make an emergency phone call for some backup.

I walk down the hall and kick the office door open without breaking stride, almost taking it off its hinges. Justin is in the far corner, standing in front of a desk. He's holding a phone to his ear with his left hand and dialing with his right. He turns and looks at me like a deer caught in the headlights. I quickly aim and fire, shooting his left hand and blowing his first two fingers clean off. He drops the receiver and screams in pain as he crouches down, holding his injured hand.

I re-holster my guns, walk over to him, and smash my right knee into the side of his face, right on the jawbone, knocking him clean out. I pick up the receiver and put it to my ear. There's a deep, angry voice on the other end.

"Hello? What the fuck's going on there? Answer me, you piece of shit!"

I smile to myself. Wilson fucking Trent...

I physically bite my tongue to stop myself from saying anything. It's not the right time. Not yet. I simply hang up and look around the office. There's minimal furnishing, with just the desk and a couple of chairs in the center of the room, and a filing cabinet against the back wall in the opposite corner. A small painting hangs on the left wall that has no business being in a place like this. It's a portrait of a woman sitting on a chair. I mean, it's not the Mona Lisa, , but come on... this is an office in a strip club, not the fucking Louvre. There's only one reason it would be here.

I walk over to it and inspect it briefly, then pull the right edge away from the wall like a small door, revealing a decent-sized safe. I walk back over to Justin and slap him hard across the face to wake him up, then drag him to his feet and over to the wall.

"Do you know the combination?" I ask, gesturing to the safe.

He groans and holds his left hand up in front of him, inspecting the wound where his index and middle fingers used to be.

"My fucking hand!" he yells as panic slowly sets in.

"Oh, relax. You still have another one, which is in perfect working order. And you can use it to open this safe. Now."

"B-but... but..."

I take out a Beretta and place it against his head.

"Don't make me ask you again. We all know Blunt and Pike are dead, which means you're running the show now. So, logic would dictate you can open this safe. Now in your own time, asshole."

He's almost crying, but he complies, using his trembling right hand to work the dial and eventually open the safe. As it swings open, I pull the trigger, putting a bullet through his head and painting the wall and door with blood, bone, and brain.

I look inside and smile.

There's a large wad of cash—maybe twenty thousand dollars' worth of twenties and fifties in bundles—and two large bags of cocaine, each containing maybe five kilos.

I've just had a brilliant idea...

I walk out of the office and down the corridor to the changing rooms. I stride in with no hesitation, ignoring the two half-naked women who are holding each other, and quickly find a backpack. I empty its contents out on the floor and, without a word, head back to the office. I clear the safe out and put everything in the bag, then sling it over my shoulder. I look around and locate the security camera, which is in the right corner of the room, level with the door. I walk right underneath it, take my baseball cap off, and stare directly into the lens, smiling. Then I raise my gun and fire, destroying the device.

I walk back out through the club, ignoring any looks and comments. I head up the steps, through the door, along the corridor, and back outside. I put the cap back on my head, squinting as my eyes re-adjust to the natural light. It's started to rain lightly. I jog across the street and open the back door to the Winnebago.

"How'd it go?" asks Josh, looking up from his laptop as I step inside. "And what's in the bag?"

I just smile at him as I rest the bag on the seating by the back window. His eyes narrow and he sighs wearily.

"Adrian, what have you done?"

11

ADRIAN HELL

Josh is worried. It's my fault; I know that.

Look, I had to make a bold statement and hit Trent where it hurts. I've managed to steal just over twenty-three thousand dollars from his club and probably ten kilos of cocaine, which I imagine has a street value of around a quarter of a million dollars or so.

That will certainly get his attention...

We left Shakes and headed straight back to our hotel in the center of the city. We're both in my suite. I'm lying on the bed with my head propped up on the pillows, and Josh is pacing back and forth.

I smile to myself at the role reversal. It's normally Josh who's calm and collected and me wearing the carpet out in frustration.

"Can I speak freely?" asks Josh after a few moments of silence.

"Don't you always?" I reply.

"You're an absolute dick."

"Huh, fair enough," I say, letting him get a much-needed vent of frustration out of his system. "What's today's reason?"

"Smiling and fucking waving at Wilson Trent!" he shouts. He glares at me, then almost immediately puts his hands up and takes a step back in apology. "Sorry," he says. "I didn't mean to scream at you."

I wave my hand dismissively.

"Forget about it," I say. "People need to let their anger out sometimes, and I'd rather you did that than let things build up and fester inside and slowly drive you insane."

"Thanks."

"But talk to me like that again, and I'm gonna have to shoot you just a little bit, okay?"

I smile, signaling a joke, which he returns with a weak attempt of his own.

I let out a heavy sigh and stand up. I walk over to the shoulder bag I brought back from the club and empty it out on the bed.

"If it'll make you feel any better, I'll donate all the money to charity and flush the drugs down the can," I say.

He closes his eyes and takes a deep breath in obvious frustration.

"Jesus, Adrian, it's not the fact you robbed him. Well, it is, but I don't care about what you took. It's the fact you took it and mocked him on a goddamn security camera. What happened to maintaining the element of surprise?"

"Look, for a moment back there, I was on the phone to the bastard. I restrained myself from saying anything to him and just hung up. But I realized that it's all well and good hitting him where it hurts and disrupting his business, but if I'm gonna get to him, I need to get inside his head.

Anonymity is no use long-term. I saw an opportunity to re-introduce myself to him, and I took it. He's gonna go out of his mind when he sees the footage, but what can he do? He has no idea where we are, or even who I am anymore. He's gonna think he's still the Big Bad, and I'm the same wannabe who ran away from him almost a decade ago. I'm gonna mock him, openly, and make sure he underestimates me. Then I'm gonna bury him." I pause. "Are you still with me on this, Josh?"

He shrugs and takes a deep breath. "It's your show," he says reluctantly. "I've got your back. You know that."

"You don't seem too happy about it, though, and this isn't the first time since we got here."

"I'm just worried about you," he says. "I'm sorry, but you're acting like you're invincible. All the years we've spent together, carefully planning hits and executing them with meticulous accuracy... y'know, all the stuff that's kept us alive? You seem to be forgetting all that, and I'm genuinely afraid that you're gonna get yourself killed. There—I said it. You're acting like you've got a fucking death wish, Adrian, and if that's the case, I want no part of this."

"So, what are you saying? That you don't think I'm capable of stopping Trent?"

"No, I'm saying the way you're going about stopping him is reckless, and I think you're blind to that fact because of the emotion driving you. I think you're running the risk of making a mistake, and we both know you can't afford to get it wrong when you live the life we do."

His words hang in the air as silence descends on the room.

Shit.

I hate when he's right. You'd think I'd be used to it by

now—ninety nine percent of the time, he knows better than me.

He paces slowly around the room before finally settling in front of the large window, looking out over the city below us.

"What would you do?" I ask finally.

He turns to look at me. "What do you mean?"

"I mean, we've been doing this my way since we left San Francisco. Like you say, maybe I'm losing control of the situation a bit—letting my emotions cloud my judgment." I sigh. It's not easy to admit when I'm wrong. "What would you do differently?"

He stands and looks out the window silently for a moment. Then he turns around with a smile on his face. "How's this?" he begins. "You want to hit Trent where it hurts, right?"

"That's the plan," I reply.

"Okay. And the guy's a businessman, so hitting his businesses seems the logical way forward."

"Like I did at the strip club?"

"Exactly. Well, sort of. But just robbing him and shooting his staff won't make a dent in an empire that stretches as far as his does."

"So, what are you thinking?" I ask with genuine curiosity.

"While your approach is good for messing with his head, there's no long-term damage. What we need is a hammer blow that will hurt him more permanently."

"I'm sensing you have just such a hammer?"

"Maybe. Going after his wallet is a good idea. We just need to think bigger. If I could hack his bank accounts, I could directly control all his assets. I could seize them, delete them, give them to the FBI. Anything, really."

"Jesus… you could *do* that?"

"Theoretically, yeah. It's not easy, but I've got a few contacts I can hit up for some help. The hard part is covering your tracks. The hacking is pretty straightforward with the right equipment, but I imagine Trent will have someone keeping an eye on all his financials. Assuming they'd be halfway competent, it'd be difficult to not get caught."

"But you'd be sat in front of a computer, not physically breaking into a bank or anything," I say. "How will they know it's you?"

"Oh, Adrian…" he replies, smiling condescendingly. "I could explain it to you, but it would be like trying to explain Einstein's theory of relativity to a five-year-old!"

I pull a face of mock offense.

"Whatever, asshole. That sounds like a great idea, though, Josh. I'll keep doing what I'm doing. It's visible and exactly what I want him to expect from me. Meanwhile, you can be arranging this in the background. He'll never expect such an intelligent and sophisticated assault to come from me, and once we've crippled him, I can make my move and take him out."

Josh nods enthusiastically. "Now you're talkin', Boss!"

We stand in silence for a moment, both happy we now have a more solid plan of attack that we both agree on completely. I think he's more relieved as well. Now that he has more control over what we're doing, I think it's put his mind at rest over my approach to everything.

"So, what now?" he asks.

I walk over to the bed and pick up the bags of cocaine.

"Wanna help me flush two hundred and fifty grand down the drain?"

He smiles. "Why the hell not?"

12

JIMMY MANHATTAN

It was just after five p.m. when Jimmy Manhattan's phone rang. He had spent most of the day in his hotel suite, working on his strategy for claiming Allentown as his own. He was happy with what he'd planned so far.

He looked at the screen and saw Tarantina's number flash across.

"Manhattan," he answered.

"Boss, it's me," said Tarantina. "Just checking in before we make our move."

"Excellent. Is everything in order?"

"Sure is. We've got teams of two or three guys stationed outside every business I mentioned to you. We've hired some outside help for the initial legwork, so we've got close to thirty guys workin' for us right now."

"That's good news. Any problems so far?"

"None—it's as smooth as silk as things stand. As a precaution, I've sent four guys over to see Johnny King. He's the guy I said might offer the most resistance, given he already owns a large portion of the city as it is."

"And what's his story, this King?"

"From what I found out, he's been around for a while. Owns a few clubs, got his finger in a few pies—prostitution mostly but some drugs too. Works out of a nightclub over on Hamilton Street. He's even got a couple of cops on his payroll. But it's nothing we can't handle."

Manhattan thought about it for a moment.

"Leave him to me," he said finally. "I think a more tactful approach would be appropriate here. I'll pay him a visit myself. You and two of our best will come with me."

"Are you sure, Mr. Manhattan?"

"Yes. I think violence and force can only get us so far. If he has as big an operation as you suspect, then he could prove a valuable ally. I'll approach with the offer of a partnership, detailing our takeover of the rest of the city. If I extend the olive branch, it might save us from any unnecessary trouble and still give us control of his assets."

"No problem, Boss. I'll pick you up from your suite in an hour."

"Make it two hours," said Manhattan. "Let his club open first. It'll give him a sense of security, having more of his own men on site. It's nothing for us to worry about, I'm sure. We're going in as friends. At least for now."

"Your call," said Tarantina before hanging up.

Manhattan regarded the phone in his hand for a moment, then put it back in his pocket. He put on his jacket and headed down to the hotel's restaurant for an early dinner.

. . .

An hour and a half later, Manhattan was finishing his second glass of red wine as he pushed the leftovers of his steak to one side of his plate. He wiped the corners of his mouth with his napkin, sat back in his chair, and took a deep breath. He was drinking a 2001 Merlot, which was a personal favorite of his. He had grown accustomed to certain luxuries over the years, thanks to the financial security his lifestyle had given him.

He checked his watch. Tarantina would be coming for him soon. Looking around, he thought about his plans for taking control of the city one last time before launching the operation. The restaurant was probably half-full and, due to the cost and reputation of the hotel, occupied by many important people. He recognized the assistant district attorney sitting with his wife a few tables over from him. And he was sure one of the Supreme Court Justices was at the back of the room in a large party. The power in the room was intoxicating, and he was eager for a taste of it.

Manhattan had somewhat of a reputation because of his former affiliation with the Pellaggios, and he knew that would assist with the transitions and help things go smoothly. Also, this would help distance him from his former dealings with that family and establish him as a big player in his own right in the world of organized crime. He smiled to himself, finally happy that he was no longer someone else's right-hand man. It would take a lot of work, setting up his own network. He had a limited knowledge of the East Coast, despite growing up there, because of his long years working over in Nevada. But he was confident and even a little excited at the prospects that lay ahead.

He looked over toward the restaurant entrance and saw

Tarantina appear. He nodded at him and signaled the waiter for the bill, which he added to his room's tab.

He left his table and walked out, greeting Tarantina as he approached him.

"Is everyone ready?" he asked him.

"Everybody's in place and awaiting the order, Boss," he replied.

"Good. In a couple of hours, we will own it all."

They walked into the lobby of the hotel, then out to the street, where a car was waiting for them. It was a rented sedan, dark blue and anonymous. There were two other men inside—one driving, one in the back. Manhattan got in behind the driver, while Tarantina rode shotgun.

Outside, the light was fading, and the streets were starting to fill up with people going out for the evening. A light rain had begun to fall, and the wind was stronger than it had been earlier in the day. In the light traffic, they made the short drive to Johnny King's nightclub in less than fifteen minutes. It was a brightly lit establishment called The Palace, which took up a modest amount of the block and already had a small queue outside.

The driver pulled up out front and everyone got out, with Manhattan leading the way. As they approached the doorman, he turned to Tarantina.

"Make the call," he said. "Tell everyone to make their move."

Tarantina nodded and quickly typed in a text message.

"Done," he said after a moment.

Manhattan took a deep breath and made his way to the front of the queue. He ignored the people lined up there and spoke directly to the doorman. He was firm but pleasant.

"Can you please tell Mr. King that Jimmy Manhattan wishes to speak with him?" he said.

The guy looked him up and down, then quickly did the same with his companions before taking out his phone and making the call. He quickly explained why he was ringing, then simply nodded in silence as he listened. After a moment, he held the phone against his chest.

"Mr. King said he ain't ever heard of you," said the doorman. "If you wanna talk to him, make an appointment or get in line like everybody else."

Unfazed, Manhattan simply smiled.

"Please tell your employer to take a moment and ask around," he replied. "As of about three minutes ago, I now run this city. My associates and I simply wish to work out a mutual arrangement that benefits both our organizations. I'm here as a courtesy and as a friend. But this is the only time I'm willing to discuss such matters. I'm sure, under the circumstances, Mr. King can spare us a few minutes?"

The doorman looked a little worried and carefully repeated the message to King on the phone. After hanging up, he made way for them.

"Mr. King says to go right in. He'll be down in a minute to greet you."

"Many thanks," said Manhattan, with a smile that said he knew all along what the outcome would be.

They strode confidently through the entrance and into the nightclub. It wasn't a standard place, catering more for the mature and refined customer. There was a small stage on the far right with a jazz musician playing some light background music on a saxophone. The tables and chairs were high-quality and well-spaced, with a small lamp on each table. Despite still being early, the club looked full. Wait staff patrolled the floor, picking up empty glasses and delivering full ones. At the back of the room was a set of double doors with a single man standing in front of them. Manhattan glanced over his left shoulder and instructed the two men accompanying him to wait at the bar. They both nodded and walked over, somewhat conspicuously, to rest on the counter.

He stopped and then looked at Tarantina.

"This is a nice place," he said. "We'll see what King's office is like and maybe base ourselves here. I like the atmosphere and it's better than The Carrington."

"It's a nice joint," Tarantina replied, nodding.

As they walked across the floor, the double doors opened, and a man walked out wearing a black pinstripe suit. Another man was on either side of him; they also wore suits, along with an earpiece.

"That's him," said Tarantina, nodding toward the man who approached them.

Manhattan had read up on Johnny King, prior to the meeting. He knew King was quite young, compared to himself at least. In his mid-forties, he had established himself more than a decade ago as the man to respect and fear in Allentown. He dealt mostly in prostitution and extortion but did earn a modest sum from importing and distributing crystal meth as a sideline. He had a tanned complexion, and his brilliant white smile touched every inch of his face, making him look more like a politician than a gangster.

Manhattan took a deep breath to relax himself before extending his hand as they met.

"Mr. King," he said. "I'm Jimmy Manhattan. It's a pleasure to make your acquaintance."

King shook his hand firmly in response. "Likewise," he

replied with a hint of skepticism. "My boy outside tells me you wanna talk to me?"

"I'd like to discuss some business with you, yes."

King gave him an uncertain look before gesturing silently for Manhattan and Tarantina to follow him, which they did. He led them back through the double doors and into the other part of the club beyond. It looked like a VIP area, with the smaller room lit by a subtle blue light all around. There was another bar but with fewer waiters. The area was far quieter and looked much more exclusive.

They followed King and his bodyguards across the area to the end, where they went through another door and up a large staircase. At the top, they turned left and walked along a dimly lit corridor, adorned on either side by contemporary works of art. At the end of the corridor was the main office. King strode in and sat in an expensive-looking leather chair behind a lavish, dark mahogany desk. His men stood either side of him, arms folded.

The room was a decent size, with a large landscape painting facing the door behind the desk and filing cabinets in either corner against the wall. A thick, expensive, dark carpet covered the floor. The walls were light beige, offering a contrast to the ambience of the room.

Manhattan sat down in one of the two chairs facing the desk without waiting for an invitation. Tarantina stood just behind him. King regarded them silently for a moment, leaning back in his chair and bridging his fingers in front of him.

"So," he began. "You have a business proposition for me?"

Manhattan smiled. "Of sorts, yes."

"So, let's hear it."

"As I mentioned to your man outside, this evening I have

absorbed the majority—in fact, almost all—of the local businesses in this city that conduct some manner of illegal activity."

King scoffed. "Are you being serious? Who the hell are you?"

"I'm a former associate of Roberto Pellaggio and later his son, Daniel. What we ran over in Nevada made this entire city look like a 7-Eleven. I've relocated my interests to the East Coast, and I have been reliably informed that you were the man in charge around these parts. Instead of dictating changes as we did everywhere else, I thought I'd extend you the courtesy of inviting you to merge your assets with mine. I'm sure we can work well together to a mutually beneficial end."

King looked at each of his bodyguards in mock disgust.

"You sound like you're trying to do me a *favor*, you arrogant sonofabitch!" He stood. "Let me extend *you* a courtesy. This is my town, you understand? And you have no idea who I am or what I'm capable of. Now I'm gonna let you walk outta here, and I'll pretend this never happened. But if I see or hear from you again, I'll fucking bury you! Are we clear?"

Manhattan sat, listening patiently, and when King had finished, he regarded him silently for a moment. Then he stood, straightened his suit, and dusted himself down.

"Mr. King," he said. "I thank you for your time and your honesty. I respect that you have been upfront with me and let me know where we stand."

Without another word, he turned and headed for the door. Sensing Tarantina's anger at the disrespect shown toward them, he placed a calming hand on his shoulder as he got level with him.

"Come on, Paulie. This is one business we're seemingly not going to add to our list of interests."

And with that, they both left King's office and headed back downstairs. They walked through the club the way they had come in, purposefully but in no hurry. Manhattan was keen to make a point that he wasn't leaving with his tail between his legs. He signaled to the two guys at the bar that they were leaving. All four of them walked back out to the street, got into the car, and drove off.

"Boss, are you really just gonna leave this asshole to run his business alongside ours?" asked Tarantina.

Manhattan smiled. "Of course not. I know just how to handle Mr. King."

13

WILSON TRENT

Wilson Trent sat in a large, brown leather chair behind his desk. His office was located in the penthouse suite on the thirtieth floor of a building he owned in the Manchester neighborhood, overlooking the Ohio River. On the first few floors were local, honest businesses which he was happy to accommodate. They masked his other, less reputable enterprises that also operated out of the building. The rest of it was luxury apartments that many of the men who worked for Trent lived in and worked out of.

His suite was spacious and sparsely decorated, giving it a contemporary, modern feel. He was fascinated with the concept of Feng Shui. So, what little decoration he had—a large plant on the right in the corner, a pet goldfish in a bowl on a small table to the left, various works of art on the walls, and rare samurai swords in a display case by the right windows—were all arranged to best accentuate a positive environment for him. Some people who worked for him joked about his strange, spiritual beliefs, albeit never to his face.

The entire wall behind his desk, plus half of either side of the room, was made entirely of glass that ran floor to ceiling, offering a beautiful panoramic view of Pittsburgh. Trent was looking out at the city, still bustling with life below him, and the river that ran purposefully next to it. Above, the night sky was dark as the moon and the stars were hidden behind the low, menacing cloud. He enjoyed the view, and he often spun around to soak it in for a few minutes while he was working.

With him was his accountant, Joseph Bernstein. He was a well-dressed man with greased, jet-black hair and a permanent suntan that made his already perfect white smile seem luminous. He sat on one of the two leather sofas that were in front of the desk, facing each other lengthways.

"So, is everything to your satisfaction?" Bernstein asked.

"It all looks in order, yeah," replied Trent. He spun around to face the room and rested his hands on his dark, solid oak desk.

As he was about to say something else to Bernstein, there was a knock at his door. He sighed wearily.

"What?" he shouted at the door.

It opened, and Duncan and Bennett entered. They were escorting a young blonde woman wearing tight jeans, knee-high boots, and a short, furry jacket.

"What's going on?" asked Trent, raising an eyebrow. He cast an approving glance over the new arrival.

"Boss," said Duncan. "Sorry to disturb you at this time of night, but it's important. This woman just showed up downstairs, said she's got something she needed to show you that couldn't wait."

Trent massaged his temples, then sighed and looked over at Bernstein.

"We're done," he said. "Get the fuck outta here."

Bernstein nodded. Without a word, he gathered his belongings and hastily made his exit past the new arrivals, closing the door behind him.

Trent looked at Duncan and Bennett in turn, then checked his watch. "It's twenty-two minutes past ten," he said. "This better be fucking good."

Duncan gestured to the woman to step forward, indicating she could talk.

"Mr. Trent," she began. "I'm Tammy. I work at Shakes, over in Hazelwood."

"And why aren't you over there right now, *working*?"

"Because of this," she replied, producing a USB flash drive from her pocket.

"And what's that?"

"The club got raided this morning," she explained confidently, like she knew she was doing her civic duty reporting it to her boss. "This guy walks in, kinda tall, cute-looking... I go over, y'know, see if he needs anything."

"Get to the point, my dear, before I lose my patience."

"Well, he starts askin' all these questions about who's in charge. I figured him for a cop at first, but then he took out Eight Ball, Mike the bartender, and followed Justin into the back. I heard shouting and shooting, then this guy walks back out. I go back to look and see Justin all kinds of dead— even had two fingers missing off his hand. Anyways, I figured you'd wanna know. This here is the security feed."

Trent clenched his jaw muscles, suppressing his anger. It wasn't the girl's fault. He was pleased she'd come to him with the information. He signaled to Duncan, who took it and walked around the desk to stand next to him. Trent gestured to his laptop, which was still open in front of him, and Duncan plugged the memory stick into it and played the video file stored on there.

Trent watched as the unknown man walked in and spoke to Tammy. He was then approached by Justin and another guy, both of whom he took out before shooting the bartender and heading to the back area. Another feed then picked him up going into the office, shooting Justin's fingers off, getting into the safe, then shooting him in the head, and emptying the contents. And then...

Staring right into the camera.

Trent's short temper took over and he exploded with rage. He slammed his fist down hard on the desk and let out a visceral growl, causing everyone in the room to jump in surprise.

"Sonofabitch!" he yelled.

"Boss, are you all right?" asked Bennett, who was still standing by Tammy.

Without answering, he stood and turned to Duncan, pointing at the laptop. The video file was paused on the screen showing the man's face in vivid detail.

"Find *him*. Now!" He walked around the desk and stood in front of Tammy. "You did well bringing this to my attention," he said to her.

She shrugged calmly. She'd worked at the club a long time and had been involved in the world that Trent ran for even longer.

"Just figured you'd wanna know, Mr. Trent," she replied respectfully.

He nodded and looked at Bennett. "See she gets home safely," he said to him.

"Sure thing," replied Bennett, ushering her out of the room.

After a few moments of pacing around his suite, trying to calm down and let his anger subside, he gave up and stormed out of the office to the elevator in the corridor outside. He took it down to the ground floor and walked out the front of the building, where his car was always waiting for him. He got in the back and slammed the door shut.

"Where to, Mr. Trent?" asked the driver, turning around in the front seat.

He rubbed his temples in frustration and anger. "Anywhere," he replied. "I need a fucking drink."

He sat back as the car drove off and looked out of the window at the lights of the city flashing by. His mind raced, and his anger boiled away just beneath the surface. He had no idea where he'd come from or why he'd resurfaced, but he was sure of one thing... Adrian fucking Hughes was a dead man walking.

14

***

ADRIAN HELL

I've left Josh working away on his idea of robbing Trent via cyberspace. I've gone for a stroll around town to find a breakfast bar. It's another miserable day that's threatening to rain. I'm walking the streets, the collar on my jacket turned up, casually navigating the tail end of the morning rush hour crowds.

Last night, since we were in such a good mood after disposing of Trent's drugs, Josh and I decided to celebrate with a few drinks, courtesy of our mini bars and room service. As a result, I'm feeling slightly delicate this morning and in urgent need of some food to make myself feel better. Josh has always been able to handle more drink than me—I think it's a British thing. Their beer's stronger than the stuff in the States, so they can down our booze like tap water.

Calling on my limited memory of the city, I remember there's a nice place not far from our hotel that used to do a nice breakfast and tasty coffee. I'm heading there to see if it's still open.

I turn a corner and walk past a furniture store, which has a huge window displaying lots of discounted sofas and chairs and tables. For no real reason, other than to occupy my mind for a fleeting moment, I glance through the window. Out of the corner of my eye, I catch a glimpse of a guy's reflection walking behind me. He's close but no closer than anyone else is at this time of a morning. But there's something about him that's immediately set my spider sense tingling. Something... familiar.

Am I being paranoid, thinking someone's following me? It could just be my mind playing tricks on me. After all, I'm going through a lot right now, and I'm probably not thinking clearly...

I need to put my mind at ease, though.

I chance one last look in the window before I pass the store and glimpse him again. He's wearing black jeans and shoes, with a long coat, fastened, that finishes just above his knees. He has a determined expression and walks with a purpose. And he's staring directly at me.

Okay, my first instinct was right. I'm not paranoid. I know a tail when I see one. My mind kicks into overdrive. Why am I being followed? And by whom? Logic would dictate it's one of Trent's men, which means he's seen the footage of me in his strip club and the game has begun. But I'm on a crowded street, and while I'm happy to get *his* attention, I don't want to get anyone else's. Not yet.

I casually put my Bluetooth earpiece in and dial Josh as I walk.

"Yo!" he answers. His trademark enthusiasm and happiness is even harder to stomach than normal due to my headache.

"Yo? Who says that anymore?" I ask.

"Just trying to bring it back, Boss!"

"Well, don't. It sounded stupid in the nineties, and it sounds worse now."

"You're touchier than usual today. Still hung over, are we?"

"No... listen—I'm being followed."

There's a moment's silence on the line.

"You sure?" he asks.

"I double-checked. Definitely a tail."

"One of Trent's?"

"That would be my guess, yeah."

"Do I wanna know what you have planned?"

"I'm not gonna kill him, if that's what you're getting at," I say. "But I *am* gonna ask him some questions when I get chance. Anything you wanna know that might help your little online robbery idea?"

"Well, I doubt we're lucky enough to have Trent's personal accountant following you, so there's not much he could do for me," he says. "But any information about how Trent's handling you being back would be helpful."

"Agreed."

"Just don't be too... y'know... *shooty* with your line of questioning."

"Too *shooty*?"

"Yeah, not every interrogation needs a gun, remember?"

"Piss off," I say with a smile as I hang up.

I take a quick look around. I can see the breakfast bar I'm looking for across the street. I'm so hungry, but food will have to wait. This inconsiderate asshole is getting in the way of my breakfast, and I'm not happy.

Up ahead there's a crossing. I use it as an excuse to casually look behind me and see where my tail is, acting like I'm preparing to cross the street, like anyone else would do. I step into a small group of people and wait for the green WALK sign to appear. And just like everyone else, I instinctively look left and right. I get a good look at the guy following me. I definitely recognize him from somewhere but can't place him.

He has to be one of Trent's men. He's trying to act as casual as I am, but he's not good at it. He might as well be wearing an A-board and ringing a bell, advertising his services as a talentless thug for hire with no sense of discretion.

I cross over and continue up the other side of the street. I see an alleyway between two sandwich bars on my right. It's reasonably wide and has trashcans piled up on either side belonging to each establishment. There are puddles on the ground and graffiti on the walls. Both doors leading into the kitchen areas of each building are open.

I make a snap decision and turn down the alley. It seems to lead right through to the street one block over, running parallel to me, so it won't have looked too suspicious—just another pedestrian taking another shortcut. I speed up a little to force my tail to break his not-so-subtle cover so that he can keep up. My plan is to lure him farther into the alley, then stop and spin around suddenly and grab him.

Simple but effective. The element of surprise is a powerful tool.

I'm over halfway into the alley, so I think now's as good a time as any. I take one last step and spin quickly on the balls of my feet, doing a quick one-eighty and stopping in a loose fighting stance.

But I'm alone.

Huh?

Maybe I *am* getting paranoid in my old age.

I wait another thirty seconds to make sure, then turn around again to head back out of the alley at the other side. I'll just double back around the block and go into the breakfast bar, like I originally intended.

I turn into a powerful right punch that hits me squarely in the face. The impact, coupled with the shock, sends me staggering backward. I eventually lose my balance and drop to one knee.

What the hell was that?

I look up and see the man I figured was following me. He must've carried on past the alley and sprinted around to the other side. He doesn't even look out of breath. His face is calm and expressionless.

I slowly get back to my feet. He stands his ground but keeps a respectable distance. I dust myself down and stare at him.

"That was your free shot," I say. "You go to hit me again and I'll break you in half."

He regards me silently for a moment.

"You're just like he described," he says with a cocky smile. "Maybe a bit smaller."

I raise an eyebrow. "You must really be sick of breathing."

"Save your threats. I'm not an enemy."

"So, why did you hit me? Who are you?" I ask, reaching behind me and taking a Beretta out of my holster, holding it loose and obvious by my side. "And before you say anything, please be aware that, to avoid getting shot, you need to make your answer *phenomenally* good."

His eyes flick between mine and my gun. He obviously knows who I am, which means he knows his life depends on what he says next.

"My name's not important," he says, remaining impressively calm. "But who I work for is. I came here to hire you."

"I already have a job," I reply with a shrug. "Take a ticket like everyone else."

"I appreciate that your services are in demand, but my employer is an old acquaintance of yours, and he's willing to pay top dollar for your services as a gesture of goodwill."

I frown. An old acquaintance?

"Who do you work for?" I ask, my curiosity piqued.

The man smiles and takes out his phone, dialing a number. When it starts ringing, he hands it to me.

"See for yourself," he says.

I reluctantly take the phone from him. "Hello?"

"Hello, Adrian. It's Jimmy Manhattan."

My eyes go wide with surprise for a split-second. I silently curse myself for letting any emotion slip out.

"So, you're not dead, then?" I ask, quickly composing myself.

"As observant as ever," replies Manhattan. "I always said you were smarter than you look."

"What do you want?"

"I want to offer you a job."

"We've been down that road before, and it didn't end particularly well for either of us. So, if it's all the same, you can feel free to fuck off."

The line goes silent. In front of me, Manhattan's man goes tense.

"Will you at least hear my proposal?" he asks me finally.

I look at his man, who's eyeballing me and trying to look menacing. I take a deep breath and sigh. I must be crazy...

"You've got thirty seconds. Then I'm hanging up this phone and killing your guy."

The guy relaxes and takes a step back, increasing his already respectful distance.

"That's fair," replies Manhattan. "Tell me, where are you right now?"

I see no reason to lie. As far as he's concerned, I'm just doing a job.

"In an alleyway in the center of Pittsburgh."

"I'm in my hotel suite at The Carrington, over in Allentown."

I fail to hide my surprise for a second time. I'm thankful Manhattan isn't here to see he's caught me off-guard again.

"What are *you* doing in Pennsylvania?" I ask, unable to suppress my growing curiosity.

"I'm currently taking over the city," he replies, quite matter-of-factly. "I've set up on my own. I'm eager to distance myself from any former association with the Pellaggios—which I'm sure you, of all people, can appreciate."

"Probably the smartest thing you've done since I've known you," I agree.

"Before I tell you the details of the job, I wanna skip ahead to how it benefits you."

"Spare me the sales pitch, Jimmy. I'm not doing a job for you."

"Humor me," he says. "Hopefully, with your help, in a few days I will have total control of this city. I have a considerable amount of assets already at my disposal, and that is increasing with each day that passes. With Allentown in my pocket, it won't be long until I'm kingpin of this state, Adrian."

"Go on," I say, intrigued. Given my reasons for being in town and what I know of the kingpins already in business, Manhattan suddenly throwing his hat in the ring may just make things a bit more entertaining.

"The way I see it, you and I are square," he continues.

"Oh, are we? How you figure that?"

"You saved my life," he says. "That cancels out all the slights against me in the last year."

I sigh heavily down the phone, resisting the urge to argue the finer points of who *slighted* whom. "Fine. So, we're best friends—why would that make any difference to my life?"

"I'm sure it won't do you any harm to have someone in my position as an ally. Certainly not in your line of work. I have a lot of resources that you may find helpful."

He has a point. I'll give him that. I don't actively associate myself with people like Manhattan; it's bad for business. But on the other hand—and I'm sure Josh would agree—having a pet gangster isn't the worst idea, especially under the circumstances. Same reason we keep a relationship with GlobaTech. Every now and then, it's nice to have some back up.

"But you're not in that position *yet*, are you?" I point out. "That's what you need me for."

"Exactly. You help me now, I'm sure I can return the favor somehow."

'What do you want?'

"There's a businessman here who is more reluctant to succumb to new ownership than other people have been. I think your particular brand of persuasion would prove most effective."

"So, you want him removed?"

"Just name your price."

I obviously don't trust the old prick as far as I can throw him, but. But maybe I could use him. If he's telling the truth, and he now effectively runs Allentown, I could use his help taking down Trent. It's unlikely he's anywhere near Trent's level, but I could definitely use what he has.

"Lemme think about it," I say.

"Excellent. You won't regret it, Adrian. I'll be in touch."

He hangs up, leaving me standing in an alleyway with one of his men, holding a phone. I click it off and throw it the man, who catches it clumsily and stares at me.

"If I see you following me again, I'll kill you," I say. Then I turn and walk off, back down the alley and toward my hotel.

I should probably talk to Josh.

09:11 EDT

"You're shitting me?" asks Josh.

We're in his hotel room. His laptop and various other pieces of equipment are scattered across his bed. He's pacing around his room as I sit, patiently, in one of the chairs by his window. He's been doing a lot more pacing than usual—almost as much as I do when I'm agitated or thinking. It probably isn't the best time to point out he's becoming more like me every day.

"Nope," I say.

"Has he heard of Trent?"

"Doesn't look that way," I say with a shrug. "There's no way he'd talk about taking over the state if he had."

"Jesus. And what are you thinking?"

"Honestly? I think having him on our side for the time being maybe isn't as sickening an idea as it sounds. Keep your friends close an' all that."

"But getting in bed with Manhattan? That's dangerous ground, Adrian. We can't trust him."

"I know," I say with an almost sympathetic smile. "But what harm would it do, compared to how it would benefit us going up against Trent?"

Josh paces some more in silence, then moves a small, hand-held radio on the end of his bed out of the way so that he can sit down.

"Fair point," he says reluctantly.

I stand and look out of the window. Light rain has started to fall, but it looks worse than it is because the wind's picked up. It's been threatening for a couple of days, and I suspect it'll get worse before it gets better, judging by the color of the clouds.

"As always, Josh," I say, turning to look at him, "we both have to agree one hundred percent on it before we do anything."

"I know," he says with an appreciative smile.

"Just look into his claims of domination over Allentown —see if there's any truth to it. If there is, we maybe look at pitching our tent in his camp for now. Agreed?"

Josh stands and nods. "Agreed."

I turn and look back out of the window one last time. I hope this is the right move. We could both get burned if I'm wrong.

15

JIMMY MANHATTAN

09:04 EDT

Jimmy Manhattan hung up the phone and tossed it on the bed. In the corner of the room, Tarantina sat reading a newspaper, which he promptly put down when the call finished.

"What did he say?" he asked.

"He said he'd think about it," replied Manhattan. "But I'm confident he'll see the benefit of assisting us in this matter."

"And who exactly *is* this guy again?"

"He's a talented and dangerous individual. I've had dealings with him in the past, and he's proved... resourceful. I'd rather have him working with me than against me. I've learnt from experience to pick my battles."

"Jeez, he sounds like a real piece of work."

"He is," confirmed Manhattan. "And if he agrees to it, I fully intend to advertise the fact that Adrian Hell will be carrying out the hit for us. Then our enhanced reputation, coupled with the mere threat of having *him* being sent after you, will deter anyone from even thinking about going up against us in the future. Nobody need know it was a one-time deal."

Tarantina nodded. "So, what now?" he asked.

"Now we wait. Go do your rounds," said Manhattan. "Check in with everyone and make sure the transitions are going according to plan."

"Sure thing, Boss."

Tarantina left the hotel suite, leaving Manhattan alone.

So far, everything was going ahead as expected. With the exception of Johnny King, everybody had relented. Manhattan now either ran their businesses as his own, or he'd closed them permanently. He kept the profitable businesses alive with his own men at the helm and killed off the rest—literally.

His next step was to secure the support of local law enforcement to make his life easier when running and expanding his empire. From experience, he knew that police officers were typically greedy but nearly always a sound investment. If he found the right cop, he could have a free run at the city. He was going to put the word out among his men to keep their ears to the ground for any potential candidates, then he would make the approach himself. He'd done it many times before and knew how to play the game just right.

But it took time to build the relationship with the law that way, and the initial resistance from King had to be dealt with sooner, rather than later. Otherwise, he'd start to lose any credibility he'd gained since arriving in the city a few days ago. He had to make a bold statement to show everyone that his way was the only viable option.

He was also confident in his plans for Adrian Hell. They

had history, the two of them. And despite Adrian saving his life not so long ago, Manhattan never forgot the people who had wronged him. He'd learned from the mistakes both generations of Pellaggios had made when it came to dealing with that man. Offering him the contract to kill Johnny King was just the first step to getting his revenge.

Manhattan smiled as he walked over to his mini bar and poured himself a small measure of bourbon. He dropped a couple of ice cubes into it, which clinked together loudly in his otherwise silent room. He sat in the chair Tarantina had occupied a moment earlier, took a sip of his drink, and looked out of the window. He wasn't concerned if it were too early to drink; he simply wanted to relax and be left to his thoughts.

It hadn't been too difficult to track Adrian down. He couldn't be found unless he wanted to be, but Manhattan was in a reasonably unique position. He had crossed paths with Adrian Hell more than once and lived to tell the tale. Consequently, he had somewhat of an inside scoop on him, which aided him greatly when it came to locating him.

It was interesting to him that he'd found Adrian in the same state as himself. He made a mental note to find out what job Adrian was working on over in Pittsburgh. If he were involved, it was likely a target of some importance, which could be a situation worth exploiting.

10:07 EDT

Manhattan's phone rang, breaking the silence in the room and disturbing his thoughts. He hadn't moved from his chair. He'd spent the time contemplating his next few moves, like playing a mental chess game, theorizing all the possible outcomes.

He walked over to the bed and answered it. "Yes?"

"Boss, it's me," said an obviously flustered Tarantina. "We've got a real problem."

"What's happened?" asked Manhattan, frowning with fresh concern.

"One of our new businesses, a launderette over in Westwood, has been hit. We've got two men dead and one injured. The place was cleaned out."

"Remind me what this business was..."

"There was a gambling house run in the back. Mostly poker. Illegal, high stakes—most visitors are our kind of people and were known players in the state looking to spend and launder cash."

"What have we lost?"

"Close to eighty large," replied Tarantina with a heavy sigh.

Manhattan's nostrils flared. His face contorted with a momentary flash of anger, then he took a deep breath.

"*Who* have we lost?" he asked.

"A couple of guys I brought into the organization. Good guys—I'd known them a long time. I ain't happy, Boss."

"I know, Paulie. We just need to handle this situation correctly. Have we been able to get anything of use from the survivor?"

"Nothing except a vague description of one of the guys who came in. The details meant nothing to me, but my guess is that it was King's men."

"That would be my assumption too, but we need to make sure. Bring me the security tapes and let me see what happened. If it *was* King, we will find the men who did this and make an example. Then send Mr. King an invoice for our missing money. This will not go unpunished."

"You got it, Mr. Manhattan," said Tarantina before hanging up.

Manhattan stared at the phone for a moment, then tossed it on the bed. He walked back over to the mini bar and poured himself a fresh shot of bourbon, much larger this time. He took a long gulp and a deep breath.

He'd expected a few hiccups along the way but nothing as daring as that. He knew he had to find out who was responsible and retaliate quickly. And if it *was* Johnny King behind it, he'd put his head on a spike for the world to see.

16

ADRIAN HELL

Josh has just spent the last hour explaining the finer details of his plan to assault Trent's bank balance, which made little sense to me. But the bottom line is that we're going to transfer all Trent's money into our bank account, which sounds pretty goddamn good to me.

We've also been discussing Manhattan's job offer. Despite the potential benefits, taking down Trent is simply more important. I don't want to lose sight of why I'm here, so we've agreed that the best thing to do is turn the job down. Plus, any dealings with Manhattan would only ever be temporary and a huge risk at best, so it really isn't worth it.

It looks like the rain outside has settled in for the duration now. It's coming down much heavier than a couple of hours ago. Despite being the middle of the afternoon, it's almost dark outside. The raindrops splash rapidly against the window of my hotel suite, the noise low and constant in the background.

Josh is sitting cross-legged on my bed, his laptop resting on his knees as he taps away, cursing occasionally. I smile. Watching him work is interesting. I can see it in his eyes—the excitement, the urgency, the intelligence.

"Right," he says, looking up from the screen. "I think I've got an algorithm that could work. It'll mask my IP address and bounce my signal all over the world before attacking the accounts, so we're pretty safe."

I nod with an exaggerated blank look on my face. "Great! I was just thinking, you'll definitely need to make sure you mask your IP address..."

He raises an eyebrow. "We both know you have no clue what I just said. Leave the sarcasm to me, yeah?"

I hold my hands up and laugh. "Fair enough. So, are you good to go ahead?"

"In theory, yes—I think so. Now we just need the details of his accounts."

"Well, let's go and get something to eat and figure out the rest of it. I'm hungry."

He closes the laptop and puts it to one side. He stretches his legs out on the bed before standing. "Sounds good to me," he says, heading for the door.

I pick my jacket up off the back of the chair and look at my guns, which are hanging underneath it in their holster.

I'm only going for some lunch. I doubt I'll need them.

I put my jacket on and follow Josh out of the room, picking up the room key from the side table as I pass. I doubled-check the door is locked behind me, then we walk to the elevator and ride it to the first floor. The doors ding and slide open, and we walk out into the lobby. Josh immediately taps my arm and subtly gestures toward the front desk. There are two police officers talking to the manager. They're holding a picture, and the manager's nodding and gesturing with his hands. We look at each other, the same alarm bells ringing in our heads. Then we stride on, quickly but cautiously with our heads down, toward the entrance.

"Oh, there he is now," I hear the manager say. I can't help but look over. He's pointing right at us. "Mr. Hughes? Do you have a moment?"

I look at the two officers as they turn to face us. They're both about the same height and build. Both are dressed the same—beat cops with their waterproof coats on. The one on the left has some stubble on his chin, while the other is clean-shaven. Their eyes narrow as they look first at us, then at the photo in they're holding. They quickly turn to each other and nod in silent confirmation, then set off walking toward us.

"We need a word with you," says the one with the stubble.

I catch a glimpse of the photo he's holding. It's a grainy, black and white picture of my face. Its poor quality tells me it's likely a printout of a screenshot from a video. In a split-second, I realize that they must've had access to the security footage from Trent's club to get that picture. If I'm to make an educated guess, I'd say these cops are in Trent's pocket, which means arresting us probably isn't high on their agenda. I have no idea how these guys found us so quickly. We're not exactly hiding, admittedly, but I kind of hoped it'd take Trent longer than this to get to me.

I instinctively reach behind me, going into survival mode and getting my guns, but I don't have them. Seriously, the *one* time I leave them somewhere...

Josh looks at me, and my jaw muscles tense. The two cops are halfway to us now, but we're closer to the entrance than they are to us.

I think that's my decision made.

"Josh, run!" I yell, breaking into a sprint and slamming through the doors, stopping momentarily on the sidewalk outside.

The rain is torrential, and I'm instantly soaked. I squint to stop the water from dripping into my eyes. Josh appears next to me; the cops are a second behind us.

"I'll go left. You go right!" I shout over the noise of the weather and the traffic. "Give them the runaround for five minutes, then meet back at the Winnebago."

"Got it," replies Josh, breathing heavy.

We split up, running off in our respective directions. I hope he's going to be okay. He's still likely feeling the effects of the wounds he sustained back in San Francisco.

There's an old saying: discretion is the better part of valor. I know I'm not a coward. I'm not running away because I'm scared. I'm simply avoiding a confrontation until I'm better prepared to win it.

I run to the end of the street, nearly slipping on the wet sidewalk. I weave and dodge through the crowd and take the first left turn I come to. I chance a look over my shoulder and briefly see one of the cops in pursuit. He isn't as fast as I am, which is a blessing. I pause a moment, giving him a good look where I'm going, then set off again. People stare at me as I run past them, obviously disturbed by the sight of a police officer chasing after someone. Halfway up the street, I spot a trashcan near the curb. I slow down enough to take my jacket off and throw it away as I pass by. I'm completely soaked and freezing. My T-shirt is clinging to my torso, almost see-through from the rain. I look over my shoulder again, but I can't see the cop. I can, however, see the crowd of people behind me parting hurriedly, so he's definitely still in pursuit.

It's a long street, lined on either side by shops and bars. I know I need to get off this main stretch and find a way to double-back to the hotel. Up ahead, I see an alleyway just after a McDonald's on the left.

Perfect!

I stop and move quickly into the doorway, turning my back to the street. I pretend to open the door, using the reflection in the glass to see behind me. I wait for the cop to run past me and set off again, chasing him now. I come up directly behind him as we approach the alley. I speed up to draw level with him on the outside. With a strong shoulder barge, I push the surprised cop into the alley. His own momentum causes him to stumble and fall to the ground.

I move in quickly after him, drag him up, and manhandle him farther into the alley, away from the street. I push him against the wall, and as he turns, I launch a straight right that catches him flush on the side of the face. He hits the wall, and I move in again, standing close and pressing my right forearm against his throat, pinning him to the spot.

His face is inches from mine. Like me, he's drenched. He's breathing heavy, gasping for air through gritted teeth as he struggles to get free from my grip, although that's a futile effort. I apply more pressure to his throat, making it harder for him to get the oxygen his body is screaming for.

"How did you find me?" I ask, shouting over the noise of the downpour.

He growls like a trapped animal, unable to get his words out as his lungs burn for more air. I ease off a little, ensuring I keep him firmly trapped against the wall.

"Answer me!" I demand.

He takes a deep breath, then another. "We—we tried every hotel in... in Pittsburgh," he says, barely managing to speak in between breaths. "Mr. Trent's got... the entire city looking for you."

I feel the look of concern creep over my face as the scope of what I'm up against hits me, and he must've seen it.

"You're... fucking dead," he rasps, smiling through his obvious discomfort.

"Whatever," I reply. "Where can I find Trent?"

"Fuck... you!"

I press down again on his throat, holding him upright as I jab him in the kidney with my left hand. "Don't be silly," I say. "Tell me where I can find Trent."

"He'll find *you* soon enough." He winces. "Why are you in such a rush to die?"

I jab him again in the kidney. "You might think you know me but let me assure you—you really don't. I'm a fucking nightmare. I'm a whirlwind of misery and suffering and hatred, and I'm here to send Wilson Trent to hell. And I will, I promise you. Now tell me where he is, or I'll leave you here, bleeding to death. Your call."

He frowns with confusion. "I'm not bleeding," he says.

"Give it a minute," I say, smiling.

For the first time, I see a hint of fear and doubt flash in the cop's eyes. He looks left and right, weighing up all his options.

"Mr. Trent owns a luxury high-rise near the Ohio River," he says finally. "The top floor is all his. If you wanna find him, that's where he's likely to be."

"Thank you." I pause to shake my head sharply to remove some of the rain that's dripping into my eyes. "See? That wasn't so hard, was it?"

I step back and, without any warning, kick him hard in the stomach with my right foot. As he doubles over, I step forward again. I clasp my hands behind his head in a clinch, pulling it down and holding him steady. I whip my right knee up and connect squarely with his face. Something gives as bone meets bone. I let him go and he drops like a stone, landing face-down in the wet, muddy alley, unconscious.

I walk back and forth, taking some deep breaths and rubbing my hands over my face to clear any rain from my eyes. At least now I know where that sonofabitch lives. I just need to plan how to get to him.

I walk back over to the cop and roll him over on his back. Christ, his face is a mess! That knee must've broken his nose and... yup, dislocated his jaw as well. He looks like he ran face-first into a brick wall.

I check his pockets and take his badge and cell phone. I look around. Happy no one can see the body from the street, I run through the alley, out the other side, and back toward the hotel. After a couple of minutes at a light jog, I make it to the parking lot, where I see Josh leaning against the Winnebago.

"What took you so long?" he asks, smiling but unable to hide the relief in his voice.

I throw him the badge, which he catches and opens up.

"Well, they were real cops, albeit on Trent's payroll," I say. "I had a little talk with him and managed to find out where Trent bases himself."

"Really?" he asks. "That's brilliant!"

I nod. "I know. Didn't shoot anyone, either..."

He scoffs. "Only because you didn't take your guns with you."

We both smile. "What happened with you anyway?"

Without a word, Josh opens the side door to the

Winnebago, revealing an unconscious police officer on the floor. He looks back at me and shrugs. "I had to improvise."

I laugh and climb in the back, stepping over the body and sitting down on the sofa against the back window. Josh climbs in after me, shuts the door, and rests against one of his worktops.

"There's something else," I say, drying my face with a cloth that was lying on the floor. "The cop said that Trent's got the entire city after me. That's how they found us so fast."

Josh let's out heavy sigh. "Damn. Shit just got real, huh?"

"Big time," I say, raising my eyebrows in agreement.

"So, what now?"

I massage my temples and stroke my three-day old beard for a moment, thinking. Only one option is making any sense to me. I catch myself subconsciously scratching the scar running down my left cheek, from just below my eye to just above my jaw. A gift from an old acquaintance...

"We need to lie low until we figure out the next move," I say, finally.

He nods, seeing where I'm going.

"Allentown?" he asks.

I sit back and rest my head against the back windshield. "Allentown."

22:27 EDT

We went back to our suites in the Hilton and gathered our things, then hit the road. We took the I-76 through Harrisburg. The weather's been horrific, with almost zero visibility the entire journey. As we slowly lost what daylight we had, the traffic has crawled to a near-standstill.

"This was meant to take five hours," Josh says impatiently. "We've been on the road for nearly eight."

"You want me to drive?" I ask.

"Nah, it's all right."

"Well, quit whining, then."

I smile as he gives me the finger.

"I just hate being stuck in traffic..." he explains. He gestures with his hand out the front windshield at the vehicles ahead of us that are barely moving.

Another car cuts across us with hardly any space to move. Josh starts punching the horn in time to his cursing.

"You! Piece! Of! Shit!" he yells.

I smile to myself, sit back, and close my eyes.

We're probably still about an hour out, and it's almost ten-thirty. I imagine we'll end up camping out in the Winnebago for the night, then go and see Manhattan first thing in the morning.

Everything lights up outside for a split-second as lightning explodes across the night sky, followed a few seconds later by a loud rumble of thunder.

"Jesus," he murmurs. "Not seen weather this bad in a while."

"Doesn't look like it'll let up any time soon either," I add.

We hear a phone ring. We both look at each other and frown.

"Is that you?" I ask.

"Not me," he replies, shrugging.

"Me neither."

I look over my shoulder into the back of the van, trying to listen and pinpoint where the ringing is coming from. I follow the sound and realize it's originating from the phone

I took off Trent's pet cop. I get up and walk over to it, picking it up curiously. I look at the screen.

"Huh."

"What's up?" asks Josh, quickly glancing over his shoulder.

I hold the phone up to show him. "It's Trent," I say.

His eyes go wide. I feel a nervous excitement wash over me.

"You gonna answer it?" he asks.

I smile and answer it, pressing the speaker button as I sit back down next to Josh.

"Yeah?" I say casually.

"What the fuck took you so long to answer your goddamn phone?" yells Trent. "What's happening? Did you find him?"

I close my eyes and take a long, slow, calming breath. I'm about to declare war, and once I do, it will only end in either his death or mine. The point of no return.

I open my eyes again. Every aspect of myself has been removed so that only my Inner Satan remains, and he's about to have a conversation he's been anticipating for close to a decade.

"Yeah, they found me," I reply.

There's a moment of silence on the line.

"Who is this?" Trent demands.

"It's the Grim Reaper, asshole," I reply through gritted teeth.

"You?"

"Me."

"Where are the cops?"

"I left one in an alleyway with a broken face. The other is bound, gagged, and unconscious in the back of my van.

Had to keep knocking him out though. Inconsiderate asshole kept waking up."

More silence.

"You're a dead man," says Trent.

"You first."

"You killed my son!"

"You killed my wife and daughter. Do you really want to start a game of who owes whom?"

"What's it been? Eight years since you ran like a fucking pussy?"

I take a deep breath, resisting every urge I have to let his words get to me.

"A lot can happen in eight years," I say.

"I'm gonna find you, and when I do, I'm gonna—"

"You're gonna what? Assume I'm still the inexperienced, wet-behind-the-ears amateur who unknowingly shot your boy in the face? Then what? You gonna shout and curse at me some more? Remind me of what you did to my family? Listen to me, you sonofabitch—you ask around, all right? Adrian Hughes died eight years ago. The monster I am now, *you* created, and I've earned the reputation that precedes me. I'm coming for you, you piece of shit, and I'm gonna bury you and anyone who dares get in my way."

I hang up, wind the window down, and throw the phone across the interstate. I take a few deep breaths to calm myself and close the door on my Inner Satan once again, then turn to Josh. He's staring straight ahead at the road, eyes still wide.

"What?" I ask.

He shakes his head. "Nothing. I just forget sometimes how much of a scary bastard you can be."

I sit back and relax.

That was nothing compared to what I have planned for Wilson Trent.

We drive on through the storm for another half-hour in silence. Then another ringing phone sounds out. This time, it *is* mine. I look at the screen. An unknown number. I look at Josh and shrug before answering.

"Hello?" I say with a sigh.

"Adrian? It's Jimmy Manhattan."

I roll my eyes and mouth *Manhattan* silently to Josh, who mirrors my reaction.

"And what can I do for you?" I ask.

"I was wondering if you'd given any more thought to my offer?"

"As it happens, Jimmy, I have. Due to some unforeseen circumstances, I have a window in my schedule to fit you in. We're driving to Allentown as we speak to come and see you. I was gonna surprise you, but we've been stuck on I-76 for hours."

"Excellent news!" he says, sounding pleased, although I detect a hint of relief in his voice as well. "I'll arrange for you to spend the night at The Carrington with me. Head straight there and we'll discuss the details in the morning over breakfast."

"Don't get carried away and start thinking we're friends, Jimmy. I'm only coming to see you to talk. I've not agreed to anything yet."

"No, no—of course. Tell the front desk when you arrive that you're there to see me. They'll show you to your rooms."

"Fine, whatever," I say before hanging up.

"So?" asks Josh, looking over.

"We have rooms at The Carrington Hotel being arranged for us, courtesy of Mr. Manhattan. We're to head straight there, apparently."

He raises his eyebrows. "Ooh, nice! See? This is how we should be living, Boss—five-star all the way!"

I shake my head and laugh. "Whatever lights your candle, Josh."

I sit back, put my feet up on the dash, and rest my head back against the seat.

What the hell have I let myself in for?

17
___

WILSON TRENT

Wilson Trent stared at the phone in his hand as the line went dead. He hated cell phones. Whenever he was angry, he could always slam the receiver on a normal phone down on the base unit. But with a cell, it was hard to express how angry he was when he simply pressed a button to hang up. He settled instead for launching it across his penthouse office into the far wall. It smashed and scattered on the floor.

His two enforcers were with him. Duncan sat on one of the sofas in front of the desk. Bennett was leaning against the wall over by the door.

"Everything all right, Mr. Trent?" he asked.

Trent regarded him for a moment. He actually quite liked him and Duncan. They'd been in his service for several years and were both capable men. They were smart enough not to ask too many questions, and they were the epitome of loyal.

"*That* was that fucking bastard, Hughes!" he shouted,

pointing at the remains of the phone. "Two of our cops found him and he took them out."

He let his words trail off as his anger superseded his ability to form coherent sentences.

"You want us to go after him?" asked Duncan, standing up almost to attention.

Trent shook his head. "No, but I want you to ask around. Find out who this guy thinks he is."

"What do you mean?" he asked.

"He said he's here to kill me, and that he's not the person I think he is. So, I wanna be ready for when he comes at me."

"You got nothin' to worry about, Mr. Trent," said Bennett, walking over to join his partner. "He's one guy, and you took out his family already. He's desperate. What can he possibly do to you?"

Trent pointed a finger at him. "Complacency is the mother of all fuck-ups," he said. "Find out who he is and why he's so goddamn confident."

He picked up a copy of Adrian's picture off his desk and threw it at Duncan, who picked it up off the floor and quickly showed it to Bennett. They studied it together for a moment, then looked up at Trent.

"Leave it with us, Mr. Trent," said Duncan. "We'll find the bastard."

They turned and left, leaving Trent alone in his office. He turned and stood looking out the window at the thunderstorm currently battering down on the city.

His city.

He wasn't afraid of the threats Hughes made. Not by a long shot. But he wasn't stupid, either. There was an old saying: forewarned is forearmed. He wanted to make sure that he was fully prepared for him when he attacked. And he believed that he *would* attack. It would be a futile attempt, of course, but he was clearly a desperate man, like Duncan had said—consumed by some glorified revenge mission. And desperate men could be capable of immense things.

Wilson Trent was an intelligent man and had gotten to where he was by making smart decisions and executing his strategies with ruthless efficiency. He'd already put the word out to the cops in the city on his payroll, and in the morning, he'd broadcast his message statewide. Every dealer, pimp, muscle, cop, and politician in Pennsylvania would have a picture of Adrian fucking Hughes, with notice that Trent wanted him—alive, preferably, but it wasn't essential. There would be a substantial reward for whoever found him.

There was a knock on his door, which interrupted his train of thought.

"What?" he shouted, without looking.

The door opened and Bennett walked in.

"Mr. Trent?" he said.

"Thought you'd gone for the night?" he asked, finally turning round.

"I had, but I figured you'd wanna hear this right away."

"Hear what?"

"I showed the picture you gave me to the men still in the building. I gave them a description and said to put the word out to their contacts in the city to be on the lookout for Adrian Hughes."

"What do you want, a medal?" said Trent impatiently.

Bennett took a breath, holding it for a moment. "Well, one of them said they know a guy who does a bit of work now and then in the killing business. Not a shooter, just a broker for information. Anyway, he rang him there and then and gave the description. His contact told him he knew

JAMES P. SUMNER

exactly who we were looking for and that we should cut our losses and, I quote, *not fuck with the guy*."

Trent frowned as he approached something akin to concern for the first time in a long time. It seemed strange to him that a low-level no-mark who gave information to hitmen would know exactly who he was looking for. It was certainly one helluva coincidence.

"How had this guy heard of him?" he asked.

"Mr. Trent, *everyone* has heard of him. When I heard his name, even *I* had, though mostly hearsay. He's a fucking ghost story, Boss."

Trent slammed his hands on his desk with frustration. "For fuck's sake, would you grow a pair? Who is he?"

Bennett swallowed hard, almost afraid to say it out loud, for reasons he hadn't quite figured out himself. "He's Adrian Hell."

The words lingered for a moment in the silence, but Trent simply shrugged. "Never heard of him."

"He's the best there is," continued Bennett. "He's legendary. Some people even say you can't kill him."

Trent looked borderline disgusted. "Don't be fucking moronic! *I'll* kill him with my own fucking hands if I have to. He's a nobody—just a rank amateur who ran away from a fight after I tore his world apart. You say he's the best? Find a professional killer who disagrees and bring them to me. I'll pay them whatever they need to take him out if that's what it's gonna take."

Bennett looked at him for a moment and nodded. "I'll get right on it, Mr. Trent."

He left the room without another word. Trent turned back to the window and looked out, his view of the city below clouded by the rain-covered glass. He knew that somewhere out there, Adrian Hughes was planning his death.

He smiled.

"I don't care who you think you are, you piece of shit," he said to himself. "I'm gonna find you, and when I do, I'll make sure your reputation gets buried as deep as you do."

18

ADRIAN HELL

The rain eased a little during our journey, and we arrived in Allentown about an hour ago. We took a swift detour to dispose of the kidnapped cop we had in the back. We left him in the doorway of a shop on a quiet street, without his phone or wallet or badge. That should keep him entertained for a while.

As advised, we headed straight for The Carrington and checked in as guests of Jimmy Manhattan's. A porter showed us to our rooms, which were as exquisite—if not more so—than our suites at The Hilton back in Pittsburgh. Josh went straight to his room and crashed, tired after the long drive.

I grabbed a shower and changed my clothes. I'm now lying on the bed, flicking through the available channels on the TV.

My room's a modest size, but the decor and furnishing are flawless. In addition to the large, flat screen TV mounted on the wall facing the bed, there's a nice, dark wooden desk and chair in the corner against the far wall, to the right of the window. A standing lamp is to the left. The door to the bathroom is just inside the room on the left, and the facilities are lavish. The shower was powerful; it felt great after so long on the road to stand under clean, hot water for fifteen minutes.

I'm not in the mood for sleeping. I've passed the point where I feel tired, and after the run-in with the cops and the phone call with Trent earlier, my mind's racing to piece together everything I want to do in order to take him down. It's the first time I've operated without a contract, without a justifiable purpose given to me by a paying customer, as Josh had put it. I'm feeling an uneasy sense of freedom, and I'm finding it difficult not to run with the situation and lose control. I'm more conscious of it happening now, after the conversation with Josh yesterday. We need to do this right, and I have to treat it like any other job. Research, preparation, and impeccable execution.

The channels on this TV suck. Sports, pay-per-view, music... I finally settle on a local news channel. There are two guys discussing Pittsburgh's upcoming NFL game, which is taking place on Sunday. Sports never particularly interested me. I don't know why. Maybe it's because I had a daughter? If I'd had a little boy, I'd probably know all about football, baseball, hockey, and everything else.

I briefly imagine what it would've been like playing catch with my son. I soon find myself remembering all the time I spent with my baby girl, Maria. She was gorgeous. She had a big, cheeky grin that always made her look like she'd been up to no good. I smile fondly, happy in a way because I still have clear memories of my family.

I close my eyes, remembering the last time I held my beautiful daughter in my arms...

09:02 EDT

The knocking on my door wakes me up. I stand, stretch, and turn the TV off before answering it. Josh barges past me into the room, looking awake and happy.

"Hands off cocks, hands on socks, my friend!" he says as he enters. "How nice is this hotel? And the shower... my God! Adrian, you *seriously* need to try to the shower."

I'm still standing at the door, half-asleep, staring into the hallway. "Morning, Josh," I say wearily. "Do come in."

I shut the door and walk back over to the bed, sitting down heavily and falling back.

"You ready?" he asks. "It's nine o'clock. I'm starving! Plus, we're meant to meet Manhattan over breakfast."

I lift my head just enough to make eye contact. "Jesus Christ, Josh, will you calm down? You sound like... a hyperactive child on Christmas morning who's seen a bicycle-shaped present under the tree."

He raises his eyebrows and laughs. "Wow... that was really random and long-winded. Fine, take your time. Whatever. Don't mind me. I only drove for ten hours yesterday without a break and—"

"Oh my God, all right, already!" I say, sitting up and stretching again. "Come on, you whiny bitch."

He punches the air and cheers. "Now you're talkin'! I'm gonna have so much bacon, I'm gonna oink."

I stand and shake my head with half-comical, half-genuine disbelief, unable to suppress a smile. We head for the door. I open it and let Josh out. I'm about to follow him, but I stop myself. I walk quickly back inside and get my guns.

I'm not making *that* mistake again!

We walk to the elevator as I fasten the holster to my back and adjust my top so that it covers the Berettas. We ride it down to the first floor and head past the front desk to the restaurant. A waiter greets us, dressed in a neatly pressed tuxedo and bow tie.

"Morning, *Jeeves*. Has Jimmy Manhattan arrived yet?" I ask as we approach him. "We're meant to meet him here for breakfast."

The waiter looks down his nose at us in disgust. "Ah, of course. You must be Mr. Manhattan's *guest*," he says in an accent so stuck-up and pretentious, he sounds more British than Josh does. "He's not long since arrived himself. If you would follow me, please, *sir*."

I don't like Jeeves.

He turns and sets off into the restaurant, so we both follow him. He leads us to the far right. In the corner, I see Jimmy Manhattan sitting alone at a table. He stands when he sees us across the room, placing his napkin on the table.

I look at Josh. "Here we go," I say.

I quickly glance around the restaurant. The tables are decorated with a white cloth and have expensive-looking silver cutlery laid out on them. The place is probably half-full with the breakfast crowd—a mixture of businessmen, couples, and families. I look at the tables close to Manhattan.

"I count six bodyguards," I whisper to Josh as we navigate our way between tables.

"Seven," he replies. "You missed the guy on his own near the fire exit."

I look off to the right, about halfway down from where we are. There's a man sitting alone, reading a paper and drinking coffee, occasionally glancing up at Manhattan.

"Well spotted," I say with a nod.

We reach the table and Manhattan smiles, extending his hand.

"Adrian!" he says. "So glad you could make it."

"I don't shake hands, Jimmy—no offence."

His smile never falters. "Of course. Please," he says, gesturing to two empty seats at his table, "join me for breakfast."

"Can I get you anything else, sir?" the waiter asks Manhattan as Josh and I take our seats.

"No, that's fine, thank you," he says, waving him away and sitting down. He looks at me and gestures to a jug on the table. "Coffee?"

I nod and he pours me a cup. He looks at Josh, who waves in refusal.

"So, what's the job?" I ask him.

He laughs. "Straight to business. I forgot how professional you can be when you put your mind to it."

"Just don't want to hang around when I'm surrounded by all your bodyguards," I counter with a humorless smile.

There's a moment's silence. Manhattan regards us both with something vaguely resembling admiration.

"Okay," he begins. "Two weeks ago, you left me in a hospital bed, having just saved my life. From there, you killed Danny Pellaggio and traveled across the country to Pittsburgh. I, however, spent a week recovering before flying here, to Allentown, where I'm doing..." He pauses and gestures around him at the opulent expanse of the hotel. "... rather well for myself."

"If you're doing so well for yourself, why are *we* here?" asks Josh.

Manhattan looks at him and smiles. "And you must be the infamous British brains behind the legendary American mouth," he replies before looking back to me. "Tell me, Adrian, is it fate that brought us both to the same state? Or something else?"

"We're not here to discuss me," I say calmly. "You got a job for me or not?"

"My apologies," he says, ever the diplomat. "Of course. As your friend pointed out, there *has* been a particular bump on the otherwise smooth road of transition. A gentleman by the name of Johnny King refused my offer of partnership and has since responded—we suspect—by stealing from one of my newly acquired businesses and killing two of my men. I'd like him removed from the picture."

"So, this is a straightforward mob hit? Not some convoluted catastrophe like the last time you tried to hire me?" I ask.

Manhattan smiles but refrains from commenting.

"Why don't you get one of your own men to do it?" I continue. "Why me?"

"I want to make a bold statement," he replies. "I want to send a message to anyone else who might one day think of testing my authority that if they do, they will be violently eradicated without prejudice. There's no denying your reputation. And I have no problem admitting my reasons for hiring you specifically are purely for some good PR."

Josh scoffs. "So, you make it look like Adrian Hell is on your side, and everyone backs off, afraid?"

"Pretty much, yes."

I stroke my stubble and think about it. I don't work

exclusively for anyone. Never have and never will. I know some people who do, and it works well for them, but it's usually something you go for when you're starting out. I don't need any help building a reputation, and I certainly wouldn't want to limit my earning options.

But... Manhattan's plan does make sense, at least from his point of view. Appearances can be deceiving. All he's going to do is make it *look* like we're best friends, and that alone will be enough to secure his position of power for a long time. No reason why I can't benefit in much the same way. It won't do any harm, especially when I'm going after Trent. If I can make it look like I've got the backing of his only legitimate competition, it might throw him off his game and force to him to look at more than just me. With him distracted, he'll be much easier to get to.

"A hundred grand, up front," I say after a moment. "Wire transfer to a numbered account that Josh will give you."

Manhattan seems surprised but recovers instantly. "A fair price. Anything else?"

"Yeah, I want to use one of your contacts to source my hardware. And I want a favor."

His eyes narrow slightly with skepticism. "What do you have in mind?"

"Nothing... yet," I say. "But when I need you, I'll make the call, and you'll be there regardless. After that, we'll be square and can start all over again."

Manhattan's silent as he thinks about my proposal. I see in his eyes that he's looking at every angle, weighing up every pro and every con—much like I would do.

"Okay," he says, finally, breaking into a smile. "You've got yourself a deal."

Josh looks at me, silently asking if I'm sure I'm doing the right thing. I nod imperceptibly to reassure him. He then looks at Manhattan and hands him a business card with my details on it.

"Here's the account information," he says. "Let me have confirmation of payment within the hour."

His tone is formal, almost off-hand, and I can tell he doesn't approve of the deal. But I also know he understands the reasoning behind it. Manhattan, who knows me well enough to know not to screw me over, is essentially the new kingpin of Allentown, and now he owes me one. I'm in the process of attacking the kingpin of the rest of Pennsylvania, so that favor will definitely come in handy. And if all I have to do is take out a low-life wannabe nightclub owner, who's told Manhattan to go fuck himself, then so be it. I'll hardly be breaking a sweat for an invaluable return.

I stand, prompting Josh and Manhattan to do the same.

"Okay, we're done here," I say to Manhattan. "You can contact Josh with the details of where I can find this King guy, and who I can speak to about some hardware for the job. Once I know the money's in the account, I'll make my preparations and carry out the hit. All goes well, I'll be out of your city in twenty-four hours."

"I'll be in touch," he replies with a nod.

Without another word, we walk off back to the elevator, meeting the eyes of every one of the bodyguards who stare at us on the way out.

"That went well," says Josh as we walk back across the foyer and past the front desk.

"You don't approve, do you?" I reply—more of a statement than a question.

He shrugs. "I know you know what you're doing, and I understand why we're doing it. I just don't trust Manhattan."

"You should always trust your spider sense," I say. "But

we both know Manhattan's too smart to try to screw us over. He benefits from this more than we do."

"Oh, I know."

We step inside the elevator, and I press the button for our floor.

"So, what's really on your mind?" I ask as the doors close.

"Just pissed off I didn't get to eat any breakfast," he replies.

10:12 EDT

After meeting with Manhattan, we both went back to my hotel room and waited for the confirmation of the wire transfer. It came through after half an hour, and ten minutes after that, Josh got the text with the address of Manhattan's contact in the city where we can go to get some hardware. The guy he uses works out of a warehouse in an old industrial complex about five miles out from the city center. We also got the details of where our target is.

We gathered our things and headed out in the Winnebago. I'm driving while Josh works his magic on his machines to find out everything we need to take the guy out.

The clouds are dark gray, and the light rain looks destined to get heavier as the day progresses—according to the local radio station we're listening to, anyway. Even if they're right, I think it'll struggle to beat the storm we drove away from in Pittsburgh last night.

I have to admit, as I navigate my way through the traffic, it's nice to take a small reprieve from my pursuit of Trent and do a normal job for a change. It's just what I need to help me relax. The driving helps too; it allows my mind to shut down and focus on the road. They say a change is as good as a rest, but I've always worked best with routine. My own order in the otherwise chaotic existence of a broken world. I can't remember a time when I didn't crave the structure and anonymity of the life I lead. Ironically, if you look down at everyone living their lives, I imagine I'd be the more noticeable one, swimming against the current.

"This Johnny King sounds like a right prick," says Josh, interrupting my wandering thoughts as I take a left turn and change lanes. "Get this: the nightclub he owns has a VIP room that's invite-only from King himself. It's reportedly frequented by local politicians and celebrities. He's criticized by local media for—and I'm quoting one magazine here—*buying his own notoriety and acting more important than he could ever hope to be.* Then in the next breath, he's praised for sizeable charity donations and fundraising in the city to raise awareness for disadvantaged children."

"Sounds to me like the newspapers are being as fickle as always," I observe. "Even though we know he's a piece of shit wannabe mobster, you can't fault all the charity stuff, I guess."

"Despite it being an obvious smokescreen to distract from the fact he's a criminal?"

I shrug. "Those kids won't care where the money comes from..."

"Yeah, fair point. Anyway, he runs all his little enterprises from his office at the club Manhattan mentioned, The Palace, so that's as good a place as any to take him out."

"Works for me. What's the building like? Is there a back way in? How many men on site?"

"Well, looking at the map, the club's on a main street with buildings opposite and on either side. However, at the *back* of the building, there's a small parking lot and some greenery boxed in by a fence. The other side of the fence is like a mirror image but leads to the back of a bus terminal. The main building has three stories and roof access."

I glance over my shoulder at him as I pull up at a red light. "Is there a clear view of King's office from the rooftop?" I ask, hopeful.

"I've got the structural blueprints of his club, and his office doesn't have any windows. But it *is* against the back wall."

I smile as my brain races around, piecing together the hit. Images link to one another like a jigsaw, and the whole thing plays out over and over again—every possible outcome.

"Sniper rifle," I say as the lights change, and I set off again. "Perfect!"

"I can go in for clean-up after you take King out?" Josh offers with a hint of excitement in his voice.

I think about it. I can't imagine there being much resistance there during the day, and it's not like he can't handle himself.

"Sure," I nod. "You can even take my babies if you want, for luck."

"I get to use the Berettas?" he asks with excitement and disbelief.

I smile as I quickly glance back at him again. I swear to God, his eyes are so wide, they might actually just drop out of his head.

"Yeah, why not!"

"Ah, Boss, you're the best!"

We both laugh, enjoying the familiar comfort of our small unit working as normal—light-hearted preparation for a violent undertaking.

I turn another corner and notice the quality of the buildings quickly declining. Everywhere looks run-down and abandoned.

"I guess we're here," I say.

Another half-mile down the road, there's a large compound on the right. A chain-link fence surrounds it, but it has no gate—just a gap where one should be. I drive straight in and pull up in the middle of the large compound. I kill the engine and check my guns are at my back. Not that I don't trust Manhattan or anything, but y'know... I don't trust Manhattan!

"You ready?" I ask Josh.

He shuts his laptop and stands up, throwing on his hooded sweater.

"All set," he replies.

We step outside and look around. There are three huge warehouses in front of us, opposite the entrance, plus two on our left and one off to our right. Each one is the width of two houses side by side, Some of them look empty. The ground around us is dark and wet, stained from the storm the night before. There are large puddles of rainwater in potholes all around.

I can't see any signs of life, but there's a medium-sized van parked out front of the warehouse on the right. I tap Josh on the arm and point to it, and we set off walking across the yard. As we approach, I see a small door embedded in the larger entrance, which resembles a small aircraft hangar. The door opens inward and man steps out and leans against the frame, watching us.

"What's the name of this guy again?" I whisper to Josh as we approach.

"Oscar Brown," he replies.

I nod and look straight at the doorman, who's set off

walking to meet us. I hold my arms out to the side, as a gesture of peace.

"We're here to see Oscar," I shout over. "Jimmy Manhattan sent us."

"What you want with Mr. Brown?" the guy replies. His voice is low and gruff, like someone who smokes forty a day.

"I'm shopping," I say, smiling.

We all stop a few feet from one another and about twenty feet from the door. The guy looks us both up and down. He's not much shorter than I am but has a barrel chest and a round gut. He's powerful, but his muscle is obscured by years of what I'm guessing was heavy drinking.

"Are you a cop?" he asks indignantly.

"Are you a retard?" I reply instinctively, immediately cursing myself for engaging my mouth before my brain. It's like an impulse at any sign of a threat.

He starts to move his right hand behind his back. I react by preparing to punch him in the throat, but a voice from over by the door distracts us all.

"You must be Adrian?" it says.

The guy in front of me visibly relaxes. I look over his shoulder at the figure that's appeared by the door. He's a short man, overweight, with thinning, greasy hair, and a smile like a used car salesman. He's grinning and leaning against the doorframe with his arms folded across his chest.

"Jimmy told me you were coming," he continues. "Forgive my friend—he's just doing his job. I'm Oscar. Welcome to my supermarket!"

"No problem," I shout back as we set off walking toward the warehouse door. I muscle into the doorman's shoulder on the way past, sending him slightly off-balance.

"Be cool, Adrian," whispers Josh next to me. I wave my hand dismissively in silent response.

Oscar ushers us both through the doorway and into a kind of reception area. He follows us inside and shuts the door behind him.

"Jimmy tells me you're in the market for some hardware," he says.

I nod. "I am. Not sure I'm in the right place, though," I reply, looking around. The room we're in consists of a desk facing the door and a battered couch against the right-hand wall. And that's it. The office area runs the full width of the warehouse, but it can't be more than seven feet deep... The actual building is massive on the outside, but inside is tiny in comparison. I look at Josh. Judging by the frown on his face, he shares my confusion.

"No offence, mate," he says to Oscar. "But for a supermarket, you've not got much in the way of, y'know... anything."

Oscar smiles, probably anticipating the reaction. I'm guessing it's not the first time he's come across it. He produces a small remote control from his pocket and presses a button.

"Don't be so quick to judge," he says.

There's a rumbling somewhere in the background as mechanisms burst into life. We turn and see the entire back wall split down the middle and slide apart like giant doors. As they part, they slowly reveal more and more of what they conceal.

I have no issue admitting that my jaw has physically dropped open.

"Fuck me..." I say quietly.

"Happy Christmas..." adds Josh.

Oscar pushes past us and walks through to the warehouse proper. "Gentlemen, if you'd care to follow me," he calls over his shoulder.

We both follow him through the doors, which have now opened fully to reveal the remaining hidden area of the building. From the floor almost all the way to the ceiling are fourteen long metal shelving units, laid out in rows. They are huge! And they're full of weapons... everything from handguns to hand grenades, from rocket launchers to claymores. You name it, Oscar apparently has it.

We walk slowly, looking all around with an odd sense of wonder.

"What d'you think?" asks Oscar, who's stopped halfway down one of the aisles.

"Impressive," I reply sincerely.

"Thanks. I have a smaller complex over in Pittsburgh, but this is my main storage facility. Now, as I'm sure you can appreciate, gentlemen, I like to conduct business quickly." He gestures around him with both hands. "What do you need?"

I look quickly at Josh, silently asking if he's happy with how we intend to carry out the job. He nods back. I turn to Oscar.

"I need a high-powered sniper rifle, good for a thousand yards," I explain. "Fifty-caliber, as I need to punch through a brick wall in one shot."

Oscar thinks for a moment, then walks back past us and down the next aisle to our left. He re-appears a moment later holding a sniper rifle. It has a long, thin barrel with a disproportionately large square muzzle and a fold-down bipod stand attached to the underside of it. He smiles at me as he holds it out for me to take.

"The Steyr HS," he declares. "It'll fire the fifty-cal Browning Machine Gun rounds happily enough. Good for sixteen hundred yards."

I take it, feeling the weight, and inspect the weapon. It's pretty light—can't be more than thirty pounds.

"Very nice," I say approvingly.

"And you're in luck—that's actually the newer M1 variant with the five-round mag attachment, as opposed to the old single bolt-action model."

"Excellent. I'll take it."

"A man who knows what he wants. You got yourself a bargain there, my friend."

"Have you got a thermal imaging scope for it?"

Oscar ducks back into the aisle and re-appears moments later holding a small, long box with another even smaller box balanced on top.

"Thermal scope and fifty-cal BMG rounds," he says.

I smile, satisfied with the hardware. This place is like Disneyland!

"Bag it up," I say, handing the rifle back to him. "That's everything I need."

"You not gonna ask how much?"

"It doesn't matter about the cost," I reply with a shrug. "I don't think you'll rip me off, given how impressive and established your business is."

Oscar smiles proudly. "You good for handguns? Can never be too prepared, y'know."

I reach behind me and draw one of my custom Beretta 92FS pistols with a blood-red devil face engraved on the butt. I hold it out by the barrel, offering it to him.

"I've got it covered," I say with a smile.

He let out a low whistle as he takes it, inspecting it with a professional eye.

"Very nice," he says nodding. "These are in great condition." He hands it back and claps his hands once with a smile. "Okay, that'll be sixty-five hundred for everything."

I turn to Josh. "Would you be so kind as to pay the man?" I ask him.

Josh turns and walks back out to the reception desk with Oscar behind him, carrying my purchases. I take a deep breath and let it out with a heavy sigh, looking around at the warehouse one last time before following Josh.

Time to go to work.

19

ADRIAN HELL

We're parked across the street from King's nightclub. We left Oscar's supermarket and headed straight here, but the journey back took a little longer than before because the streets were busier, crammed with shoppers and commuters and family sedans. I'd driven here while Josh worked away on his laptop in the back. I wanted to get a feel for the place before heading for the bus terminal and settling in for the kill. After sitting at seemingly every red light in the damn city, we finally arrived here a few minutes ago.

"Looks closed to me," I say, looking at the club.

"Must just be strip joints that cater for the desperate midday crowd," Josh offers without looking up from his computer.

I smile. "You sure you're okay with going in on clean-up duty after I take care of this King asshole?"

Josh closes the laptop and looks across the street for a moment, then turns to me. "Of course," he says with a smile.

"I'm looking forward to it, and I wanna help. Not just sit here and talk you through everything like always."

I notice a look in his eyes. A twinkle, almost. I've not seen it since we'd arrived in Pittsburgh a few days ago. He looks like his old self—not the worrying, vaguely depressed old woman I've managed to turn him into over the last week. It's great to see and it gives me a boost as well. It's good to be on a normal job, back in the old routine, away from the self-inflicted drama of Wilson Trent. It's not just therapy for me; it's something I think we're both long overdue.

I reach behind me and unfasten my holster, handing it over to Josh. These are my pride and joy... my babies. I used to have the 92A1 variants, but I lost them. These were a gift, replacements from a friend back in San Francisco.

Christ... my time there feels like another life entirely.

The guns sway back and forth gently as I hold them up, presenting them to Josh almost like a badge of honor.

"Be good to them, and they'll be good to you," I say.

Josh reaches over and takes them from me. "I feel like we're missing the bright light shining down through the clouds, illuminating the power I now hold in my hands," he says, laughing. He looks me in the eyes. "I've got your back, Boss."

"I know," I say. "Come on, you sentimental old woman. Let's go get into position."

We switch seats and Josh starts the engine. He pulls away from the curb and drives us around the block to the staff parking lot at the back of the bus terminal, which over-looks the back of King's club. I climb out, stretch my arms and back, and crack my neck. Then I pause to take a good look around.

The back of the parking lot has a chain-link fence around its perimeter. Across from it is the rear entrance to

The Palace, separated by a small alleyway which runs in between the properties. There are a couple of trees around but nothing to obscure my view. Behind me is the main office building of the bus terminal, which is three stories high and has access to the roof by way of a fire escape that climbs up the wall facing the parking lot. From the rooftop, I'll have an unimpeded view of the club.

I open the side door of the Winnebago and take out the sports bag containing my recent acquisition. I feel a rush of adrenaline as I sling it over my shoulder, feeling the comfortable and familiar weight of the weapon inside. Not counting my little escapade on Alcatraz, it's been a long time since I've used a sniper rifle for a hit. There's something oddly satisfying about watching your target drop from a thousand yards away, having never seen the bullet coming.

Josh has fixed the holster in place and is putting his earpiece in as he walks over.

"All set?" he asks, handing me an earpiece of my own.

"Good to go," I say, taking it from him and putting it in place.

We quickly check that our comms are working, and then set to work.

"Wait at the back entrance for my signal," I say. "Once you're inside, don't take all day. Sweep quickly and cleanly up to his office, confirm the kill, and get outta there. Clear?"

"Crystal, Boss. Don't worry about me, okay? I got this."

And I believe him. We've been through a lot together over the years. He wasn't always my own personal nerd. He was—and still is—a capable soldier. And like he said to me a few days ago, practice doesn't do anyone any harm.

We bump fists and head our separate ways without another word. I take a quick look around. Seeing there aren't too many people nearby, I sprint over to the fire escape. I notice just the one security camera, which is covering the back door to the building. It's static and easily avoidable, so I'm confident no one will see me. I hadn't expected much in the way of security. I mean, who in their right mind would want to break into a bus terminal?

Luckily, the ladder on the fire escape is already down, so I climb up and make my way to the first platform. It doesn't take long. As I step onto it, I look across the parking lot and see Josh scaling the fence behind the club. He drops down into a crouch, waits thirty seconds, then heads over to the back door, keeping low.

I smile to myself and carry on. I move quickly along the platform and up the next flight of steps, then again until I come out on the rooftop. Despite the heavy cloud and the high mist that indicates a pending shower, I have a good view all around me. I pause for a moment to soak it in. There's a closed maintenance door on the roof leading into the building.

I'm all alone up here.

I crouch down at the edge of the roof, looking across to King's club. I can see Josh in position, waiting patiently, ever aware of his surroundings. I set the sports bag down and unzip it, taking out the Steyr HS rifle. I look at it approvingly for a moment. I take out the thermal scope and carefully attach it into place, making sure I don't remove the lens cap until the last minute, to avoid any flare-up that might give away my position.

You never know who's watching...

Next, I load a clip of ammunition with the fifty-cal rounds and slide it into the horizontal receiver on the barrel, slamming it firmly into place. I push the bipod stand down into place and lie down on my front, adjusting myself until I'm comfortable.

I might be here a while.

I lift the rifle into place in front of me. I tuck the stock into my shoulder and flip the lens cap up, so I can look through the scope. I use my left hand to adjust the focus and activate the thermal imaging. The world goes dark, and the heat signatures of everyone around me appear in my line of sight in a blur of reds, blues, and yellows. I look at Josh crouching by the exit.

"I see you," I whisper into my earpiece.

"Good," he replies. "Any sign of life?"

I look up at the back wall, where I know King's office is, and scan the area. "Nothing yet. We just need to play the waiting game now."

"Copy that."

An important part of this job is patience. Ironic, given my general lack of it. But when I'm working, it's different. If need be, I might have to wait hours for King to show.

12:21 EDT

"I've got movement," I say to Josh. "Two targets are in the office now—one standing, walking back and forth, the other sitting down."

"The guy sitting down has got to be King, right?" he replies.

"That would be my guess, yeah, but I'll take them both out to be safe."

I take a long, slow breath, steadying my heart rate and composing myself. I line the crosshairs up on the colorful image of King's head, adjusting slightly for the wind.

"Got him in my sights," I confirm, tweaking the focus slightly.

I take another deep breath, and everything slows down around me. The individual background noises sound off to me in turn. I can hear the chaotic bustle of the traffic on the Boulevard... the gentle roar of the water from the river... a bird squawking overhead, lost in the clouds. After each one registers in my ears, it disappears from my radar, eventually leaving an unnatural silence. It's in this moment when I prepare myself, focusing on the task at hand.

The sound of the shot will be loud—especially a fifty-caliber round—but it shouldn't attract too much attention. I'll be long gone before anyone tracks down the source of it anyway.

"Ready when you are, Boss," Josh says.

I move the scope subtly back and forth, practicing the shot. King's head—BANG! Quick to the right, second target's chest—BANG! Job done. I replay it almost a dozen times. I'm maybe eleven hundred yards away. At this distance, I need only move the barrel of the gun a millimeter or so. The movement is so precise, the slightest error in judgment on my part and I'll miss my shot by ten feet.

I re-focus on King and line up the shot once again. My finger tightens on the trigger. I slow my breathing down, steady my arms, and push my weight forward, planting my feet into the ground so that I have a firm base.

One breath, in and out.

A second, in and out—slower this time.

The third, in... and out as I squeeze gently on the trigger. The gunshot's louder than I anticipated, and the recoil slams the stock into my shoulder. The bullet traveled the distance in a fraction over a second, punching through the wall and into the back of Johnny King's head. I see the figure through the scope slump to the floor, motionless; the heat signature slowly fades away. I quickly line up and fire at the second target in the next breath, hitting him in the chest. He, too, falls to the floor.

I take a deep breath and let it out with relief.

"You're up," I say to Josh.

I place the rifle down and get up into a crouch as I watch him enter the building. I pack everything away, then hastily make my way down the fire escape and back over to the Winnebago. I put the sports bag in the back and get in behind the wheel. I sit and focus on my breathing, urging the adrenaline rush to subside. I tap my fingers on the wheel impatiently as I wait for Josh to come back out.

Five minutes pass. I'll admit I'm starting to worry. I've not heard any gunshots, but I'm not sure I would from this distance anyway. Finally, a few moments later, he appears in the back doorway. He walks casually toward the back of the parking lot, clears both fences with an ease not befitting his age, and climbs into the passenger seat next to me.

"All good?" I ask.

His face is solemn and his eyes are serious. I was expecting him to look more... I don't know—*alive* after coming out of there.

"I think we just cemented ourselves in the annals of history as being the two most unlucky bastards ever to walk God's green Earth," he says.

I sigh.

"Of course, we did. What's happened now? It wasn't King we killed, was it?"

"Oh, yeah, you took out King—great shot, by the way. Manhattan will be well pleased. I swept the building, managed to take down the three other guys in there without firing a shot."

"Nice."

He shrugs modestly. "Thanks. I got to King's office, saw him and another guy dead, and thought, great—a nice, clean hit. I figured I'd have a look at his papers and on his computer, to see if there was anything of interest. May as well, while I was there."

"Can't hurt," I agree, nodding.

"I found a lot of accounts information, which I'm sure Manhattan will be glad of. I downloaded them to a flash drive I happened to have on me. I always carry one just in case I ever need it."

"So, what's the problem?"

"I had a quick read through his financials," he says. "Johnny King used his club for many things, most of them illegal. Including but not limited to laundering money for various gangsters and corrupt politicians within the state."

"Right..."

"Want to have a guess which gangster in particular was his biggest client?"

His words hang there for a moment as a painful silence descends.

"Johnny King worked for Wilson Trent..." I say, closing my eyes and massaging the bridge of my nose in frustration.

"He basically ran Allentown for him, which accounted for a sizeable percentage of Trent's overall income," Josh confirms. "And we just killed him. Well... *you* just killed him." He turns and pats my shoulder. "Nice going."

I laugh, more out of disbelief than humor. "For fuck's sake..."

20

WILSON TRENT

Wilson Trent had hardly slept the night before. He was too angry to think about resting. All he could focus on was Adrian Hughes and how much he wanted to kill him. And what made things worse was that everyone seemed intimidated by the guy. They seemed to have forgotten it was *him* they should be scared of. They had forgotten what he would do to them if they failed to bring him Adrian's head on a silver platter.

Trent sat eating his lunch in a small restaurant not far from his personal skyscraper. It was busy, due to the lunchtime crowd, but he was a regular and... well, he was Wilson Trent. He had a table to himself at the back of the room, with three men guarding him. The waitresses knew to give him a wide berth, only approaching his table to deliver food and take empty plates away.

It was a nice place, well decorated with a slightly overpriced menu. Trent enjoyed the seafood pasta dish they served there and had been a regular customer for a several years.

He'd instructed Duncan and Bennett to put the word out and find a contract killer who was up to the task of taking that sonofabitch Adrian Hughes down, and he'd yet to hear back from them.

He had, however, been contacted by the manager of the Hilton hotel, which was only a few blocks away from where he was sitting. He'd informed him that two police officers were there the night before, looking for a man who was staying with them, fitting Adrian's description. They'd approached him, and they gave chase when he ran, but he hadn't seen either the police or Adrian since. This just added salt to the wound for Trent. He knew perfectly well what had happened to the police officers he paid a small fortune to, having spoken with Adrian himself the other night.

Trent took some solace in the fact that at least the hotel manager was doing his job and reporting to him, but that still did nothing to subdue his anger or reduce his blood pressure to a healthier level. If anything, it actually made matters worse. He knew *exactly* where Adrian was now but still couldn't do anything about it. He needed someone professional to go after him.

Send a snake to catch a snake.

Just then, the door opened and Trent happened to look up as a woman walked in. She looked around the place casually before setting off across the room.

She was exceptionally beautiful and emitted an aura of confidence in her leggy stride. She had long, dark hair and an olive complexion. Her tanned skin gave her an Eastern look. As she passed by the tables, every man in the restaurant stopped and stared—even those sat with other women. Her tight jeans were tucked into brown knee-high boots, and the cropped tank top she wore revealed more than it covered. As she approached Trent's table, one of his body-guards stepped forward to meet her. He was a tall, broad man wearing a suit and an earpiece.

"Hold up," he said, holding his hand up to her. "This is a private table."

She eyed the three men in turn before directing her gaze at Trent. He looked her up and down.

"Help you, sweetheart?" he said, leaning to the side slightly to look past his bodyguard at the woman.

She smiled a strange kind of half-smile—almost a smirk —that made her look even more attractive. The more he stared, the more Trent's guard dropped. He was smart enough to acknowledge it was a clever tactic, but he wouldn't allow himself to fall victim to it.

"If your boys here let me sit with you, I think you'll be very interested in how *I* can help *you*," she replied.

The guard in front of her turned to Trent for instruction, who simply nodded. He stepped to one side to let her through. As she strode past him, she ran her hand slowly down his chest, causing him to stare straight ahead and take a deep breath.

"Thanks, big boy," she whispered with a smile.

She slid into the chair opposite Trent, sitting side-on to the table so that he could see her crossing her long, toned legs slowly. She rested her elbow on the table and leaned her chin on the back of her hand.

"So," said Trent, "how can *you* help me?"

She remained silent for a moment, then said, "I hear you're looking for a professional to dispose of someone."

Trent let out an involuntary laugh before composing

himself. "Sweetheart, I don't know who you think you are, but I'm after an assassin, not a hooker. I might have a job for you in one of my clubs, though."

She smiled at him, but this time there was no humor or flirtation.

"I'm here looking for work, so I'm going to let that one slide," she replied. "But if you insult me again, I'm gonna slit your throat open, then reach inside and pull your balls out. We clear?"

Trent raised an eyebrow and regarded her for a moment. He liked her attitude. Maybe he had jumped the gun a little with his first impression...

"What's your name?" he asked.

"Dominique."

"Okay, Dominique. How did you know where to find me?"

"I'm good at my job," she said matter-of-factly.

"Okay," he said after a moment. "You're hired. Your target is staying in the Hilton not far from here. I want him dead. And his friend. Leave me your details, and I'll wire one point five million dollars to your account, up front. Just get it done."

She raised an eyebrow. "Who's the target?"

Trent shook his head impatiently. "It shouldn't matter who the target is. Just kill them. I've told you where they are, so go and do the job you came here to apply for before I change my mind and have you removed from my table."

She rolled her eyes and was about to say something, but Trent cut her off.

"And just because you waltz in here with your sexy strut and your attitude, don't think that counts for anything. You can make all the idle threats toward me that you want, but

One Last Bullet

make no mistake, sweetheart. I'm the worst kind of bad guy, and I'll gut you like a fucking fish and string you up by your insides. Do not fuck with me."

Dominique paused, then nodded. "Consider it done," she said before standing and walking off past the body-guards. As she did, the one who stopped her when she first arrived smiled at her menacingly.

"How's about me and you have some fun later?" he said with a wink.

She stopped in her tracks and looked at him over her shoulder. She thought for a minute, then smiled and walked back toward him. She stopped in front of him. They were almost the same height because of the heels on her boots. She placed her hand on his chest and slowly moved it down, tugging lightly on his belt before resting on his crotch. She moved her hand up and down slowly.

"You mean... *this* kind of fun?" she said playfully.

He smiled and nodded.

Then, in a flash, her smile faded. She grabbed him hard, squeezing her hand tightly. He gasped loudly, his eyes going wide in pain as she twisted her hand slightly, applying more pressure to his most sensitive area. Some people turned to stare for a moment but hastily looked away again when they saw it was at Wilson Trent's table.

"You men are all the same," she said, looking at Trent, who was watching with bemusement. "If I were you... any of you... I'd think twice before fucking with *me*!"

She let go of the guard, who immediately bent over in pain. As he did, she brought her knee up and smashed it into his face. He grunted at the impact, then slumped forward to the floor, unconscious.

She smiled at Trent and winked before turning and

walking off, looking as confident as before, through the restaurant and out the front door.

The remaining bodyguards looked at Trent, who simply shrugged and smiled.

"I like her," he said.

21

ADRIAN HELL

We decided to ignore the unexpected link to Wilson Trent. We left King's body for his people to find, fulfilling the terms of our contract and sending a clear message on Manhattan's behalf.

It's late afternoon and the first drops of rain have begun to fall as we head back to Pittsburgh. I'm staring out the window while Josh drives, my mind rushing in a million different directions simultaneously. The morale boost was short-lived, and we're back where we started—us versus Trent, with us on the back foot.

What is it with Wilson fucking Trent anyway? Everything we do seems to lead back to him. I know his empire is far-reaching, but I had no idea he's so embedded in everyone's lives and interests. Even Manhattan's found himself on Trent's radar now, thanks to our efforts a few hours ago.

Not that I've told him yet.

I need to get to Trent before he gets to me. I can't afford

to let myself go on the defensive. I have to attack. Get my retaliation in first, so to speak.

Josh glances at me with a brief look of concern, as if deciding to try to distract me from my thoughts.

"So, do you wanna break the news to Jimmy, or shall I?" he asks.

I let out a heavy sigh. "I'll call him later and tell him," I reply, distant.

I drift off, my eyes locked on something far enough in the distance that they lose focus and the need to blink. The world flashes in front of me in an anonymous blur as I stare at absolutely nothing. Occasionally, a drop of rain draws my focus as it slashes across the window, bringing me back to the here and now, but I quickly zone out again.

"What the hell do we do, man?" I ask Josh, finally returning to the conversation. "Trent's everywhere, and it's just us trying to go against him. Talk about an uphill struggle."

"Hey, we'll be fine," he says. "Like it or not, we've got Manhattan fighting our corner for now. I'm still working away at assaulting his finances, and there's no one he can throw at us that we can't beat. We just need to pick our fights, choose our moments wisely, and not get caught out. It's a numbers game, and it's sometimes easier to win five small fights than one big one."

I rub my temples, then massage the base of my neck, where a tension headache that feels like a thousand knives has settled in for the long haul.

"Yeah, you're right," I acknowledge. "I'm just frustrated because whatever direction we seem to turn, that bastard has already made his presence felt, meaning we're poking an already pissed off bear."

We fall silent again. I figure Josh probably feels the same

way I do. We're just going around in circles and accomplishing nothing except giving our enemy more reason to want us dead.

Another twenty minutes pass before Josh speaks again.

"Okay, we've been traveling long enough that I can tell you, and there's nothing you can do about it," he says.

I look over at him, confused. "Tell me what?"

"We're taking a detour."

I frown and look out of the window again—this time paying attention to where we are and trying to figure out where he's taking me.

Josh remains silent as I look around for road signs. We're still on I-76. Given how long we've been traveling, I would expect us to be turning off for I-376 any time now. Except we're not. He's keeping left, which means we're staying with the '76, all the way toward the Allegheny River.

I sigh. I know exactly where he's taking me.

"Josh, you don't need to do this," I say.

"I think I do, Boss," he replies. "I know this is hard, but I think you need reminding why we're here and to get your head back in the game."

17:22 EDT

Josh pulls over and stops opposite a large white and grey house, on a quiet street roughly thirty minutes from the centre of Pittsburgh. I stare out the window, feeling numb as I look at the house I lived in with my family.

It feels like a lifetime since I was last here.

Josh gets out of the Winnebago without a word and stands on the sidewalk, looking at the house. It takes me a minute to join him; a flurry of emotion explodes inside my head like a thunderstorm.

I haven't seen the house since the day I left. Not since the day I found my wife and daughter murdered on the kitchen floor.

I take a deep breath.

"You all right?" he asks me.

I nod.

"You pissed at me?"

I shake my head and smile weakly, momentarily lost for words as the occasion proves too much for me.

"Good, because this... this is why you're here, Adrian," he says, pointing at the house. "No matter how shitty things might look, we both know you will not let your girls down."

My whole body relaxes. As I stand staring at my old home, a numbing sensation washes over me. I look at the windows, in desperate need of cleaning... the car parked on the drive with a baby seat in the back... the front lawn with the same rosebush that I planted the day after Janine and I moved in, still growing strong...

Josh has paced away slowly and aimlessly out of respect, giving me a moment or two alone. As I stare at the place, the image of how it used to look when I lived there bleeds through from the depths of my mind. It gives me a glimpse into the past; a happier time before my demons consumed me... before I was so passionate and serious about being a killer.

When I had genuine love in my life.

A voice drifts into my thoughts, causing the image to evaporate in front of my eyes.

"Huh?" I say absently.

"Adrian? Is that you?"

I shake my head to regain total focus and turn to my

right. There's an old man standing next to me, staring at me with a look of disbelief. He's much shorter than me, with thin gray hair and light brown eyes. He's easily eighty years old and dressed in suit pants, with a sweater vest over a white shirt and striped tie.

I frown at him for a moment, confused. Do I know him?

Oh, shit—yeah, I do. He's my old neighbor! Jesus... he remembers me?

What the hell was his name?

"It *is* you, isn't it?" he asks again, his voice frail and cracked.

"It's me," I confirm after a moment.

"Well, I'll be... we thought you were dead," he says. "After what happened, there was a lot of talk from folks around here for a long time afterward."

He lets his words trail off before extending his hand. I look down and shake it.

He nods to me. "It was a goddamn tragedy what happened here. I'm truly sorry for your loss."

I take a deep breath before letting go of his hand.

"Thank you," I say eventually. "I appreciate that."

"If I may," he starts. "What happened to you? The police were around here for weeks after they found... well, no one knew where you were. I think you were a suspect at first, but then word got around that you'd died too. Over time, the matter was simply dropped. Another unsolved crime."

"I bet," I reply, unable to hide the disdain in my voice. "I left town when I found them. I... I knew who was responsible, and I knew the police wouldn't do anything. I got scared and I ran."

The old man purses his lips together. Then he holds a finger up at me and leans forward slightly to speak.

"Don't you dare feel fuckin' sorry for yourself, son."

I can't hide my surprise at his candidness, and he undoubtedly sees the look on my face.

"Everyone knew who was to blame," he continues, gesturing to the houses around him. "I tell ya, he thinks he fuckin' runs this state. Goddamn police in his pocket, literally got away with murder." He spits on the ground, then takes a breath and coughs. "Makes me sick!" He looks me up and down, as if he's judging me. "You back to bury that sonofabitch?"

Josh appears next to me, and I quickly look at him before answering.

"What makes you think I'd be able to do something like that?" I ask cautiously.

"Ah, don't gimme that crap," he says, making a dismissive gesture with this hand. "I've lived here nearly sixty years. Seen all kinds'a things and all kinds'a folks. I never miss nothin', Adrian."

I know what he's saying without him having to spell it out to me. He knew all along what I did for a living and why Trent attacked my family. I don't know how he knows—I guess he's observant.

I hold his gaze for a moment but say nothing. After a moment, he simply nods.

"Good. That bastard deserves everything he's got coming to him. So, where you staying? Somewhere local?"

"A hotel in the city, yeah," I say. "I've just been seeing an acquaintance over in Allentown while I was around these parts."

"Well, if you're ever around here again, you make sure you call in for a coffee. Or something stronger."

"That's very kind of you," I say, extending my hand, which he shakes. "But to be honest, I don't think I'll be back around here again for a long time."

He looks at Josh briefly, giving him a curt nod, and then walks uneasily back to his house.

"What was that about?" Josh asks.

"My old neighbor was giving me his blessing to kill Wilson Trent," I reply.

"Ha! Well, now we know *he's* all right with it, we can go ahead!"

I laugh. "Come on," I say, walking back to the Winnebago. "Memory lane isn't what it used to be."

As I'm about to open the door, my old neighbor re-appears on the sidewalk, shouting my name.

"Adrian," he says. "Hey, Adrian. I got somethin' for ya."

He walks over to us, out of breath, and hands me a small photograph. It's from a Polaroid camera and shows a young man standing with a beautiful woman holding a baby in her arms.

My eyes go wide and my mouth opens in shock as I look at the picture of me with my family, taken in a different time... a different life.

"I had this picture of you," he explains. "I found it on the street when the police were searching your house, after they found them. I thought you might want it before you go."

"Thank you," I say, lost for words as I stare at the picture of everything I've lost.

"And just you remember," the old man continues. "There's that saying about a man on the road to vengeance digging two graves. You just watch yourself, ya hear?"

I look him in the eye. "You're gonna need a lot more than two by the time I'm finished."

22

JIMMY MANHATTAN

18:41 EDT

Word spread quickly of Johnny King's demise. Jimmy Manhattan knew the few hours after his death were crucial. That was when panic set in and people instinctively looked for someone to turn to. When they found no one, that's when the fighting would start. And by the time the dust had settled and the victor had emerged, enough would've been destroyed in the process that they ended up being in charge of nothing. He'd learned from his time working with Roberto Pellaggio that it's best to act swiftly and decisively.

Upon hearing King was found dead in his office, Manhattan immediately sent Tarantina and three other men to The Palace to establish his presence and quash any concerns people there may have had. He gave Tarantina instructions to kill anyone who challenged their authority without hesitation.

As expected, it was necessary to make one or two examples, but the rest fell in line soon after. Tarantina had stayed at The Palace, organizing the newly acquired businesses and personnel. And that was that. Manhattan now completely ran Allentown without opposition. After a few moments to allow everything he'd accomplished to soak in, he set to work figuring out how to get the rest of the state.

The first and most obvious hurdle to get over was the discovery that the rest of Pennsylvania was owned and run by a man named Wilson Trent. A quick look through King's financial records told Manhattan that he laundered money through his nightclub for Trent.

Manhattan had done some digging and made some calls. It turned out that Wilson Trent wasn't exactly a hard man to find out about. Any aspect of the city worth controlling, or illegal enterprise worth starting, Trent did it years ago.

He'd actually heard the name many years prior, when Pellaggio was still completing his takeover of Nevada. Trent had always been a player, but he was never in the major leagues. It was only in the last decade or so when he really came into power, and he did so in a big way.

It hadn't taken long to get a good idea of how far and wide Trent's reach stretched. But what was interesting was the discovery of Adrian Hell's relationship with him. A former employee of Johnny King's had proven most helpful in detailing why Trent was so irate that Adrian had resurfaced on the East Coast after a prolonged absence. And the more Manhattan learned, the happier he became.

If he had one regret in life, it was hiring Adrian Hell for that job back in Heaven's Valley. It made perfect sense to do so, given he was the best hitman money could buy. But he was... different. He asked questions. He thought too much. It made him great at his job but also a major pain in the ass for anyone hiring him. Manhattan had hated him ever since, and the only memories that made him smile were the ones where he was causing that bastard pain.

He had played the diplomat with him earlier in the day, as it was good for business, and it had proven a wise choice. Within three hours of giving him the contract, Johnny King was dead. Tarantina subtly leaked the fact they'd hired Adrian to do it, so everyone in the city now associated him with Manhattan. So, now he was untouchable. People would be too afraid to cross him because he'd let Adrian Hell loose on them.

Or so they thought.

But by sheer coincidence—or fate, if one believed in such things—that relationship with Adrian had now put Manhattan firmly in Trent's crosshairs. Both he and Adrian Hell now had a common enemy. His only viable option was approaching Trent as a businessman and appealing to his sense of enterprise. And Manhattan would be the first to admit that he didn't like his chances of success.

Adrian Hell, however, wasn't known for his diplomacy. From what he'd heard, he seemed intent on tearing the world apart for an opportunity to kill Trent, and justifiably so.

Like a chessboard, Manhattan was positioning all the pieces, ready for his final assault on the king. He knew that if he played things right, he could help Adrian take out Trent—which he figured was the favor he had mentioned to him that morning over breakfast. But he needed to do it in such a way that he was also setting him up at the same time, so when Trent was gone, Manhattan could step in, take out Adrian, and take control of the throne of Pennsylvania.

He could see it all so clearly in his mind. His trick was to start with the endgame and work backward, looking at every possible scenario that could come before and what preceded that... and so on, until in the end, he was left with the perfect place to start.

He had a good idea of what path Trent would take, as they were similar people. And he'd had vast experience with Adrian's frame of mind. Coupled with what Manhattan assumed he would be feeling at the moment, he was predictable to the point where he almost felt sorry for him. He wondered how long it would take Adrian to tell him about the link to Wilson Trent. He must be aware of it himself by now, and the fact he hadn't been in touch already to discuss it just proved he couldn't be trusted. All the more reason to make sure he was taken out of the picture once and for all.

Manhattan was sitting at a table in The Carrington's restaurant, eating a lobster salad and drinking a glass of champagne. He couldn't help smiling to himself at how well things had fallen into place. And, more to the point, how much better he was doing now that he was in charge and not taking orders from someone else.

His phone rang, interrupting his musings.

"Yes?" he answered.

"It's me," replied Tarantina. "Just wanted to let you know everything's in order over here. I've given the books to our accountant, who's distributing our new funds accordingly across our businesses. Some of the new recruits are asking questions, but it's nothing I can't handle."

"That's excellent news, Paulie. You've done well today."

"Thank you, Mr. Manhattan. You ain't done so bad your-self. How's it feel owning the city?"

He paused to take another sip of champagne.

"It's but a small step on a much longer road," he said. "But today we can celebrate."

"Drinks are on you, Boss."

Manhattan smiled and hung up.

23

ADRIAN HELL

I made Josh stop for some food and a few drinks on the way back to our hotel. He didn't want to, but I figured he owed me and he wasn't about to argue. It's been a long and eventful day, and we've got plenty to think about. Not going to figure this out on an empty stomach.

We waited a few minutes before getting out of the Winnebago to make sure no one had followed us or was scoping the place out. Happy we were in the clear, we crossed the street and headed inside.

"I'm gonna grab a shower and crash," I say to Josh, as we stand outside our rooms. "Come and get me in the morning. We'll grab some breakfast and plan our next move."

"Sounds good," he replies.

I take my keycard out of my pocket and move to swipe it on the keypad next to my door, but I notice my door's already open, standing slightly ajar. I instantly reach behind me for my guns, but I've left them in the Winnebago...

Shit! I *really* need to stop doing that!

"Josh," I whisper.

He's halfway into his room when he stops and turns. I silently point to my door. He nods once and instinctively takes up position on one side of the doorway. I lean against the wall across from him. We communicate in silence using our hands. On the count of three, I'm going to push the door open and dash inside, dropping low and moving to the side of the bed for cover. Josh will follow, staying high and ducking just inside the bathroom, using the door for protection.

I count on my fingers...

One...

Two...

Three!

I move in front of the door and kick it open. I run in and dive at the side of the bed, quickly scanning the room. I hear Josh coming in behind me. I can't see that anything's been visibly disturbed or stolen—not that I've left many belongings in the room anyway. The only thing different from what I remember is the chair by the window. It's not empty anymore.

Sitting in it is one of the most extraordinarily beautiful women I've ever seen in my life. She's sat with her legs crossed, smiling at me with amusement and curiosity. I stand slowly, keeping eye contact with her.

"Josh, I think we're fine," I call out.

He appears from inside the bathroom and steps out into the room, standing next to me.

"*Very* fine!" he says, smiling, looking at the mystery woman with an approving eye.

She tilts her head slightly. Her smile changes to an inquisitive smirk that further accentuates her beauty.

I hold my hands out to the side, showing I have no weapons. My palms are open as a passive gesture, signaling that I pose no threat.

"Are we good here?" I ask her.

She stands and draws a gun from behind her with a speed I don't mind admitting I'm impressed by. She holds it professionally in both hands and aims it first at me, then at Josh. When she speaks, her sultry voice has a strong accent that I can't quite place. That intoxicating smile on her face hasn't faltered once. She raises an eyebrow.

"We're great."

She's quite tall, maybe five-ten, with long, dark, straight hair that's shining like a shampoo commercial. She has skin-tight jeans tucked into brown, knee-high boots that have impractically high heels on them. Her tank top is a couple of inches too short, exposing her toned midriff, and the neckline is low enough to show off her ample breasts. It's like a car crash—as much as I don't want to look, I can't help it.

Come on, Adrian. Get it together. You're acting like you've never seen a woman holding a gun before!

I take a deep breath and focus. That accent... where's she from? If I can figure that out, I might be able to work out who she is. My gut's telling me she's in the business.

"I know you, don't I?" Josh says, breaking my train of thought.

I look over at him, surprised. "Josh, you sly dog... you kept this one quiet!"

She raises an unimpressed eyebrow at me and turns to look at him. She regards him impassively for a moment. Her eyes narrowing slightly as she tries to remember if she's met him before.

Without warning, she swings her gun round and pulls the trigger, shooting Josh in the arm, just below his left shoulder. He falls to the floor, letting out a grunt of pain as he lands. Blood spreads slowly across the carpet from his wound. He clutches at it, applying pressure with his right hand to stem the bleeding.

"Josh!" I yell. I immediately rush toward her, but she quickly takes a step back, adding distance between us, and re-aims her gun at my head with ruthless efficiency. I stop in my tracks and put my hands out to the sides again.

"I'm all right," he says through gritted teeth. "It's just a flesh wound and only hurts... a lot, actually."

"Okay, enough," I say to the mystery woman. "Who the fuck are you? And why are you in my hotel room?"

"Your friend's right," she says. "He *does* know me. We briefly crossed paths a few years ago. However, *we've* never met, Adrian."

I look over at Josh, who's managed to sit himself up against the wall. His hand's stained with dark crimson from his wound, and he's fading in and out of consciousness, presumably due to blood loss.

"Well, he never mentioned you," I say. "You couldn't have been that memorable."

She laughs. "Oh, your words hurt me. Your trademark verbal offense, as advertised. I'm truly in the presence of greatness!" She sits down again, never taking her gun off me. The barrel is steady and aimed perfectly between my eyes. "It is an honor to meet the *legendary* Adrian Hell."

Ignoring her obvious sarcasm for a moment, I have to admit it *is* nice when my reputation precedes me. It proves I've been doing something right all this time, I suppose. But still, when a strange woman breaks into my hotel room and shoots my best friend... pleasantries aside, she's skating on thin fucking ice.

I look her up and down again—this time with a more

professional eye. She has toned legs, and the skin-tight jeans accentuate her well-developed muscles. She's in great condition. Those thighs could probably crush a man to death.

Her skin is like silk, blemish-free and tanned. She's covered up pretty well, despite the obvious fashion statement with her breasts. But her arms are the key—again, muscular in a delicate kind of way. But I can just about make out part of a tattoo on the top of her right shoulder, which I'm assuming runs down her back or side. It looks like a dragon...

My initial instinct was right—she's a trained killer. And she has to be in the business because she knows me. I thought she might've been Iranian at first, but having heard more of her voice, I think she's Israeli. She's younger than I am but probably older than she looks. I'd say maybe late thirties. Possibly former Mossad or Shabak. Either way, she's definitely had extensive training.

"Listen, I'm sure this is a very big day for you," I say. "Meeting me... waiting in my room for me like a horny little groupie. Your whole life has likely been building to this very moment. But for me it's just Saturday. And you just shot someone close to me. So, I suggest you drop the gun and start talking. Otherwise, you might find yourself prematurely giving up breathing."

She's still smiling. As nice as it is to look at it, it's starting to get a little weird. She also seems confident and comfortable pointing a gun at me. And given she knows who I am, that actually speaks volumes.

"You talk a lot," she says, seemingly unfazed.

"Yes... yes, I do."

"You think you're smarter than everyone else."

"And funnier. And more talented."

"Your little routine probably works on most people, right?"

"More often than not."

"I'm not *most people*."

"Yeah, I figured that out already."

"But have you figured out who I actually am?"

"If I were to guess? I'd say a professional assassin, hired to either kill me or capture me. The smart money would be on Wilson Trent signing your paycheck, given I don't have many other enemies."

"Ha!" she scoffs. "I find that hard to believe, Adrian."

"No, it's true. Mostly because all but two of them are dead. I don't take too kindly to people who try to kill me."

"Well, I am not your enemy."

"In that case, your impression of a friend is fucking terrible."

"No, I simply mean I have no personal hatred toward you. I'm just doing a job, end of story. Is that any comfort?"

"Not really, no."

She shrugs. "Oh. Well, I tried."

I smile humorlessly, tiring of trading verbal blows with her. "So, what now? You gonna shoot me?"

She pulls an oddly cute face as she pretends to think about it. "Hmm... I'm not sure. I *do* get a lot of money if I do..."

"Really? How much?"

"One point five to make you dead."

"Million? Is that it? I'm hurt that my life isn't valued higher."

She rubs her temple with the barrel of her gun, seemingly frustrated. "You're a very strange man, Adrian."

I shrug. "So people tell me. What's your name?"

She stands and flashes me a smile that I'm sure has

broken many men's hearts in the past. And probably their necks.

"I'm Dominique Tevani," she announces.

I raise my eyebrows with genuine surprise. I've actually heard of her, purely by reputation. She's a damn good killer if you believe the rumors. Never met her or seen a picture, though. She's certainly attractive, which I figure is a well-utilized weapon in her arsenal.

Trent isn't messing around if he's gone looking for someone of her caliber. There are only a few people in the business better than her, by all accounts. Luckily for me, I'm one of them.

"What if I offered you two million to go back and say you never found me?"

Her smile finally fades. Her expression changes to one of confusion and something resembling disappointment.

"Adrian Hell, bartering for his life? Definitely not what I'd expect from someone with a reputation such as yours..."

I smile. "I'm not bartering for anything," I reply casually. "I hope you realize that I could've killed you at least twice already if I'd wanted to. But I like to know everything and cutting off a prime source of information would be irresponsible."

She raises an eyebrow, presumably not believing a word I've just said. "So, why the bargain?"

"Do you know why Trent wants me dead?"

"Because he hates you?"

"Well, yeah... but he hired you because he's scared of me. I'm on a job, just like you. He knows I'm coming after him, and he's scared of what I'm gonna do to his entire world when I make my move."

She says nothing, but she lowers her gun ever so slightly.

I'm not sure if she's aware that she has. But I can see the doubt in her eyes. And the curiosity—the intrigue.

Who needs a gun when you've got a brain?

"Ask yourself," I continue. "When was the last time you heard of anyone being hired to kill one of our own who's simply working a job? Plus, I consider two million an absolute steal if it means I can get valuable information about Trent and maybe mess with his head a little."

She looks over at Josh, who has slid sideways and is now lying unconscious in front of the door. He'll be fine. He's survived much worse. He's just milking it for the audience, the big British pussy.

"And what do I get out of it?" she asks, sounding sincere.

"You mean, besides the two million dollars?"

"You know as well as anyone, I can't go back on my contract."

"Would you help me if you weren't obligated to Trent?"

"Not sure. Under any other circumstances, the opportunity to work with you would be too good to pass up, I guess. Plus, you are quite handsome..." She looks me up and down approvingly, which makes me feel more uncomfortable than the gun she has pointed at my head.

"But," she continues, "we only have *these* circumstances."

I briefly see the muzzle flash, but I don't register the sound of the gunshot. I feel like I've just been hit in the shoulder by a sledgehammer. I feel myself falling backward...

??:??

I can hear muffled voices around me.

I'm definitely lying down, but I've no idea where I am or how long I've been here...

Am I still on the floor of my hotel?

God, I hope not—that would be embarrassing!

I'm definitely breathing, which is a good start. I'm pretty sure Dominique shot me in the arm...

I try to move my arms and legs. They all work, but my left shoulder is throbbing and sore.

Okay, she *definitely* shot me in the arm. That's fine—I can live with that.

Right, let's see where I am...

I open my eyes slowly. A blurry world rushes toward me and gradually falls into focus. I look around. I'm in a hospital. All the classic signs are here—people in white coats, beeping, generic color on the walls and ceilings, the smell of disinfectant...

I wiggle my fingers, then my toes. I flex my wrists and crack my neck. I've not looked, but I don't seem to be restrained in any way, which is nice. If I've ever blacked out in the past, I nearly always wake up tied to something...

My life sucks sometimes.

I lift my head, and the white coat next to me starts to pay attention. I look out the window and see darkness. I have no idea what time it is, but it must be late.

"Where am I?" I ask, confused.

"Just relax," says a soothing and professional voice. "You're in the hospital. You've been shot. But you were lucky. There's no serious damage. It was just a deep flesh wound. You'll be fine after some rest."

I frown as I try to remember exactly what happened. It suddenly comes back to me like a highlight reel...

Hotel room... Dominique... Gun...

It wasn't luck. If she wanted me dead, I would be. She shot me exactly how she intended to.

Oh, shit... Josh!

I turn to look at the white coat standing on my left, next to the bed. "Hey, where's—"

"Your friend's fine," interjects the voice, cutting me off. "He lost a little more blood than you did, but he only suffered a flesh wound too. He's lying right next to you."

I sigh heavily with relief and look to my right. Josh is indeed lying next to me, looking much the same as I imagine I do.

"You good, bro?" I ask.

He tries to laugh, but it comes out as more of a groggy wheeze. "I hate you."

I lie back and relax. Yeah, he's fine.

The white coat next to me is looking at a clipboard. He seems normal and reasonably smart, so I'll let him go about his business without bombarding him with questions.

"You're both doing really well. The stitching is top-notch, and you should heal up good as new in a few weeks. But... the police will want a word with you. Standard procedure after receiving a GSW in your hotel room, I'm afraid. You boys feeling up to it? They're right outside."

My jaw muscles clench as much as they can. The cynic in me doesn't believe for a second the cops outside aren't on Trent's payroll. And we're both sitting ducks lying in here.

"Gimme a few minutes to wake up, would you?" I ask.

"Sure thing," he replies. He replaces the clipboard on the edge of my bed and walks out of the room.

As soon as the door closes, I swing my legs over the side of the bed and test my weight on them. I manage to stand with no issues. There's a clip on my left index finger, which I remove. I look quickly at the wound on my left shoulder, which is exactly as advertised by the good doctor. I'll barely notice it after a couple of painkillers.

I'm wearing what I had on pre-bullet wound, and my T-shirt has a new hole in the short sleeve. I sigh, stretch, and look over at Josh.

"We need to get out of here," I say.

"Figured you'd say that," he replies as he completes the same ritual.

We both stand and regard each other silently for a moment. He seems reluctant to speak but finds the words he's looking for after a moment.

"So, is this it?" he asks. "Is this the moment where you get pissed off beyond comprehension, Hulk up or whatever, and go and kill everyone?"

He doesn't ask with any humor. He just sounds tired, almost defeated—like he just wants it all to be over.

"Josh," I say. "I'm not sure what the next move is yet. I might be wrong, but I think Dominique did this on purpose."

"No shit, Sherlock!"

"No, I mean, she shot us and left flesh wounds on purpose. She didn't intend to kill us. She intended to let us get away and make it look convincing."

"I don't follow," he says, shaking his head and sounding frustrated.

"She was paid one-point-five million dollars by Wilson Trent to kill me. I offered her two million to not kill me and say she did. She knew me by reputation, and I think she might have taken my offer."

He's silent for a moment, staring at me in disbelief. When he speaks, he gestures wildly with both arms—then with just one when he remembers his bullet wound.

"Are you out of your tiny, stupid, American mind?" he asks. "She wouldn't go back on a contract, Adrian. Same way you wouldn't!"

"Actually, Josh, I kinda did once, remember? Extenuating circumstances, et cetera..."

"Oh, sorry, Mr. *Exception to Every Rule*! Look, I'm sick of the dancing around and the mind games and the uncertainty, okay?" He points to his arm. "I'm sick of getting shot! Whenever I'm with you, I get shot. It's like you're a magnet for random gunfire for Christ's sake!"

Without warning, he slaps me hard across the face with his good arm. We both stand there in silence—equally shocked but I imagine for different reasons. After a moment, he speaks again.

"Will you please, for the love of all things Holy, just kill this sonofabitch, so we can all go home?"

My eyes are wide with shock. I understand and share his frustration, and I know he's trying to rally me into action, but in all our years together, he's never laid his hands on me. And vice versa.

But I'll admit, it's worked.

I feel a rush of unbridled rage explode inside me, tearing through my body like wildfire through a dry forest. I look around, not knowing how to handle the sudden influx of fury. It's a small room, empty except for the two beds, a couple of monitors, and a window. And the door. Beyond which are two cops who are most likely on Trent's payroll.

Either way, I can't afford to waste time on them.

Like lightning, my right arm flies out and grips Josh by his throat. My Inner Satan is behind the wheel for a moment. It's like I'm looking on from the outside, like an out-of-body experience or something.

"Touch me again and I'll kill you," I snarl through gritted teeth. "Now stay close—we're leaving."

I release my grip and he massages his throat, taking in some deep breaths. But he looks calm. He's not angry with me, and he isn't afraid. I think, if anything, he seems relieved.

"Atta boy," he says quietly.

I quickly check that I have everything with me and walk toward the door. As I reach for the handle, it swings open and a man walks in, stopping in the doorway. He isn't a cop, and he isn't a doctor. He's a good height, around six feet tall. He's not fat, but his middle-age spread has gone unchecked around his waist and chin. He needs a shave. With his thinning gray hair and old, stained, knee-length raincoat, he could easily be confused with a homeless person.

But he's not homeless. At least he wasn't the last time I saw him, which was close to ten years ago. He looks like shit, but I guess that's to be expected. He'll be close to fifty now, and the last decade is unlikely to have been good to him.

"Adrian?" he says, his voice like gravel and his breath like whiskey. "So, it's true... you *are* back."

I take a step back, my rage quickly subsiding and making way for shock. I've got no idea how he found me, but the conversation I figure I'm about to have has been a long time coming.

"Hey, Frank," I say.

Behind me, I can sense Josh quietly figuring it all out. I don't think these two have ever met before, but he'll know who he is, I'm sure.

"Frank?" he says out loud behind me, to no one in particular. "Jesus... you're..."

His words trail off, so I fill in the blanks for him.

"That's right. Josh, meet Frank Stanton—my brother-in-law."

Silence descends on the increasingly awkward reunion for what feels like hours. Frank's hand disappears inside his pocket and comes back out holding a small pistol. I flash a quick glance at it. It's a Taurus 605, which fires .357-caliber magnum rounds. He aims it at me, the tiny barrel just inches from my face.

"My sister's dead because of you, you heartless bastard!"

His voice is icy calm and laced with venom. I imagine he's rehearsed that line a million times in his head, waiting for his chance to face me and seek whatever answers he needs for his own peace of mind.

I take a step forward, allowing the barrel to touch my forehead. I push against it lightly.

"Frank," I say. "My *wife's* dead because of me. And my daughter. Whatever pain you're feeling... whatever hatred's been driving you... trust me, I've been there and bought the T-shirt. Please..." I hold my hands out to the side, palms open—total surrender. "Please... can we talk about this? I'll tell you everything you want to know, I promise."

His breathing gets more erratic. His eyes narrow and his lip curls as he battles his own inner demons. After a tense few seconds, he lowers the pistol, which I immediately snatch out of his hand and throw on the bed behind me. He takes a step back in shock.

"You left her..." he says. "You let them die."

I sigh, massaging my temples as I look at the floor. While he's probably spent the last God-knows-how-long picturing this moment, I've honestly never even thought twice about seeing him again. And for him to show up randomly right now has really thrown me off my game. I have no idea what to say to him, but the truth is really the only option I have. And it's not going to be an easy conversation.

"Frank, can we do this somewhere else? You've kinda caught me at a bad time."

He looks at me, then at Josh. He sees our wounds and frowns. "Why would someone shoot you both?"

"Same reason you were about to," mutters Josh, who's sitting on his bed and watching everything unfold.

"It's... a long story, Frank," I say.

"I've got all the time in the world," he replies.

"I'm sure you have, but unfortunately, I don't. Not right now. There are two cops out there who are more likely to wanna shoot me than ask me questions. As it stands, I suspect I have the entire state of Pennsylvania trying to kill me. I'm tired and sore, and the longer I stay here, the greater the chances are of me getting dead. Can we *please* do this later?"

He seems to think about it.

"Come on," he says with a heavy sigh. "I'll give you a ride wherever you wanna go. Then me and you are gonna have a long talk."

I nod. "Absolutely."

He goes for the door, but I grab his arm to stop him.

"Are there definitely two cops outside?" I ask.

"Yeah, at the end of the hall."

"Okay, let me go first."

I leave the room first and step out into the hallway, followed by Frank, then Josh. The buzz of the fluorescent lights overhead is loud in the near-deserted hospital. My footfalls echo on the permanently buffed tiled floor. I look left and see more rooms; to the right are the front desk and the elevators. And the cops.

"Come on," I say over my shoulder.

I stride purposefully toward the reception area. The cops are standing side by side talking to the nurse on night duty. As I step out into the waiting area, they turn and stare at me.

A few questions, my ass.

Making a conscious effort not to use my injured arm, I rush over to them. Before they can properly react, I throw a straight right and catch the cop on the left flush on his jaw, sending him sprawling to the floor. As the second moves to draw his gun, I swing my right elbow back and smash into his nose. Using my momentum, I turn and kick his knee with my left foot. He overbalances and drops to the floor.

Both cops are down and neither is in any state to follow me, which is good. I've made sure they're not seriously injured, either, just in case I'm wrong about them working for Trent.

The nurse standing behind the front desk is staring at me, eyes wide, jaw open. I avoid any prolonged eye contact with her, so I'll be less memorable if she gets questioned later. I head for the elevators, press the button, and wait. Frank and Josh appear next to me. Josh has a bemused look on his face. Frank, on the other hand, is dumbstruck. He looks behind him at the cops, then back at me.

"Who the hell *are* you?" he asks.

The doors ding open and we all step inside. I hit the button for the first floor, and as the doors close again, I turn to him. "All in good time, Frank," I say. "All in good time."

24

WILSON TRENT

October 5, 2014 — 04:30 EDT

Wilson Trent's phone rang, disturbing him from his already restless slumber. He leaned over and clicked on his bedside lamp, rubbing his eyes until they adjusted to the sudden brightness. He looked at the clock and groaned when he saw the time. He picked it up and looked at the display.

Unknown number.

"What?" he said as he answered.

The voice on the other end was female, deep and alluring.

"It's me," said Dominique Tevani.

"Is it done?" he asked, finding it difficult to hide just a hint of excitement from his otherwise cold voice.

"You never told me it was Adrian Hell you sent me to kill."

"I gave you the location of your target and told you how much money you'd be getting. Why the fuck should it matter who it was?"

"I'm a professional," she replied. "I like to know everything about my mark, so I can prepare for every eventuality. He's the biggest fish in the ocean, and the fact I had no idea he was going to walk into that room left me unnecessarily vulnerable. The added risk is going to add to the price."

"How much?"

"An extra half a million," she said.

Trent was silent for a moment, angry that someone had the audacity to try to negotiate with him. But under the circumstances, he relented.

"Whatever," he said. "Is it done?"

It was Dominique's turn to fall silent before talking. Then she said, "I put a bullet in him, yes. And his weird little British friend."

He was beginning to lose his temper.

"Is that fucker *dead*?" he shouted, pausing slightly after each word for emphasis.

"It's true what they say, y'know?" she began, ignoring his question. "You should never meet your heroes. I'm not saying he was my hero or anything, but I always admired his work. I mean, that guy was a legend in our business, y'know? Yet, when I was face to face with him, it turned out he was incredibly easy to put down. He just kinda stood there and talked at me until I shot him..."

It was like she was talking in general, as opposed to directly to Trent. Her words trailed off, sounding like she was heavily distracted.

Trent stared at the receiver in disbelief before speaking again.

"Do I need to hire someone else to dispose of yet another assassin who's begun to annoy me? Is that piece of shit dead? Yes or no?"

Dominique was silent for a moment longer before answering.

"Yes," she said.

"Good," he replied. "Then it won't be a problem delivering his head to me, will it? Midday, my office."

He hung up and threw the phone across the room. He heard it smash against the wall, then turned his light off and closed his eyes once again.

10:07 EDT

Later that morning, Trent sat behind his desk in his penthouse suite atop his office building in downtown Pittsburgh. With his chair turned around, he looked out the window at the expanse of the city around him.

His city.

It was still quite dark. The low, gray cloud circled around in the sky menacingly, preparing to assault the city with another downpour.

Facing his desk, sitting on one of the sofas, was his accountant, Joseph Bernstein. He was wearing what looked like the same suit from the other day. His briefcase was open on the table in front of him, and he was shuffling through some papers as he spoke.

"I also need to explain the one-and-a-half million dollars you transferred yesterday to an account in the Caymans. How would you like to handle that?" he asked.

Trent didn't turn around and was silent for a few moments. He had gotten to where he was by being a ruthless and savvy businessman, as well as a notorious gangster. He ran most of Pennsylvania because he invested heavily in the major cities within the state. He bought and expanded local businesses, creating income and employment opportunities. He financially supported local officials and state senators in their campaigns, helping them get elected. He gave to charities so that the people loved him. Then, once each city was in the palm of his hand, he clenched his fist, tightening his grip on their lives and squeezing them with extortion, prostitution, arms dealing, drug trafficking... even funding terrorism, if he saw an opportunity to profit from it. He was extremely frustrated that one man had attempted to threaten everything he'd built.

He spun around in his chair and looked at Bernstein.

"It's two million," he corrected. "It was a personal investment. Explain it however you want."

Bernstein simply nodded and let the matter drop. He'd been Trent's accountant long enough to know when to stop asking questions and when to gloss over certain details.

Trent pressed a buzzer just underneath his desk. Moments later, Duncan and Bennett came in. They strode side by side across the room and stood behind the sofa opposite Bernstein.

"Find the woman," Trent said to Bennett. "Dominique. I don't trust her. Follow her and make sure she brings me Adrian's head. And once she has... bring me hers."

Bennett simply nodded, then turned and left the room.

Trent looked at Duncan. "I intend to take this afternoon off," he announced. "I'll be going to watch the Steelers game later from my box. Make the necessary arrangements."

"Will do, Mr. Trent," replied Duncan. "You think they're gonna win today?"

"They'd better fucking win! I'm not in the mood for failure."

Duncan nodded and took his leave, having learned over the years how to read Trent's moods.

A moment later, as Bernstein was preparing to leave, Duncan re-entered the room, talking animatedly on his phone.

"What happened to fucking knocking?" asked Trent.

Duncan put his hand over the phone and held it away from his head to respond.

"Sorry, Boss, but you're gonna wanna hear this. Gimme a minute."

He resumed his conversation as Trent looked on with impatience and curiosity.

After a couple of minutes, Duncan ended the call and looked at Trent. His eyes betrayed his fear. "Mr. Trent, that was one of my guys over in Allentown. They just got word that Johnny King's been taken out."

Trent slammed his fist on the desk. His eyes were so wide they bulged against their sockets and threatened to pop right out of his head.

"What?" he yelled. "How?"

Duncan took an involuntary step back, seemingly reluctant to answer.

"Was it him? Was it Adrian fucking *Hell*?" Trent asked, practically spitting the name out with disgust.

"We don't know who pulled the trigger yet," he replied. "But it happened yesterday afternoon. We asked around, and there's a new player in Allentown who's taken over everything except what King ran for you. My guess... it was him."

"So quickly? Christ. Who? Anyone we know?"

"His name's Jimmy Manhattan. Word is he made a helluva name for himself over on the West Coast. He's old school, like you, Boss. Big reputation and his new outfit is growing fast over there."

Trent sighed heavily. He stood and turned to look out of the window once more.

"If you no longer need me..." began Bernstein.

"Get the fuck outta here," said Trent without looking around.

Not needing telling twice, Bernstein left the office.

"Bring me this Jimmy Manhattan," he said finally as he turned to face Duncan, who was shifting nervously on the spot. "I don't care how you do it, but he's gonna be standing right in front of me before the Steelers kick off. Am I clear?"

Duncan nodded, then headed for the door.

Trent looked at his watch. It was just over ten hours until the Steelers game started. He took a deep breath and sighed heavily again.

He had a feeling the day was going to get worse before it got better.

25

ADRIAN HELL

Frank drove us to a motel on the outskirts of town. We'd all checked in and headed to our rooms, having agreed to meet back up after a few hours' sleep. It's a typical place—big neon sign and basic single rooms with a double bed, generic bathroom, and questionable carpets. I've only managed a few hours. My mind's going a hundred miles an hour, processing everything over and over again.

I'm sitting on the edge of the bed, gently massaging the area of my lower back that had a rogue mattress spring sticking in it while I was asleep. I walk to the bathroom and turn the shower on. While I wait for the water to heat up, I look at my reflection in the small mirror above the basin.

I look old.

Am I old?

No. Forty-three isn't old, is it?

I don't know.

I don't *feel* old... but I damn sure look it.

Old and tired.

No, worse than tired... I look *beaten*.

I'm not—Hell, I *know* I'm not... but that doesn't change the fact that I look like shit.

My eyes are sunken slightly, carrying big, black bags below them. My eyes have always been a stark blue, like ice, but now their piercing color seems dull, almost subdued, by minimal food and sleep and high levels of emotional stress.

I'm long overdue a shave. As I rub my hand quickly across my face to wipe away the cobwebs, the scar below my left eye itches.

That reminds me—I still need to call Manhattan and tell him about Wilson Trent. I let out a heavy sigh. Shower first... then the awkward conversation.

I step under the hot water, appreciating the feel of it on my skin. It's almost like it's washing away my troubles. If only that were true. Nevertheless, after five minutes, I turn the water off and dry myself down. By the time I'm dressed again, I feel like a new person.

I cross the room to my bed and pick up my cell phone. I select a number from my recent contacts list and dial.

"It's me," I say when the call's answered.

"Good morning, Adrian," replies Jimmy Manhattan. "What can I do for you?"

I pause and take a deep breath. I have to give him as much information as I can without telling him my role in everything. I need to choose my words carefully.

"Step forward, all those who *aren't* completely fucked..." I say. "Not so fast, Jimmy."

"Is there a problem?" asks Manhattan innocently.

"Well, I took out King for you. No issue there."

"I know, and you were paid rather well for it."

"Indeed. However, before we left, we checked his office and found that he actually worked for someone else."

There's a brief moment of silence on the other end of the line. "That's of no concern to me, Adrian. My only interest was in getting him out of my city, and thanks to you, that's a job well done."

"Actually, Jimmy, it does concern you. Ever heard of Wilson Trent?"

More silence. I wait a moment to give him chance to respond, but he says nothing.

"I'll take that as a *yes*," I continue. "King worked for Trent. In fact, King ran most of Allentown for him. Do you need me to draw you a picture of how truly boned you are right now?"

"Why are you telling me this?" he asks after another few moments of silence. "Why do you care if Wilson Trent has an issue with me?"

"I have my reasons—most of which are none of your goddamn business. But after taking that job for you, I now have a vested interest in you and your little organization's well-being, seeing as you owe me one. Wouldn't want anything to happen to you before I can cash in my favor, now would we?"

"Okay, so what would your advice be? You seem quite well-informed, so I'm assuming you have an opinion on the best course of action here?"

"I do... prepare for war."

I hang up and head outside to the parking lot, where Josh and Frank are waiting for me. Without a word, we climb into his car—a rusty, light brown sedan with torn leather seats and an engine that sounds like a dog chewing a socket wrench. Frank eases out onto the road and sets off to find somewhere to eat.

It takes less than five minutes to find a diner that looks adequate. We pull up in the parking lot around the back and head inside. It's a small place, not a franchise, and looks nice enough, despite needing to be cleaned. There aren't many seats, but we spot a table at the back for the three of us. As soon as we sit down, a waitress comes over with a pot of coffee. We all order a cup, as well as food. Josh and I opt for the pancakes, while Frank asks for toast.

Josh has brought his laptop with him, and he's sitting silently, looking through all the information downloaded from Johnny King's computer. I regard him for a moment, watching him work. He looks as tired and old as I do. I sigh, feeling guilty for dragging him along with me. He'd have been so much better talking to me on the other end of the phone, out of the firing line. But I suppose he'd just say he volunteered to watch my back, and he'd never hold me accountable for anything that happened while he was with me.

I smile, but Frank's gravelly voice interrupts my train of thought.

"So..." he says. "You mind telling me exactly what the hell's going on?"

I look at him. I can see a cocktail of doubt, confusion, and disdain swirling around in his eyes as he stares back at me.

"Where to begin?" I reply, genuinely unsure.

"Start with why my sister and niece were killed."

So, I do.

11:15 EDT

. . .

After our food arrived, I spent a good half-hour telling him everything that had happened in my life since leaving the military—becoming a hitman, taking the Darnell Harper job, Wilson Trent's retaliation... everything.

I'm not sure how I expected him to react, but I'll admit to being surprised at how calm he remained. He didn't nod or ask questions or give any sign he was actually listening to me. He just sat there and let every single one of my words hit him.

"So," I conclude, "after San Francisco, I realized I was ready to avenge their death... ready to finally put them to rest. And here I am."

I imagine it's a lot to take in all at once. Out of the corner of my eye, I see Josh crack a slight smile, but he says nothing. Frank finally nods, slowly, having absorbed as much of what I just said as I suspect he could.

"You're a hitman?" he asks.

"Yes."

"Are you any good?"

The question throws me a little. After everything I've just told him, *that's* the first thing he thinks to ask?

"He's the best," answers Josh, without looking up from his laptop.

"Okay," says Frank. "If you're so good, why isn't Wilson Trent already dead?"

I smile humorlessly. "I'm working on it. These things take time if you want to do them right."

He nods again.

"So, what's your story?" I ask him. "Start with how you found me."

"That's easy. Your old neighbor called me after you'd spoke to him. He said you'd told him you were staying in Pittsburgh, so I checked all the hotels and hospitals in the city, starting in the city's center and working out. It didn't take long."

"That's pretty smart," I say, impressed.

He shrugs humbly. "I'm a P.I.," he declares. "Pretty basic stuff, really."

"Holy shit, really?" I ask, unable to hide my surprise.

He nods. "Yup. Set up on my own not long after..." His words trail off, and he stares vacantly at the table for a moment before continuing. "I just wanted to do something. I wanted to know who was responsible and why. So, I've dedicated every second of my life since to finding out what happened. And now, a thirty-minute conversation with you has filled in every blank I had."

"You're welcome," I say.

"I wasn't thanking you, asshole. I'm *blaming* you!"

"Hey!" says Josh, finally looking up from his work. "That's a bit unfair, isn't it?"

"It's all right, Josh," I say. "I blame myself too. I have all these years, and the weight of all the guilt has finally become too heavy to bear. That's why I'm here. I realized it wasn't my fault they died. It was Wilson Trent's. And I will have my vengeance."

An uncomfortable silence descends on our table. Josh retreats to his laptop. I hold Frank's gaze until he looks away. He seems to be wrestling with his conscience over something, but I don't know what.

Josh was right, and it feels good to finally say it out loud.

I wasn't to blame.

I *wasn't* to blame.

Frank slips his hand inside his long coat and takes out a folder, which he puts down on the table and slides across to me.

"What's this?" I ask.

"Everything I've managed to put together on Wilson Trent in the last nine years or so," he replies.

Josh pushes his laptop to one side and takes the folder before I get the chance to pick it up. "Let me see that," he says, flicking through the concise dossier.

"It didn't take long to find out it was Trent behind the murders," Frank concedes. "The big gap in the story was why and how you fit into it. Did Janine know what you did for a living?"

I shake my head. "My cover was that I was a consultant to a private security firm," I reply. "It made sense, given my military background, and explained the good money."

"Smart..." he says reluctantly.

"Frank, this is amazing," says Josh, whose growing excitement is starting to bring out the British in him once again. It's good to see. "You've got evidence linking him to all kinds of shit!"

"I asked around, followed the right people... it took a long time," he says. "I finally started making some progress, but I never had enough damning evidence to take to the cops. It was always circumstantial or from anonymous sources. Basically, it was all stuff that could be explained away or buried by the people on Trent's payroll."

"Well," I say. "Maybe if we combined our efforts, we might have more luck... but I have to ask, Frank—how badly do you want to take him down?"

"I wanna see him rot," he replies instantly. "Why?"

"Because, as *we* have discovered—" I gesture to Josh and myself. "—you have to do things you wouldn't normally do when going against someone like Trent. And trust me, there aren't many things I take issue with. But I'll admit I've pushed the boundaries a little more than I usually would, and I don't want to involve you in my world if you're not ready for it. That wouldn't be fair."

"Pushed the boundaries?" asks Josh, briefly looking up from the folder. "That's putting it mildly, isn't it?"

"Not now," I say with a half-smile.

Before Frank can answer, Josh shouts, causing what customers are in the diner to turn and stare at us. "We've got it!"

"What?" I ask.

"Our way in... our way to get Trent... we've got it!"

"Care to calm down and elaborate?"

"There's mention here of Trent's accountant, Joseph..."

"Bernstein," adds Frank. "Yeah, a slimy little prick who meets with him a couple of times a week. So what?"

"Adrian, if we can get to the accountant, we can get to his accounts..."

"...and with his accounts, you can do your online robbery," I say, finishing his sentence.

"Okay, what?" asks Frank, his head in his hands with frustration.

I stroke my chin for a second, thinking. Putting more of the pieces into place...

"Josh is planning to rob Trent by stealing all his money over the internet. Hit him where it hurts and cripple his empire before I face him. He's got the tech side of it ready. We just need details of all his business accounts. And we might just have found a way to get them."

It's Frank's turn to show signs of life and excitement, probably for the first time in a long while. "I can take you to his office," he says. "I've followed him a few times, and I know his routine. It's Sunday, right? He'll have been to see Trent this morning, like he always does."

I look at Josh, who's staring at me with a big smile on his face.

"This would be that break we've been trying to catch all week," I say.

"Let's rock and roll," he says, picking up his laptop. He stands and sets off for the door.

"So, that's it?" asks Frank as I move to follow Josh. "You get an idea and two minutes later you're off?"

"Pretty much," I say with a slight shrug. "That's kinda how we do things. I don't have time for hesitation or doubt. That shit will get you killed. Now this is your last chance, Frank. If you take us to Bernstein, there's no going back. You're in this with us until the end..."

He stands and steps in close to me, holding my gaze for a moment.

"Come on, you're wasting time," he says.

He strides out of the door, leaving me standing there.

"The game is on," I murmur to myself. I throw a couple of twenties down on the table for the food we ordered and join them outside. Josh is leaning against the trunk of the car. Frank's already behind the wheel, waiting for me; the engine's idling.

I climb into the passenger seat and Josh gets in behind me.

"Let's go," I say.

Frank presses play on the CD player and sets off, turning right out of the parking lot.

"Hang on, hang on—what the hell is *this*?" asks Josh, gesturing to the stereo in disbelief.

"It's the Beach Boys," says Frank, in a tone that clearly indicates he can't see a problem with it.

"Oh, no, that won't do at all. We're on a mission now, Frankie! We need mission music. We need to feel inspired, motivated, alive! This makes me feel like I'm a depressed stoner in a rowing boat..."

Josh reaches into his laptop bag and pulls out a CD. He passes it through to the front and hands it to me.

"The emergency music?" I ask, having heard the CD he keeps on him at all times.

"I can't listen to this shit. I'm sorry."

I change the CD over and press Play.

"Sorry, Frank. Rules are rules."

He shakes his head in disbelief as the opening chords of *Ace of Spades* by Motorhead sound in the car.

"What the fuck have I got myself into?" he mutters.

I laugh. "Welcome to my life, Frank."

26

ADRIAN HELL

11:42 EDT

The drive didn't take long. Apart from the loud music, the twenty or so minutes passed mostly in silence. Frank's pulled up across the street, opposite the accountancy firm where Joseph Bernstein works.

O. B. D. Accountants is a modest building on Center Avenue. It has a glass front with the name of the firm printed across it. The closed blinds give the impression they're not open for business, as it's Sunday, but I know any firm who has clients like Wilson Trent will be open twenty-four hours a day, seven days a week.

We sit in silence for a moment, all looking across at the office.

"What's the move?" asks Josh.

"Worst case is that the office is full of accountants doing overtime," I say. "But I'm not worried about that, really. What are they going to do? Attack me with their calculators?"

Josh chuckles, but Frank shifts uneasily in the driver's seat. I turn and look at him.

"What's on your mind?" I ask.

"Bernstein manages the books for the biggest crime lord in the state," he replies. "Do you honestly think there won't be any security in that building?"

Huh. He has a point, but it still makes little difference to me. I can see why the idea would make him slightly apprehensive, though.

"Good point," I say. "You wanna wait here? Me and Josh can go in, find Bernstein, and get the information we need."

"And how are you going to do that, exactly?"

"Frank, don't ask questions you don't want to know the answer to, okay? You had your chance to walk away from all this, and you decided you were with us all the way. Don't be getting cold feet on me now."

He sighs heavily, torn over what he should do.

"I get it, Frank. I really do," I continue before he has chance to speak. "I've spent eight years coming to terms with what happened and what I've become as a result. You're trying to do the same thing in twenty-four hours, and it won't happen. I can't offer any words of comfort or advice on how to make this less awful, but I can promise you this: Wilson Trent is going to die. His world is going to turn to ash, and when it's all said and done, we will all have some much-needed closure. But until that happens, we have to be prepared to get our hands real dirty."

I feel Josh punch the headrest of my seat behind me. "Fuck yeah, Boss!" he yells. "That's the inspirational, ass-kicking Inner Satan shit I've been waiting to hear from you all week!"

Frank looks over his shoulder at Josh, then back at me.

He holds my gaze longer than most people would, then nods. "Just don't kill anyone, okay?"

"I'll do my best," I reply, holding up my right hand as if swearing on a bible.

Frank gets out of the car and stands on the sidewalk, staring across the street.

"You think he'll be okay?" asks Josh.

"Vengeance is a powerful tool," I say. "I think he'll be fine."

"It's kinda sweet that he thinks you'll be able to do this without pulling a trigger," he says with a smile.

"Kiss my ass, Josh," I say, getting out of the car.

He makes an exaggerated smacking noise with his lips as he climbs out behind me.

We all cross over and stand in front of the building, looking somewhat conspicuous. I take a quick look around. No surveillance that I can see. I glance through the window, but there's no one on the front desk. Maybe admin staff isn't required for weekend work.

I try the door, but it's locked.

"Kick it down or try the back?" asks Josh.

Before I can answer, Frank pushes past me, reaches into his coat, and retrieves a lock-picking kit. He crouches down, puts the two long, thin metal pins into the keyhole, and moves them expertly for a few seconds. The door clicks open. He stands, puts his kit away, and pushes the door open. He faces us both and winks, gesturing for us to walk in, like a doorman.

"Nice," says Josh, smiling as he heads inside.

I take one last look up and down the street and follow him in. Frank comes in behind me and shuts the door quietly.

Inside, the carpet's a neutral color, the walls are white,

and the desk and chairs look like they're from IKEA. Two sofas form a reverse L-shape in front of the window and against the right-hand wall, acting as the waiting area. The front desk covers the top right corner of the room, with a door leading to the offices beyond in the top left, facing the entrance.

Frank walks over and listens at the door. "Seems quiet," he whispers.

I nod. "Let's go."

We head through and into the main office area. A central bank of empty desks stretches to the far wall. Along the right-hand side are four small offices, all of which are empty. They have floor-to-ceiling windows and fitted blinds, with a door to the left.

"So far, so quiet," whispers Josh.

I point to the staircase in the back left corner. "I guess we go up."

We cross the office space and climb cautiously up the stairs. Halfway up, they wind to the left. As we turn, I hear voices. They're low and relaxed, with the occasional chuckle of meaningless conversation. We creep up the rest of the way, pausing just before the staircase opens out in the middle of an open-plan vestibule on the second floor. The layout is identical to downstairs, except there are offices against the left wall too, on either side of the staircase. Also, before the main office area starts, there's a circular desk, like a security station, dead ahead in the center of the room. Three men are behind it; two are sitting down, and one is standing and resting his crossed arms on the counter.

I peer around the corner. From where I'm standing, I can almost see beyond the desk into the office. The main floor is deserted, and every door along both sides is standing open. All except one, against the far wall in the left corner.

"Bernstein must be in his office," I whisper over my shoulder.

I take a step forward but feel a hand on my arm. I look back at Josh.

"Adrian," he says. "You want me to handle this? You can't talk your way out of anything. We both know that."

"I'm not intending to talk at all," I say.

Frank goes to say something, but I pre-empt his objections. "And no, Frank—I'm not gonna shoot them. Just... disable them for now."

He lets out a sigh of obvious relief and nods, as if giving his approval.

The security guards haven't looked up. I'm thinking the best way to take them out is quickly and head-on—surprise them and attack before they know what's happening. This tactic works best when a large group's all together. If you're outnumbered and they're spread out, more often than not, they'll come at you individually or in pairs, which is easy enough to handle. But when *you're* approaching *them* and they're close together, you run the risk of being mobbed. The trick is to hit hard, hit fast, and hit once.

I look over my shoulder and signal to Josh and Frank to wait here, just out of sight. I step out into the office and walk briskly toward the desk. After a few steps, as expected, they look up, initially confused. The guard that's standing is a tall, dark-skinned man wearing a charcoal-gray suit and no tie.

"Hey!" he shouts to me. "Who the fuck are you?"

Without a word, I run at the desk. I jump as I reach it and place my hands flat on the counter, using my momentum to lift me up and over. As I bring my legs up behind me, I swing them round, kicking the first of the two guards sitting down in the face. He falls backward off his chair. As I land, I deliver a strong right punch to the guard next to him, who also flies off his seat and lands next to him.

Before the remaining guard can react, I swing my left leg low as I turn to face him, kicking him firmly on the right knee. He loses his footing and drops to the floor. I kick him again, squarely in the face, and knock him out cold.

I signal Josh and Frank over and set off toward Bernstein's office at the back. Without waiting for them or breaking stride, I raise my right foot and kick the door clean off its hinges. I walk straight in and take the handset off Bernstein, who looks startled and confused, and slam it down on the receiver. I stand in front of him, letting him look me up and down and process what's happening.

"What the... what's going on? Who are you? Where's our security?" he asks, the panic evident in his voice.

"*I* am Adrian Hell... *you* are Wilson Trent's money man... and your *security* is out cold," I reply. "Which means you and I are going to have a real good talk."

His eyes go wide. I'm not sure what's worrying him more —me, or the thought of what Trent will do when he finds out I've been here. Either way, he's terrified.

"I d-don't know—" he starts.

"What I'm talking about?" I offer, interrupting. "Sure, you do, Joe."

"But you're supposed to be dead..."

"Ah, yes—the beautiful assassin Trent hired to kill me..." I show him my arm. "She missed."

I reach behind me and draw one of my Berettas, which I aim at him.

"Now this can go one of two ways. One option is that I ask questions, you answer them honestly and with vast detail, then I leave you alone, unharmed."

"What's the second option?" he asks.

"Pretty much the opposite of the first one."

Behind his desk, he plops down heavily in the chair. He looks around nervously for a moment, then sighs with resignation.

I smile. "Atta boy, Joe."

Frank and Josh walk in behind me. I stand in front of the desk, which is clear, save for a few pieces of paper and a computer. Josh walks around and stands behind Bernstein's chair, resting on the back of it. Frank stays by the doorway, a little unsure of himself. I'm happy to take the lead with the interrogation. I lower my gun slightly before talking.

"So, we want the inside scoop on Trent. You have access to all his money, and we know you were with him this morning, so you're our golden ticket. Start talking."

"Do you have any idea what he'll do to me if he finds out I've spoken to you?" he asks.

"Yes. And I honestly don't care. But if it's any consolation, if you give us enough juicy details, I'll make sure he's too dead to take anything out on you anyway."

He takes some deep breaths, trying to stay calm. Like a typical numbers man, I see in his eyes he's weighing up the odds, deciding on his best course of action.

"What do you want to know?" he asks, concluding that my way is the only way, which is smart.

I look up at Josh, who takes his cue and spins the chair around slightly, so Bernstein is facing the right-hand wall, looking in between the both of us.

"I need information on all of his personal and business accounts," he says, leaning over the chair.

"I c-can't give you that!" he exclaims, turning to me. "That would basically give you full access to every cent he has!"

I smile. "Why else would we ask for it?"

"You're insane. Do you even *know* Mr. Trent? He'll kill you, your family, and everyone you've ever cared for if he finds out what you're doing."

"Joe, that ship has sailed—trust me. Trent won't do shit to me. His time's running out, and I'm gonna take everything from him. Understand? Everything. Now before you get me all the account information my colleague has asked for, tell me more about where he lives. This big penthouse apartment he works from."

Bernstein shrugs. "What's to tell? He works on the top floor of an apartment building. Everyone who lives there works for him. He runs some businesses out of the apartments there too."

"How tall is the building?" I ask.

"Thirty stories, I think."

"What kind of protection does he have?"

"I've only ever seen his two bodyguards, Duncan and Bennett, by his side. But there's a lot of muscle in that place. Scares the shit outta me every time I go in there."

Frank steps forward, level with me. He glares at Bernstein for a moment before speaking. "If we wanted to get to him, how would we do it? Doesn't sound like knocking on his front door is really an option..."

"I have no idea, honestly. He doesn't confide in me and I'm not privy to any of his movements. I just make sure his money is all accounted for and in the right place. Please, you have to believe me!"

Frank takes another step forward, his face turning red and his eyes going wide. I can relate to his frustration. I put my hand on his arm. He looks at me for a moment, then walks away, out of the office.

I look at Josh, then back at Bernstein.

"Get the account details for my friend," I say, leveling my gun at him once more.

He nods hurriedly and starts typing on the keyboard in front of him. A few mouse clicks later, the screen flashes as spreadsheet after spreadsheet loads up.

"There," he says. "That's all his financial records for the last six months."

Josh grabs him by the neck and forces him out of the chair. Then he sits down and reviews the information on the screen.

"Adrian, this is the bloody jackpot!" he says. "We've got it all here—bank details, recent transactions... you name it."

I allow myself a small, silent celebration. This is our first significant step forward since arriving here, and I can finally see some light at the end of the tunnel. We still have a long way to go, but this is a big win for us.

"Brilliant," I say. "Now that we can hit him in his *wallet*, we need to find a way to hit him in his *face*."

"Well, I might just have the answer to that as well," says Josh, engrossed. "There's a transaction here on one of Trent's personal accounts for a Pittsburgh Steelers season ticket."

"The Steelers are playing today..." offers Frank, who has reappeared in the doorway.

We all look at Bernstein, who's holding his silence in the corner as Josh works at his desk.

"Joe," I ask, "you hear any mention of this when you were with him today?"

I see his hesitation.

"Joe..."

"He did mention a game this morning, yes," he sighs. "And I know he has a private box at the stadium..."

Josh and I exchange a glance. I smile as our next move becomes obvious.

"Fancy going to a football game?" I ask him.

"That still ain't football, Boss man, but I could sure use the R and R," he says with a smile full of excitement and menace.

He quickly downloads all the account details to a USB drive and puts it in his pocket. "We're done here," he announces as he stands.

"Frank, is there anything else you want to know?" I ask, turning to him.

"Not from him," he replies, nodding at Bernstein.

"All right, then."

I raise my gun again and pull the trigger. The bullet hits Bernstein on the neck, causing blood to spray across the back wall with a squelch. He clutches at the wound as he slumps to the floor. He starts to shake as blood pumps over his hand and down his suit, forming a dark, crimson pool on the floor around him.

"Jesus Christ!" yells Frank behind me. "Are you insane?"

I look at him impassively. "You honestly think he wouldn't have called Trent the moment we left here?" I ask.

"Well, maybe... but you didn't have to shoot him!"

Josh walks around the desk and heads for the door. He stops next to Frank and pats him on the shoulder.

"You've got a lot to learn, Frankie," he says with a humorless smile. "Adrian's never finished an interrogation without putting a bullet in someone."

Frank looks at me, but all I can do is shrug. Sadly, Josh has a point.

I look down at Bernstein, who's stopped breathing. I put another bullet between his eyes, to make sure, and then leave the office.

We all walk back to the car in silence. Frank gets in behind the wheel and sets off. "So, what's next?" he asks after a moment.

"It looks like we're finally ready to launch our attack," says Josh. "That right, Adrian?"

My jaw muscles tense as I nod slowly. "Fuckin' A."

27

WILSON TRENT

It had been an increasingly stressful day for Wilson Trent, and since Bennett had arrived back at his office, it had only gotten worse. After asking around, he'd found out that the woman he'd hired to kill Adrian Hell had lied to him. That piece of shit had left the hospital earlier that morning with nothing more than a flesh wound. And that was after assaulting two police officers. They weren't even on his payroll. He assumed Adrian was feeling extra paranoid, which was a good sign. It proved he was getting to him.

He wasn't interested in why she'd lied; he was only interested in making sure Adrian Hell was dead. And Dominique Tevani was still the best option he had.

She just needed a little persuasion.

It hadn't taken much time or effort for Bennett to dig into her life and find her weakness. And now that it had been exploited, he simply needed to remind her that he wasn't someone she should betray.

He picked up his cell phone and called her.

"Hey, big boy," she said as she answered. "You got more work for me?"

"Cut the crap, Dominique," replied Trent. "You care to explain why the fuck Adrian Hell walked out of a hospital earlier today with a bullet hole in his shoulder?"

She fell silent.

"I don't believe you're that bad of a shot," he continued. "So, I wanna know why, and I wanna know when you intend to finish the job I paid you exceptionally well to carry out."

"Look, Willy, like I told you before, you should've said it was Adrian Hell you were sending me after in the first place."

"What difference would it have made?"

"I'd have told you to go fuck yourself," she said. "Aside from who he is, professional killers work to a code. And one of the rules of that code is that you never take a job to kill one of our own."

"Don't give me that code of honor crap," said Trent, losing his patience. "I doubt more than a couple of you psychopaths ever adhere to that so-called *rule*—the money's too good. Now you either finish the job, or you'll find your-self just below Adrian fucking Hell on my shit-list!"

She laughed down the line.

"Listen, *Willy*, you don't frighten me. You can have your money back. I don't care—I'm not going after Adrian."

Trent took a deep breath, struggling not to lose his patience. "I figured you might say that, so I took the liberty of finding something to encourage you..."

He nodded to Bennett, who left the room, then returned a moment later dragging a young girl by the arm. She was fourteen years old and dressed in jogging pants and a hooded sweater. Her eyes were red from crying and her long, dark hair was messy from the struggle she'd put up when Bennett took her from her home a few hours ago. He marched her up to Trent's desk and held her still.

Miley Tevani stared at Trent, her anger and hatred matched only by her fear.

"I've got someone here who'd like to say hello." He placed the phone on speaker and held it in front of the girl's face.

"H-hello?" she said nervously.

"Miley? Sweetie, is that you?" said Dominique, her voice cracking with emotion.

"Mom? Oh my God, Mom! Help!" she screamed.

"Baby! Oh, God! Baby, it's okay—Mommy's gonna come get you, okay? Just be brave, sweetie!"

Trent took the phone off speaker and nodded to Bennett, who escorted her back out of the office. When he spoke to Dominique, he was smiling from ear to ear.

"I'm sure I don't need to spell this out for you, you stubborn bitch. Bring me Adrian Hell's head, or I'll send you your daughter's in the fucking mail!"

"I swear I'm gonna blow your goddamn brains out!" she replied, unable to suppress her anger. "If you hurt a hair on her head, I'm gonna—"

"No, you're not," he interrupted casually. "You're gonna go and kill Adrian Hell, then you can pick your daughter up. She won't be harmed as long as you do what you were paid to do. Making threats to me won't get you anywhere, sweetheart. Now I don't wanna have to remind you again. Go and do your fucking job!"

He ended the call and threw his cell phone across the room with frustration. It shattered against the far wall just as Bennett re-entered, narrowly missing his head. He ducked instinctively before closing the door. As he approached Trent's desk, he glanced at the remains of the phone.

Christ... that's the third time this week, he thought.

"Everything okay, Mr. Trent?" he asked.

Trent sighed heavily. "Why do people insist on pushing me?"

Bennett remained silent, sensing the question was rhetorical.

"Is the girl secure?" asked Trent.

Bennett nodded. "A couple of the guys are watching her down the hall. She's tied up and not going anywhere."

"Good. I want you to go and keep an eye on Dominique. Make sure she does her job this time, will you? And if she doesn't, kill her."

He nodded again but hesitated before leaving, as if wanting to speak but unsure if he should. Trent noticed.

"What?"

"If I have to kill her, what do we do about her kid?" he asked.

Trent held his gaze without a word, then simply turned his back on him. He stared out the window of his office at the gray skies outside.

Bennett sighed and took his leave, having been given the answer to his question without any words needed.

Trent didn't think of himself as a monster, despite having done some truly monstrous things in his life. He classed himself as a businessman, nothing more. And he would do whatever it took to ensure the success of his business. If Dominique betrayed him again, he'd have her executed in a heartbeat. As for her child... well, Trent hated loose ends, but he could always find a use for her. In a few years, he could put her to work in one of his clubs, maybe. But then he'd have to look after her until she was ready, which would be time-consuming and a hindrance.

No... he'd just kill her. He would bury her with her fucking mother.

28

JIMMY MANHATTAN

Jimmy Manhattan was sitting at a table in Walkers Sports Bar, cradling a double whiskey in his hand. Next to him, Paulie Tarantina was sending a text message to some of the guys on their payroll, issuing instructions to their respective businesses.

Manhattan looked around. The bar was mostly empty, save for the three men that Tarantina insisted follow them everywhere; the bartender, who was cleaning some glasses behind the bar; and one patron, who sat in the corner facing the door, drinking a beer and reading the newspaper.

He looked at the stairs leading up to the room above. It seemed so long ago that he climbed them, fresh out of hospital, and put in motion his plan to take over the city. In truth, only four days had passed. But in that time, he had indeed taken over nearly all illegal activity in Allentown. It was an impressive feat, and it made a bold statement to anyone who would challenge him.

Except Wilson Trent.

He cursed himself for neglecting to consider the bigger picture when making his plans. He looked at things one city at a time. But what he should've done was consider the entire state before making his move. Still, he couldn't help bad luck. He just needed to make sure he was ready for what was coming.

He thought back to his conversation with Adrian Hell earlier that morning. He smiled at Adrian's weakness. He'd called him to tell him about Wilson Trent, warning him about his discovery like a friend or colleague would. He allowed himself a moment of pride. His plan to play Adrian was working better than he'd expected. He had his own issues with Trent, and his involvement would likely cause enough of a distraction that he'd be able to capitalize and take over once Trent had been killed. He knew enough about Adrian Hell to know that people were unlikely to survive if they were in his crosshairs. But it wasn't just Trent who'd be distracted by this. When the time was right, he'd take out Adrian himself.

He smiled to himself as he took another sip of his drink and remembered, somewhat fondly, slicing his face with a scalpel. He remembered him saving his life in San Francisco. And now he'd called up with a warning of a potential attack from one of the biggest crime lords in the United States.

But Manhattan was way ahead of him. As soon as he found out about Trent, he'd prepared himself for retaliation. But for his plan to work, he needed to keep his cards close to his chest. Even from those closest to him. If things went as he expected they would, he'd need people's reactions to be as believable as possible, to keep up appearances.

"What now, Mr. Manhattan?" asked Tarantina, placing his phone on the table and picking up his glass of water.

"We're in no position to go up against Trent," Manhattan replied. "Diplomacy is our only move. I have a feeling our new ally is looking for ways to get to Trent as well, so we just need to bide our time and wait for our moment."

Tarantina nodded as he sipped his drink.

"I had no idea Trent was this powerful," he said after a moment.

"Me neither," conceded Manhattan. "Of course, I'd *heard* of him, but back when I was running the West Coast with Pellaggio, Trent was nothing compared to what he is now. He was a real slow burner—he took his time and played the game, and now he owns everything. You've got to admire that."

"Do you think we can do everything we want to with him in the picture?"

Manhattan took another sip of his whiskey and shrugged. "Honestly? I think we could, but there's no way he'd sit back and make it easy for us. That would lead to a turf war, and it costs a lot of money if you want to win one of those."

"So, what did Adrian Hell say to you?"

"He said to prepare for war. Trent's after our blood since we ordered the hit on Johnny King."

"Can we not make it look like Adrian acted independently? Shift the blame away from us? From what you said, those two clearly have history, so Trent might buy it. Then we can bypass the confrontation and seize more power in the aftermath."

Manhattan smiled. "I've always said you were smart enough to run your own business, Paulie. I've not forgotten what he's done to me in the past, and I will make sure he pays for it all. There's obviously something between him and Trent, and I'm keen to find out what that is. Maybe an opportunity to exploit whatever history those two have will present itself soon, and I'll be ready if that happens. But until then, we play this smart and patient, and focus on what we *do* know, which is that Wilson Trent will be looking to us for payback. We need to make sure we handle him correctly. We have the back-up plan of blaming Adrian, should it make sense to do so, but I think we need to focus on working *with* Trent, not against him."

Tarantina nodded slowly, as if taking notes from a teacher, and then silence fell between them. Ten more minutes passed without a word, both men enjoying a rare moment of relaxation.

The door swung open, and four men walked in. One walked in first with the other three behind him in a loose semi-circle. The man in front was tall and well built, wearing a tight black t-shirt under an open jacket. The men behind him were all dressed in suits, with no ties. They were a little shorter, but of similar stature.

They all scanned the bar before their eyes settled on Manhattan and Tarantina.

"Boss..." said Tarantina.

Manhattan looked up and silently signaled to the two bodyguards standing near them and the one over by the bar to do their jobs. They all quickly moved to intercept the new arrivals.

Both groups of men squared off to each other, threatening with evil looks and puffed chests, as only hired muscle could do. Manhattan watched for a moment before speaking.

"Can I help you, gentlemen?" he asked.

The man at the front looked past the bodyguards,

directly at Manhattan. He wasn't intimidated in the slightest. If anything, he was a little bemused.

"You Jimmy Manhattan?" he replied.

"Who wants to know?" said Tarantina, standing and joining the group of men. He stood directly in front of the man who spoke. He was a lot shorter, but what Tarantina lacked in height, he more than made up for in violence. When it came down to it, if he was let off his leash, Tarantina was an animal.

Manhattan suppressed a smile. "Easy, Paulie," he said. "I'm sure we can avoid any unnecessary conflict here." He turned to the new arrivals. "I am Jimmy Manhattan, yes. And you are?"

"My name's Duncan. I'm here because Mr. Trent has requested I take you to see him."

Manhattan nodded slowly. *Just like Adrian said,* he thought.

"Can I politely decline his invitation?"

"If he was inviting you, you'd have the option, sure," he replied with a shrug. "But this ain't an invitation—it's an order. So, get to it, Pops."

Manhattan allowed a smile. "You do realize I'm about the same age as your employer? I think *Pops* is a little below the belt, don't you?"

In the blink of an eye, Duncan swung his right hand, catching Tarantina on the side of the face. He staggered backward, completely unprepared for the attack, and over-balanced, crashing into the three bodyguards. Duncan side-stepped to his left, out of the way, while his three men all drew their pistols and opened fire, riddling Manhattan's men with bullets. Tarantina caught one in his shoulder but managed to stay standing, moving slowly over to Manhattan's side.

It was over as quickly as it had begun, and an eerie silence descended on the bar. The smell of gunpowder was strong in the air. The bartender had ducked down behind the counter, and the lone customer sitting near the door had fled the bar when the shooting started.

Duncan stood in front of his three men, arms folded across his chest, facing Manhattan, who had remained seated throughout. He had expected some sort of display of dominance—an extreme message sent early and quickly. He knew how to handle the situation. He'd played the game many times before.

He stood, slowly, placing his empty glass on the table.

"You've made your point," he said nonchalantly. "Let's go and see Mr. Trent, shall we?"

"Word of advice," said Duncan. "Drop your gentleman act. You ain't made that much of a name for yourself yet. You should be very afraid right now."

Manhattan smiled. "Not at all," he replied. "Mr. Trent and I are similar. We're both businessmen at the end of the day, and I'm sure he'll understand it's in his best interest to do what's good for business. I have no issue with him, and there's no reason he should have an issue with me."

"That's for you and Trent to talk about. I'm just the delivery man. Now move your ass." He grabbed Manhattan by the arm and ushered him to the front of the little posse as they made their way out of the bar. He looked over his left shoulder to one of his men, nodding toward Tarantina. "Bring that piece of shit too."

A few minutes later, they were both bundled into the back of two separate black four-by-fours with dark tinted windows. Duncan sat in the back with Manhattan in one of them, and two of the men took Tarantina in the other.

As they set off on the journey back to Pittsburgh,

Manhattan relaxed against the black leather seat and smiled to himself.

So far, so predictable, he thought.

"What're you smilin' at?" asked Duncan.

Manhattan didn't reply. He just stared through the window at the passing traffic, playing the chess game over and over in his head, planning his next few moves.

29

ADRIAN HELL

We're all in my motel room. Josh is sitting at the table by the window and working away on his laptop, planning his digital bank robbery. Frank's sitting on the bed, leaning forward with his elbows on his knees and his head in his hands. I'm pacing back and forth impatiently. I'm so close to this all being over. I hate all the waiting around. But I know we need to do this right.

"What time will the game kick off tonight?" I ask.

"About eight," Frank replies without looking up.

"Okay," I nod. "We'll need to make sure we're in place about seven."

"You've got a plan?" Josh asks, his head still buried in his laptop. "That's not like you…"

"Desperate times, desperate measures," I say with a half-smile.

I know we've only got one real chance of the plan work-ing. Trent will be expecting us to make a move soon, so he'll have increased security. Josh needs time to make sure the online heist goes off as planned, so I have to rely on Frank's help to get ready for the game later this evening.

"Where are we up to?" I ask Josh. "Are you good to go?"

"Now I know where all Trent's money is, I have to program my virus to infiltrate all the different accounts simultaneously, then transfer the money into the single account I've set up in the name of a dummy corporation. Then I'll use a different algorithm to re-transfer the money in small amounts, no more than a dollar, to random bank accounts across the country. The algorithm will continue to run, moving each individual small amount every half-hour into a new account, making it practically impossible to trace the money once it's left Trent's accounts."

Frank finally looks up. "Jesus Christ, you can do that?" he asks, taken aback by how extravagant the plan sounds.

Josh nods. "It's not easy, but I can," he says. "I've been putting together the code since we arrived on the East Coast. Only thing missing was Trent's financials. Now that we have them, the final piece is in place."

"Can the origin of the code be traced?" he asks.

I raise my eyebrows, surprised that Frank seems to understand at least half of what Josh is saying. I'm completely lost, and I'm happy to sit thinking about how it'll all play out once we get to the Steelers game.

"I'm using every encryption I have to bounce and mask my signal. It's not unbreakable, but it'll take a lot of people a long time, and that's all that matters. Once Trent's dealt with, the algorithm can stop, and we can simply put the money where we want it and ride off into the sunset as rich men."

"How much money does he have, exactly?" I ask.

"Close to quarter of a billion dollars."

"Christ..." mutters Frank.

I let out a low whistle. That's some serious change. I'm not doing this for the money—I've got plenty of my own. But someone like Trent shouldn't be allowed that amount of money or the level of power it grants.

"Nothing can replace what I've... *we've* lost," I say, looking at Frank. "But you have to admit, that's a helluva compensation payout."

He nods absently, lost in his own thoughts.

"You want anything to drink?" I ask them both. "I'm just gonna go to the vending machine in reception and get a bottle of water."

"Pepsi, please," says Josh.

"I'm good, thanks," Frank replies.

I open the door and step outside. The sky's gray and filled with low clouds. It's stayed dry for most of the day. It's starting to darken, and the temperature's dropped a little as the light starts to fade.

I look around quickly. The parking lot's empty, apart from Frank's sedan, which is in the middle, directly facing the row of three rooms we've rented.

I shut the door behind me but immediately stop, alert.

What was that?

I just heard a low, hollow whooshing noise. It sounds far away and is worryingly familiar. It's the same noise I heard over a week ago, in San Francisco. It's the unmistakable sound of someone firing a rocket launcher. I quickly look around for the source. A small, bright light appears from directly opposite the motel complex, seemingly from the rooftop of a nearby building. Everything slows down as I see it rushing toward me, far too late to be able to do anything. I stand watching with dumbfounded horror.

"Guys! Hit the deck!" I shout as loud as I can, hoping they hear me from outside.

The rocket hits Frank's car, which disappears in a thunderous explosion and a brilliant flash of light that sears my eyes. The force of the blast sends me crashing backward and through the door, taking it off its hinges.

I'm lying flat on my back, on top of the door on the floor of my motel room. Every time I blink, I see flashes of white. My eyes are sore from the blast. My ears are ringing too, and I'm disoriented as I prop myself up on my elbows.

"Is everyone all right?" I ask, hoping for a response.

I sit up and look around the room. Frank's lying face-down on the floor on the other side of the bed. Josh is still sitting at the table, his hands frozen over the keyboard of his laptop, his eyes transfixed on the now open doorway and his jaw hanging loose.

"What the..." he starts. "Adrian!"

"I'm all right," I say, holding a hand up and waving it slowly. "Did anyone see who or what hit us?"

"No. We heard you shout, then everything went boom."

"Frank, you okay?" I shout over.

He grunts, which I take as a sign he's fine, albeit a little shocked and disgruntled that his car's just been decimated.

I stand slowly, blinking and rubbing my eyes to clear my vision. I look out of the doorway at the parking lot. The sedan is a flaming wreck. Car parts litter the area. I step outside, feeling the heat from the explosion on my skin. I can't see anything or anyone, but as the ringing in my ears subsides, I hear a motorcycle approaching from the left. Behind me, I hear Josh shout something to Frank, but the words are drowned out as a black Ducati turns into the parking lot and stops just inside the entrance. A leather-clad figure climbs off it, dressed completely in black. They have a rocket launcher, loaded, over their shoulder and a gun belt around their waist with a pistol attached. They walk toward me, undoing the chinstrap on their helmet. As they lift it off, long dark hair falls out and rests on their shoulders.

"Hey, big boy," says Dominique Tevani. She drops the helmet on the ground and draws her pistol in one swift motion. "You miss me?"

"Oh..." I say, trying to hide my surprise and displeasure. "It's you. I kinda hoped you and I had developed an understanding after we last met?"

She smiles that killer smile but without any of the playfulness I saw before.

"That was a momentary lapse of reason," she says. "Nothing more."

She fires off a few rounds in succession. I run to the right, staying low, and dive for cover behind the bushes that border the parking lot.

Without a moment's reprieve, I hear her drop the pistol, swing the rocket launcher around on its shoulder strap, and aim at my room.

"No!" I yell, but it's futile.

She pulls the trigger and fires. The rocket makes its whooshing noise again—only it sounds much louder this time. A second later, my room and the ones on either side of it explode in a shower of brick and fire.

I look over from my cover as flames billow out in all directions. My eyes are wide with a mixture of fear, anger, and sadness. I don't know what to think. As my brain fights to kick into survival mode, I just about manage a single word.

"No..."

. . .

16:32 EDT

I'm kneeling behind the bush, staring blankly at the remains of the motel for what feels like hours. But my brain finally kicks into gear and tells me I've only been there a few seconds, and I need to take out my Berettas and fight.

So, I do.

I reach behind me, drawing both guns simultaneously, and then stand. I walk purposefully toward Dominique, firing round after round at the beautiful bitch that's just blown up my best friend and my brother-in-law.

She's standing, still holding the rocket launcher, looking on with proud satisfaction at the carnage she's caused. My bullets distract her and she dives to her right, dropping the launcher. She retrieves her own pistol and returns fire.

We both zigzag and run and dive behind whatever we can, trading bullet for bullet. I'm squeezing the triggers in sheer anger. I'm not even aiming at her. I just want to fire at her over and over again, to let my pain and hatred flow out of me with every round.

She clicks on an empty chamber a second before I do. We both stare at each other for a moment, catching our breath, feeding off the adrenaline and feeling the heat from the flames. In the distance, I hear sirens. All kinds of emergency services will be arriving in a few minutes.

I throw my guns down and run at her. She does the same, and we meet in the middle near her motorcycle. Against someone like her, leading with an attack is be a bad move. So, I anticipate her first punch, which is a right hook to the kidney, and lead with a block with my left arm. Positioned correctly, she punches the bend of my elbow. She doesn't miss a beat and immediately counters with a swinging left hook aimed high at my left temple.

I see it coming, so I duck and roll under it to my right. Then I launch my own—a straight right punch—at her face, which connects sweetly on her left cheek. As she rocks backward from the impact, I step through and push my right foot through the kneecap of her back leg. The angle is perfect, so it doesn't break, but it knocks her further off-balance and sends her crashing to the ground. I take a step toward her but hesitate. My survival instincts take over from my emotions, protecting me. I let her get back to her feet. She's favoring her right leg after the kick to her knee, but she isn't fazed at all.

"Screw you, Adrian!" she yells over the noise of the crackling flames. "Just accept it—you've got nothing left. I'm doing you a favor by taking your life. What have you got to live for?"

I raise an eyebrow. It's a classic attempt to knock me off my game psychologically. I was trained a long time ago to stop myself from reacting to mental attacks like that. I'm surprised at how quickly she's resorted to what we in the business would consider a last resort tactic. Is she really getting *that* desperate so quickly?

I smile back at her and slowly shake my head. "Nice try."

She charges at me again, leading with a roundhouse kick from the right that's aimed at my side. I hook my left arm under her leg, catching it and absorbing what little impact made it through. I'm going to drop my right elbow down across her extended leg, as it'll cause farther damage to her knee. But as I'm about to, she jumps up with her left leg and hooks it around, kicking it into my right temple. It takes me by surprise, and I let her go as I drop to my knees.

My head's spinning from the impact and it momentarily disorients me.

She lands on her front but bounces back to her feet and pounces on me immediately. She delivers a knee to my jaw, which I just about manage to get my hands in front of, but I do little to parry it. It sends me sprawling backward to the ground. I have no comprehension of my surroundings as I lie spread-eagled on the parking lot, looking up at a sky black with smoke and alive with the glow of the blaze.

I grunt in pain as she leaps on me, straddling my chest. Her thighs tighten, gripping my sides like a vice and squeezing the air out of me. I buck once with my hips, as hard as I can, but she holds on and rains down blow after blow on my face. I get both my arms up, and my forearms take the brunt of the punishment, but I'm in serious trouble if I stay where I am for long...

I thrust my hips up again, this time dislodging her slightly. Sensing a way out, I buck one last time and roll to my left. She loses her grip and falls to the side. I continue to roll over and wind up on top of her with her legs on either side of me, resting on my hips. She manages to keep me at a distance by pushing down with her legs, forcing my hips back, but I land a couple of good shots to her head and body.

She winces in pain but fights on. Her stunning features contort with rage and desperation as we each struggle to gain the upper hand. I throw a straight right, aiming for the bridge of her nose. If I connect, it'll break it and make her eyes water, blurring her vision and restricting her ability to take a deep breath. But as I throw the punch, she catches my arm with both her hands and holds my wrist, pulling me toward her and wrapping her legs around me. She crosses her feet behind me, trapping my head and right arm completely in the triangle formed by her legs. She squeezes with every ounce of strength she has left and pulls me toward her. The pressure on my throat is tremendous, and I'm instantly constricted.

I can feel myself losing consciousness...

...

...

...

I re-focus on her as the world fades back to life.

I must've slipped away then...

...

...

...

...and again! Shit! I need to get out of this. The bitch is killing me!

I frantically hammer her left side with small hook shots from my free arm, but I can't get enough momentum behind them to do any significant damage.

My mind races to think of a way out. I look around as much as I can, but there's nothing nearby I can use.

It's getting harder to breathe as she tightens her grip around my neck and shoulder. I've given up trying to fight my way out with my free arm. There's only one thing left to try...

On my knees, being pulled forward by Dominique, I slowly bring one leg forward, then the other, so I'm in a low squat. I grip one of her wrists with my right hand as much as I can, then grab her waist with my left and squeeze, sliding my hand underneath her body. Then, with one insanely difficult gulp of air, I use every last ounce of energy I have to stand up.

The strain on my legs and arms is intense, and it momentarily causes her thighs to tighten even more, but I somehow manage to stand up straight. I hold her above me, her toned stomach pressing against my face. She's no longer pulling me by my right arm—I have a hold of her instead of the other way around. My left hand is underneath her ass, holding her steady for a split-second; the scene is frozen in a violent, almost sexual position.

Then I use everything I have left to slam her down on the blacktop. I bend forward and put all my momentum into pushing her through the goddamn parking lot. Her back and head connect first with a sickening thud. She lets out a grunt of pain as I fall forward, landing on top of her, exhausted. Her body twitches once as my weight crushes her, then she remains still.

I push myself off and fall back, so I'm sitting down, facing her. There's an expanding pool of blood flowing slowly out from underneath her head as she lies motionless.

I gasp for air, remembering I've just been starved of oxygen and I've asked my body to use much more than it had available.

My surroundings bleed slowly into focus. The heat from the blast, the darkness of the sky, the noise of the sirens...

Shit!

I scramble to my feet, coughing as I massage my throat. The police and the fire department will be here any moment, so I have to make myself scarce. I gather up my guns and holster them. I stand staring at my decimated motel room for a moment.

Josh...

"Adrian!"

I frown.

Josh?

"Adrian!"

What the...

"Josh?" I shout, unsure if the voice is even real.

I look around. Over to the right, close to where the reception building is, I see Josh and Frank looking on.

I walk over slowly, relieved but confused. "How the hell did you…"

"We ran out after the first explosion," Josh explains, "just before that crazy bitch blew up the motel. I'm guessing you didn't hear me shouting?"

I shake my head. "I thought you were both dead…"

Josh raises an eyebrow. "Were you upset?"

I shrug, keeping my face deadpan. "I paused for a whole thirty seconds to mourn you before I moved on with my life. I almost shed a tear…"

A smile creeps over both our faces at the same time, and we laugh out loud. But before I can say anything else, a voice behind me interrupts our short-lived reprieve.

"Adrian!"

I turn and see Dominique staggering toward me like an extra from *Dawn of the Dead*. How the hell is she still alive?

"Adrian, I… I have to kill you. You don't understand!"

She's completely helpless and has no chance of even raising a hand to me. I almost feel sorry for her.

"Dominique, it's over," I say. "Get out of here and don't look back."

"I can't!" she continues. "You… have to… die!"

Before she can take another agonizing step toward me, I hear three loud gunshots from behind me. I freeze and close my eyes instinctively, tensing my entire body. Despite the noise all around, the next few seconds pass in silence.

I open one eye… then the other. I turn and see Frank standing with his legs wide apart and his Taurus 605 held out in front of him with both hands, smoke twirling from the barrel.

I relax and look at Josh, who's standing with his mouth open, staring blankly at me. I slowly turn back and see Dominique lying on the ground, blood pumping from three bullet holes in her chest.

I look back at Frank. Josh is slowly pushing his arms down. He's in shock at having just pulled the trigger.

I walk over to them both hurriedly. "We need to leave... now."

Frank doesn't answer, or even take his eyes off Dominique's body.

"Frank!" He turns to me. "We need to move."

He nods vacantly and turns to follow Josh, who has set off running past the reception area and over the small wall to the road beyond. We catch up with him and cross the street.

"We'll split up here," I say. "We're only about fifteen minutes from the city's center on foot. We'll all meet up in half an hour outside the Hilton, okay? We'll lie low in the Winnebago."

They both nod.

"Frank, are you okay?" I ask.

"Yeah, I'm fine," he replies unconvincingly.

I nod again, letting the matter drop, and we all set off in different directions.

I take one last look behind me as I set off, looking at Dominique's motionless corpse with the fire burning fierce and bright behind it.

What a goddamn waste.

30

ADRIAN HELL

17:01 EDT

We all arrived back at the Hilton hotel within minutes of each other, and we've congregated in the parking lot around the Winnebago. Frank looks out of breath and Josh seems frustrated, but we're all in one piece, which is a blessing.

"Everyone okay?" I ask.

Frank's leaning forward, his hands resting just above his knees. "I haven't done that much exercise in years," he replies.

Josh remains silent, pacing up and down for a few moments.

"Josh?" I say.

"My laptop's fried," he says eventually. "Damaged beyond repair in the blast. I salvaged what I could and downloaded it to a USB drive, but I don't know if I've got enough to launch my virus and attack the accounts."

I sigh heavily. If that's the case, it's a massive blow to us. Dominique's attack was completely unexpected, and I'm lucky to still be alive after fighting with her. I just hope Josh can still work his magic with what he has. He hates it when his toys get damaged...

We all clamber into the back of the Winnebago. Josh turns on a spare laptop and sits down at his makeshift workbench in silence. I sit on the old sofa along the back and rest my head against the pillows. It's been a long few days. I feel tired, I'm sore from various fights and gunshot wounds, and the light at the end of the tunnel has just been moved a little farther away than it was before.

I look over at Frank, who's shifting uncomfortably on the spot, like he's unsure if it's okay for him to sit down. His hands are trembling a little, and he's sweating. And not, I suspect, purely because of the run to get here.

"You did great back there, Frank," I say. "Are you all right?"

He smiles half-heartedly and gives a weak nod. He looks like he's uneasy at receiving a compliment for having just taken a life—probably for the first time. He's nervously looking around and fidgeting with his hands.

"Ever fired that gun before?" I ask.

He shakes his head.

"You're a great shot," I say with a smile, trying to help him relax and take his mind off the pending onset of shock.

Again, he forces a weak smile.

"Frank, it's never easy taking a life..."

"Says the professional killer?" he scoffs.

"Yeah, says me. I'm speaking from experience. It's never straightforward squeezing that trigger, and you should be thankful that you feel as bad as you do."

"Thankful? Why the hell would I be *thankful*?"

"Because if you didn't feel bad, or uneasy, or scared... if you felt complete indifference to the fact someone is no longer breathing because of you... you'd be me. And you wouldn't want *that*, trust me. Being me sucks."

He regards me for a moment in silence, then turns and walks through to the front. He sits down in the passenger seat and stares out across the parking lot.

"Halle-fucking-lujah!" Josh shouts.

"Good news?" I ask.

"I was able to use what I saved from my laptop, and we're good to go, Boss. I press this button, and we steal a quarter of a billion dollars from Wilson Trent and hide it in plain sight across the country until you wanna keep it all in my bank account!"

I look at him with a raised eyebrow.

"Okay, *your* bank account..."

"Better..." I say with a smile. I check the time. Despite the unexpected setback, we're still on track for my plan to work. "Do it."

Josh smiles, then looks down at the Enter key on his laptop. After a brief moment of ceremony, he presses it.

"Boom!" he exclaims. "You now have two hundred and fifty million dollars! Drinks on you?"

I laugh and we bump fists. This is a huge victory for us and much needed, given the last couple of hours. But we still have a long way to go.

"C'mon, we need to get moving."

"Where?" he asks.

I smile. "I'll fill you in as you drive."

17:42 EDT

. . .

Josh is driving with me next to him. Frank's sitting on the sofa in the back in silence. I figure it's best to leave him be and let him deal with things in his own way. The poor guy has really been thrown in at the deep end, and the last twenty-four hours have been tough on him.

Having called ahead for directions, we pull up outside Oscar Brown's other warehouse complex—his smaller one in Pittsburgh. Well, I say *smaller*, but the place is still huge. There are two massive buildings directly in front of us, which look like aircraft hangars. There's another, smaller building over on the left, which Oscar told me to head for.

We get out and make our way across the broken, wet concrete. I check the time on my phone. I hope to God that he's here. There are no signs of life, and we're cutting it fine as it is.

"Where are we?" asks Frank as he climbs out behind us.

"Second home of the world's first illegal arms supermarket," I reply.

"Sorry I asked..." he mutters to himself.

As we approach, the door in front of us opens. Oscar Brown appears with a big smile on his face. "You found it okay?" he asks.

"Yeah, thanks," I say. "Sorry to drag you halfway across the state on short notice, but time is of the essence. I need a... specialty item."

He regards me for a moment, sensing the tone and the mood. "Step into my office," he says, beckoning me with his hand.

I turn to Josh. "You wait here with Frank," I say. "I won't be a minute."

"What you got up your sleeve, Boss?" he asks with a frown.

I smile and follow Oscar into the warehouse.

. . .

18:25 EDT

We're parked outside the service entrance at the back of Heinz Field. I've just finished explaining my plan to Josh and Frank, and they seem impressed, despite some initial concerns.

"You're crazy," says Frank, shaking his head in disbelief. "You're actually certifiable, you know that?"

"It's been pointed out to me once or twice, yeah," I reply. "So, are you in?"

He gestures with his arms in mild exasperation. "Why the hell not..."

I smile and turn to Josh, raising an eyebrow and silently asking him the same question.

"I just don't understand... when did your Inner Satan start making insane, yet beautifully intelligent schemes like this one?"

"What can I say?" I reply. "I got inspired, I guess. Unique circumstances... unique approach."

"Unique? Good—because it's really weird not being the brains behind this outfit!"

We laugh and get out of the Winnebago. I instinctively check my guns at my back by tapping both barrels. Josh stretches and cracks his neck and shoulders, as if he's limbering up for a workout. Inside, Frank lowers the window, having slid into the driver's seat, and leans out.

"I'll park over there," he says, pointing to an empty area of the parking lot. "See you on the other side."

"Thanks, Frank. I appreciate your help with all this."

He nods and gives me a tired half-smile before driving off, leaving Josh and me standing side by side.

"You ready?" I ask.

"Ready," he replies.

We bump fists and walk over to the service entrance, where security and catering companies come and go during game days. The door's open, and we can see one security guard just inside. Ahead of us, two men wearing red T-shirts enter, flashing the guard the passes they have attached to a lanyard that hangs around their necks.

"I'll handle him," I say, striding forward ahead of Josh.

"I bet you will..." I hear him say behind me.

I walk through the door, and the security guard stands up from the stool he was sitting on. He holds out his hand to stop us. He's a tall, dark-skinned man and broad—just on the overweight side of well-built. He has short black hair and a thin moustache. He's dressed in jeans and a navy-blue jacket.

"Got ya pass?" he asks.

"Y'know, I've gone and left it in my car,' I say, patting my pockets as if searching for it. "But I'm running really late. Can you just let me past, and I'll come and get it on my break later?"

The guard's face is expressionless, almost bored. He's probably heard it all a thousand times before. "No pass, no entry."

I sigh. Why doesn't anyone ever just accept the story I tell them? Why do they always have to give just enough of a shit about whatever they do to make me have to resort to plan B?

Without another word, I leap forward and smash my forehead into the bridge of his nose. He's about my height, which means I'm able to get the perfect angle as my head arches forward. I connect sweetly, and the guard falls backward like a tree and sprawls out on the floor.

Josh appears behind me and steps over the unconscious body with an exaggerated lunge.

"Smooth..." he says.

"I did try the subtle approach," I reply defensively. "He just wasn't buying it."

He turns around and starts walking backward as he speaks. He holds his arms out to the sides and laughs.

"Well, I guess you get points for effort!" As he turns back around, he bumps into a caterer coming out of one of the rooms on the left. "Ah, jeez... sorry, man."

The caterer waves him away as if to say it's no big deal. But as he's about to walk off, Josh grabs his arm and holds him in place, looking him up and down. He looks over at me with a smile, then turns back to the caterer.

"Okay, this is gonna sound weird, but... I need your clothes, your boots, and your motorcycle."

The guy looks horrified and immediately tries to make a run for it, but Josh trips him up and punches him in the face on the way down, knocking him out cold. I walk over to him, exaggerating the step I take over the body of the unconscious caterer.

"*Smooth...*" I say with a smile.

"I learned from the best," he replies. "You not impressed with the Arnie quote just then?"

I shrug. "I've heard better."

He drags the guy into the room he'd just come out of. As the door is swinging shut, he sticks his head back out, his expression deadpan.

"I'll be back."

I roll my eyes. "If you say, *Get to the chopper*, I'm going to shoot you. Now hurry up, will you?"

He disappears inside, and a few minutes later walks out dressed as a caterer. The shirt's a bit too small for him, and he can't tuck it in properly at the back, but it won't make much difference. He looks believable, which is the main thing.

"Put your hair in a ponytail," I say. "They wouldn't let you wear it down if you were serving food and drinks to people."

"No probs," he says, tying it up.

On the wall down the corridor is a large, laminated floor plan of the stadium and seating. We walk over to it and find the exact location of where Trent's private box is.

"You sure this plan of yours will work?" he asks me.

"Nope... but it's a really good plan, and if it *does* work, it will be a brilliant way to get rid of Wilson Trent once and for all."

"He certainly won't see it coming."

"No one expects me to think this much about something. That's why."

"No kidding!"

"Screw you," I say with a smile. "Right, you go find some props. I'll wait for my cue."

We set off in different directions, knowing that in little under an hour, this could all be over.

31

WILSON TRENT

Wilson Trent sat at a table in a small restaurant close to Heinz Field, the home turf of the Pittsburgh Steelers. When the opportunity arose, he liked to indulge himself by going to watch the team he'd supported since he was a child. It was the one thing he took time out to do just for himself. He worked hard running the empire he'd built over the last thirty or so years, and football was his own little reward. He was proud of the fact he could see the stadium from the window of his penthouse suite as well.

He was a creature of habit, and before every game, he came to the same restaurant for something to eat. He was surrounded by his own protection detail. There were two men by the door, one at the counter, and two on either side of him, one at each table. The rest of the place was mostly empty. That's why Trent liked it so much—all the crowds heading to the game went to the bars nearby, or for pre-match drinks and food in the stadium itself, meaning he could enjoy his meal in peace before surrounding himself with the noise of the fans.

The door opened and Bennett walked in, striding purposefully toward Trent. He approached the table and cleared his throat, announcing his arrival. Trent didn't look up from his food.

"I hope you have good news for me," he said.

Bennett shifted nervously on the spot for a moment before replying. "I did as you asked, Boss," he said. "I followed the assassin."

"And?"

"She fired a rocket launcher at Adrian's motel room. She blew up their car, then fired again and blew up half the motel."

Trent half-smiled. "You've got to admire her approach."

Bennett took a deep breath before continuing. "But she didn't kill him, or either of his friends. She had a pretty brutal fight with him, and he drove her head into the goddamn parking lot—split her skull wide open. To her credit, she got up and went after him again, but some guy shot her dead."

Trent put down his knife and fork and dabbed the corners of his mouth with his napkin. He took a small sip of his water before finally looking up at one of his most trusted enforcers.

"She failed?"

Bennett nodded.

"So, Adrian fucking Hughes—Hell... whatever he calls himself—he's still alive?"

He nodded again.

"How *fucking* hard is it to kill someone?' Trent yelled,

causing the few customers and staff in the restaurant to fall silent and turn to look at him.

He took a deep breath as he felt his anger swirling around inside of him, like he was trying to contain a tornado in a coffee mug. He paused, then stood and grabbed the knife off his plate. He walked over to the nearest occupied table, where a young man and woman were sitting. They both looked terrified and couldn't take their eyes off him. Trent grabbed the man by the hair and yanked his head back, then thrust the knife into his exposed throat. Once... twice... and a third time. He left it sticking out as blood spurted in a thick, crimson fountain all over the table and the young woman. She started screaming. Trent picked up the man's fork and stepped around the table. He grabbed the woman by her hair and drove her face into the table. Once... twice... her nose burst open and blood gushed down her face. Then, holding her head back, Trent jammed the fork into her right eye and pushed her aside, causing her to fall to the floor.

Nobody screamed. Nobody moved. Everyone froze.

Trent walked back to Bennett.

"See how fucking easy it is?" he said, frighteningly calm after his moment of explosive rage. "Why can't anyone kill Adrian Hell?"

"I don't know," he said.

Trent looked at each one of his men individually before turning back to Bennett.

"I'm going to the game," he announced. "You are going to find that sonofabitch and bring me his head. Or I'll take each and every one of yours."

He left the restaurant, hastily followed by all his men, except Bennett, whom he left standing there.

. . .

19:14 EDT

Trent stepped into his private box in Heinz Field, which was behind the goalposts at one end of the ground. He had a slightly raised, unobstructed view of the entire field. He sat down and looked out, relaxing and forgetting all of his troubles. The view alone was well worth the thousands of dollars he paid each season. Floodlights beamed down on the field below as the players warmed up, ahead of kick-off.

Inside the booth was a small, waist-high wall, then a double-glazed window, which could be slid open if required. He preferred having the window open, weather permitting, to soak up more of the atmosphere. He leaned forward and looked up at the evening sky, which was all but black and threatened another downpour. He hoped the weather would hold off long enough for the game to finish.

Surrounding him were the five men who had been with him in the restaurant, all standing in a loose semi-circle behind him. There was a knock on the door, and a caterer came in, pushing a cart with a bottle of champagne in an ice bucket on it. It was a vintage Krug Brut, which was Trent's personal favorite, and it cost around two thousand dollars a bottle.

"Drink, sir?" asked the caterer.

Trent nodded silently without taking his eyes off the field. The Steelers were warming up, and he was genuinely looking forward to seeing them play for the first time since the new season had started.

"How do you think the Steelers will fare this season?" asked the caterer.

Trent frowned at him with a mixture of confusion and

disgust. The caterer seemed unfazed, oblivious to who Trent was.

"You ask me," he continued. "I think they've got a good shot at it. Although, I'm not really much of a fan, myself. Never quite understood the appeal of the game. Like, for one thing, why do they call it football? They hardly touch the ball with their feet. And it's not even a ball, really. It's not round..."

Trent held up his hand to stop the caterer talking. His eyes narrowed as he looked him up and down. His long blond hair was tied back in a ponytail, and his white shirt was creased and partially untucked. He threw a quick glance to one of his men, who understood the silent command instantly and reached into his jacket, gripping the butt of the gun he had holstered inside. The other men quickly took note and followed suit.

"Do I know you?" asked Trent. "Because you're a real talkative guy and way too comfortable in my presence. So, do we know each other, or do you just dislike breathing?"

The caterer put the champagne bottle down slowly and held his hands up in silent apology. "No, sir. I don't think we've met before. I'm new to the job."

Trent stood and squared up to him. "Where are you from? Your accent sounds British."

The caterer nodded slowly. "I'm from London."

"And how long have you worked here?"

He checked his watch before answering. "About twenty minutes..."

"What?"

Trent's men all took a step toward their boss, sensing the need to offer protection. But the door burst open, kicked in from outside. Everyone turned round to see who was in the doorway. The caterer stepped in close to Trent and pressed a knife against his kidney.

"Yeah, we haven't met, so let me introduce myself. My name's Josh. I believe you know my friend?"

Josh nodded to the doorway, where Adrian Hell stood, a Beretta in each hand and an evil smile on his face.

32

ADRIAN HELL

I'm leaning against the wall just outside Trent's box, listening at the door as Josh plays his part beautifully. He's simply to wind Trent up enough for him to get distracted, so I can make my entrance and put the next phase of my plan into action. And from how it sounds in there, I figure the room's just about ready for me...

I draw both my guns, checking the magazines are full and the safety switches are off. I stand in front of the door and take a deep breath. Everything we've done over the last few days... everything I've done in the past eight years... it's all served as a prelude to this moment. I'm about to come face to face with Wilson Trent.

I can feel my Inner Satan snarling and spitting, pulling on its restraints and begging for freedom, so it could unleash its fury on the world.

Not quite yet...

I kick the door open so hard that it almost flies off its

hinges. I stand in the doorway and quickly survey the room. There are five bodyguards, each with their hands tucked inside their suit jackets—presumably reaching for their guns. Behind them, Josh is standing just behind Wilson Trent, close to his side and holding a knife to him.

"Yeah, we haven't met, so let me introduce myself," says Josh. "My name's Josh. I believe you know my friend?"

Trent and I hold each other's gaze for a moment. How easy it would be to put a bullet in his head right now. But that's not the plan. Besides, it could easily go through the glass and out into the surrounding crowd, and I'm keen to avoid any unwanted casualties... or attention.

"Not interrupting, am I?" I ask with a wicked smile.

"You!" seethes Trent through gritted teeth.

"Me..."

One of the bodyguards twitches; his gun hand moves a millimeter inside his jacket. I have both guns on Trent, but I move the one in my right hand and aim it at him.

"Don't be doing anything silly now, boys," I say. "Your lives depend on it."

I look over at Josh and nod imperceptibly. He moves away from Trent and stands between the bodyguards and me.

"All right, ladies, hands where I can see 'em," he says. It takes a moment, but they comply, much to Trent's dismay, though he remains silent.

Josh moves to each one individually, lightly frisking them and taking their guns. The first one he takes, he slides into his waistband at the back. The other four, he throws across the box into the corner.

"All clear, Boss," he announces after a few moments.

I haven't looked away from Trent since I entered the room. My entire body is tense and on edge. It's not that I'm not relaxed, but I have to physically restrain myself from rushing over and blowing Trent's head off. That's not the plan. The plan is to break him. Make him suffer.

And suffer, he shall.

"Good man," I reply. "Now Trent... where should we start?"

His unwavering gaze does its best to bore a hole of hatred right through me, but I see in his eyes that he knows he can't intimidate me, even if he doesn't fully understand why.

"How about I kill you with my bare hands, you arrogant prick?" he snarls.

I smile. "Don't confuse arrogance with knowledge. I'm confident because I know things about this situation that you don't. The fact that I'm better than you in every single way is beside the point."

It's Trent's turn to smile. I know what's coming. He's going to antagonize me, try to force me to make a mistake. I'm not going to like it, but I've prepared for it beforehand—as has Josh.

"I did it, y'know?" he says. "Pulled the trigger, I mean. I put a bullet into your wife's face and made your daughter watch. Then I made her beg before all my men emptied their clips into her. I tell you, she bounced around that kitchen floor like a ragdoll after every shot..."

My jaw muscles ache as I clench and tighten them. He's standing in front of me, grinning with fond recollection of how he murdered my family. I can feel my blood boiling underneath my skin, succumbing to an anger and rage I've never even dreamed of being capable of. My face must be telling quite a story; the five bodyguards and even Josh all take a step back, giving Trent and me some room. They all exchange worried glances with each other and then look at

Josh, who simply shrugs. He has a vague idea what's going to happen next, and he knows to stay out of the way.

With both my Berettas aimed squarely at Trent, I can feel myself starting to shake as I struggle to hold back the demon within. I take some long, deep breaths, trying to settle the kick of adrenaline that's surging through me.

"And to think," Trent continues. "That all happened... because of *you!*" He points his finger at me, jabbing the air as he explains. "*You* got your family killed because you took my son away from me!"

"Oh, give it a rest, will you?" I reply, breaking my silence with a calmness that even surprises me. "You didn't even *know* your son. He hated you and wanted nothing to do with you. He didn't even have your name. I did my research. You hadn't seen him since he was three. You banged some random whore one night and got her pregnant, then walked away from her and Darnell Harper when she demanded you help raise him. Let me guess—you killed her and left the boy in foster care? A victim of this country's broken system. No wonder he grew up to become such a worthless little bastard. I did the world a favor by blowing his goddamn head off. And yet you use him as justification for killing my wife and daughter, whom I loved with every ounce of my being. You want the truth? Yeah, you broke me. You took my soul and killed Adrian Hughes in the process. After a couple of years of searching, Adrian Hell found me and turned me into the monster I am today. I can end you with a click of my fingers, you fat piece of shit."

Trent looks both angry and, for what I imagine is the first time in his life, a little afraid. But he holds his ground and my gaze and speaks without skipping a beat.

"You don't intimidate me, Adrian. I've been around a long time, and I've seen it all. I don't even think you're that good a hitman. That bitch I hired to take you out came damn close more than once. If you were as good as you think you are, she'd never have gotten near you." He chuckles to himself, gaining confidence with each word he utters. "And you're gonna what? Click your fingers and finish me? Surrounded by sixty-five thousand witnesses? Go right ahead, you fuck!"

I smile. Then I slowly holster one Beretta, followed by the other. I put my left hand in my pocket and lean left against the doorframe. I casually look over at Josh, who's doing his best to hide his excitement over what's coming.

"You got anything you want to say to any of your boys here?" I ask, gesturing with a nod to the five men in the room.

"Ha! Why? You intend to take them all out with your bare hands?" he replies.

I look over at the five bodyguards, who are shifting nervously on the spot. I look each one of them in the eye with an apologetic expression. Josh takes a small step away from them, leaning against the far wall of the box. I look back at Trent. He frowns at me in disgust, not buying into the little show I'm putting on for him at all, which makes this whole thing even sweeter...

I wink at him and click my fingers on my right hand. His five bodyguards instantly drop dead on the floor.

Trent's jaw hits the floor a moment after the bodies do. I stand up straight and draw one of my Berettas again, taking aim at him. Josh steps over the pile of corpses and stands by my side.

"Wha... how... what the fuck just happened?" asks Trent, completely dumbfounded.

"Simple," I reply with a casual shrug. "I just killed five of your men by clicking my fingers."

"Oh, oh, can I have a go?" asks Josh excitedly. He makes a point of moving his hand around like a magician and then clicking his fingers. Trent frowns with more confusion.

"And what the fuck are you supposed to have just done?" he asks, regaining some of his composure.

"Me? I just robbed you of two hundred and fifty million dollars," replies Josh with a smile.

Trent's eyes go wide. I think under normal circumstances, if someone had said that, he'd have laughed them out of the building. But given what he's just seen me do, he's probably more inclined to believe him.

"You've *robbed* me?" he asks him.

"Of every last penny, you sanctimonious nutsack!"

"You see, Trent," I say, "this is what happens when you make an enemy out of me. I don't just get my revenge—and Lord knows I've been dreaming of doing *that* for the last ten years of my life—but I also beat you. I outplay you every step of the way and take everything you've ever had in this world away from you. Your power, your money, your bodyguards... everything. I've systematically picked you apart, and now you're standing in front of me, an absolute nobody with nothing to live for."

That is a no holds barred lesson in antagonizing someone, and he just got schooled.

He lets out a cry of unbridled fury, like a warrior on the battlefield standing over a fallen adversary. Given his height and weight, I'll admit his rage is an impressive sight. I can see out of the box, and in the general crowd, a section has stopped and turned to look, to see what the noise is.

I expected some kind of retaliation from him, obviously. But I honestly never thought he'd react like I would. He charges me, ducking down to his left and dropping his right shoulder as he does. Despite his size, he's fast, and he's on top of me before I realize he's moved. He slams into my gut and sends us both flying backward out of the box and into the corridor. He's knocked the wind out of me, and I'm lying flat on my back, coughing. My gun's flown out of my hand and is out of reach.

Trent leaps to his feet and runs back into the box, tackling Josh as well. I sit up, regaining my composure as I look on. Despite the few blocks he's managed to get in the way, Trent has overpowered Josh, slamming his large fists into his head and body before grabbing him by the throat and hurling him almost single-handedly through the glass and out of the box, into the crowd below. That's a good ten-foot drop! I hear screams from the crowd outside, which grow louder and louder like a wave.

"Josh!" I yell, scrambling to my feet and running at Trent, who turns around just in time to catch the right elbow I'm throwing at full speed. It connects with his jaw and sends him crashing to the ground.

I can't afford to give him a moment's reprieve. I'm sure Josh can handle himself for now.

I pounce on Trent, straddling his barrel-like chest in a full mount position, and hammer down blow after blow on his face and chest.

"Fuck you, Trent!" I scream. "This is for my family. Do you understand me?"

I emphasize every other word, timing them with my punches for added effect. I unload punch after punch until my knuckles bleed. His face is starting to swell underneath his eyes. His nose is broken and a couple of his teeth have gone flying out of his mouth, but I'm still bombarding him with my assault. I grit my teeth, ignoring the pain in my hands, determined to pummel his head into a bloody pulp.

My arms are tiring, and I'm out of breath, so I pause and

let out a similar, guttural war cry to what Trent had done moments before. I sit up straight and look up, resting back on my haunches. I close my eyes as I try to catch my breath.

I fly forward, feeling a pain in my back. Trent must've brought his knee up and slammed it into the base of my spine. It takes me by surprise, as I didn't expect him to have any more fight left. I hit the wall beneath the window with a grunt.

"Shit..." I murmur.

I drag myself to my feet and turn just as Trent charges me once more. I have no idea how he's even still standing, let alone fighting back. He tackles me again, and we both topple over the edge and fall out of the box, down into the crowd.

We land among a large group of people, which cushions our fall somewhat. But this causes a domino effect, and innocent football fans fly in every direction, falling down the steep steps that lead to the different levels of the stand. It's a total frenzy around me, and it takes a moment to fight my way through the masses of people just to get to my feet.

As I stand, Trent does the same. Shards of glass are sticking in my back and legs from the fall, but I quickly pull them out, ignoring any pain. I've got more important things to deal with.

Our eyes meet across the crowd, and we charge for each other once more, as best we can in the chaos. Over Trent's shoulder, on one of the other stands, I catch a glimpse of security guards running toward us. A quick glance across the field at the large TV screen shows our fight is being broadcast to the entire stadium. Over the screams of people nearby, I can faintly hear the cheers and jeers of people urging us to keep fighting.

It's always confused me how people can have such a

blind fascination with violence, seemingly to the point where they'd happily endanger themselves purely to get a glimpse of it.

We thunder toward each other and meet in the middle on one of the staircases that separates the rows of seats, about halfway up. I think he'll lead with a desperate straight right punch, so I immediately duck. A right hand flies over my head, and as his momentum carries him past me, I stand and step to the left, throwing a left hook into his ribs, just under his armpit. The impact knocks him off-balance and he falls, prompting more screams from the crowd as they watch his body tumble and bounce down the concrete steps, coming to a sickening halt as he hits the wall at the bottom rolling down the steps. People are simultaneously trying to get out of my way as I walk slowly down the steps after him and trying to stay close enough to me to see what's going to happen next.

I reach the bottom and stand over Trent, looking down at his battered body. His face is a crimson mask, with blood flowing freely from a gash he's sustained on his forehead from the fall. It looks like he's broken his ankle too, given the shape of it. From the quick, ragged way he's breathing, I suspect he's got a couple of busted ribs on top of all that.

He's done.

I reach behind me and draw my remaining Beretta. I aim at his head and feel every ounce of pain and guilt that I've carried on my shoulders for so many years just... float away. He looks up at me, and I see regret in his eyes. And fear. Wilson Trent is afraid of me.

"Any last words?" I ask him. "Any more insults you want to throw at me? Do you want to brag some more about killing my family, perhaps?"

He closes his eyes slowly, taking as deep a breath as he dares.

"Go to Hell... Adrian," he rasps.

I smile. "Been there, bought a vacation home..."

My finger tightens on the trigger as I prepare to end this miserable bastard's pathetic life, but I feel a hand on my shoulder that stops me. I spin around to see Josh standing there. He visibly winces with every deep breath he takes. His right arm is hanging loose, close to his side, which looks to me like a dislocated shoulder. He has blood around his mouth too, and coupled with his painful breathing, I suspect he also has busted ribs and some internal bleeding to go along with it.

"Christ, you look like shit," I say.

"Thanks," he replies with a weak smile. "Listen, Adrian... you can't do this here."

I shake my head. "This ends right here, right now, Josh. Everything we've been through has led me here. It's over."

"And I completely agree—this *is* over. But you can't blow his fucking brains out while you're on TV."

He points over to the big screen that, sure enough, is still broadcasting the drama and giving the security guards my exact location. Outside the ground, over the screams of the crowd, a cacophony of sirens grows louder by the second.

I sigh and curse to myself. I'm *this* close, but I still can't end the prick.

I look down at Trent, who's slowly crawling back up the steps, pausing every few seconds to cough up some blood. The crowd has given us a wide berth now. I know that the stadium security isn't far away, with the cops close behind.

I walk over to him and crouch down over him, pressing my gun to his temple as he lies face-down on the steps.

"Open your mouth," I say to him.

His eyes widen in horror as he realizes what my intentions are.

"Oh, Jesus..." I hear Josh whisper behind me.

But I don't care. I can't fire my gun? Fine. But Wilson Trent is dying before I leave this stadium, one way or the other.

"I said, open your fucking mouth!" I repeat.

Reluctantly, he does, biting the step beneath him and closing his eyes tightly. I stand up and take a look around. People have fled the immediate area, but the rest of the crowd are on their feet, trying to see what's happening while security do their best to usher them away to safety. On the field behind me, even some players have stopped their pre-match training, wondering what all the commotion is.

My eyes meet Josh's uncomfortable gaze. We stare at each other for a moment, then he slowly nods, giving me his unspoken blessing before walking off up the steps.

I take a deep breath. An image of Janine and Maria flashes into my head. They're running together in a park. The sun's shining and they're laughing together. They both look so beautiful. But the image soon disappears and everything is black and empty.

I step forward and, without breaking stride, bring my boot down hard on the back of Trent's skull. The force drives his head forward. With his mouth open, the step splits his head horizontally, taking his jawbone almost clean off and killing him instantly.

There are no screams of shock and horror around me. No mad rush or panic to flee the area. There's just... silence. Every person in the crowd who just witnesses Trent's demise is standing and staring at me.

I have no idea what I thought I'd feel like when I finally

killed him. I guess I figured I'd feel relief, or happiness maybe. But I feel... nothing.

I walk up the steps toward the exit, where Josh is waiting for me.

"You okay?" he asks.

I nod silently as a wave of numbness slowly wash over me.

"You feel you got the closure that you wanted, though?"

I regard him for a moment, trying to thinking of the honest answer. But I come up with nothing. There's just an empty void where my soul should be. No closure, no celebration, no regret... nothing. I just feel dead inside, and for the first time in my life, I'm afraid. Without saying anything, I simply walk off, leaving Josh standing there, surrounded by the carnage I've created.

33

ADRIAN HELL

I quickly retrieved my other gun from Trent's box. Then we managed to make it back out to the parking lot and into the Winnebago, where Frank was waiting, with minimal fuss. We navigated the panic-stricken hordes of fans rushing to the nearest exit simply by feigning the same fear, blending into the masses and easily dodging any security guards.

The real police are arriving just as we're driving off. We sit in a queue, anonymous, like any other vehicle scrambling to get away from the horrors inside the stadium, so no one gives us a second thought as we drive past.

"Is it done?" Frank asks after a few minutes of silence.

"Yeah," I reply, sounding vacant.

"And did everything go down like you'd planned?"

I reach into my left pocket and pull out a small box, no larger than a USB drive, with a switch on it. I hold it up for him to see. "Like a charm."

He shakes his head in disbelief. "I still don't get how it worked..."

"They're basically an EMP over Wi-Fi," I explain absently. "I bought a handful of them from Oscar. They're the size of a button and expensive. A standard EMP will let out a blast that disables all electrical equipment but is essentially harmless to humans. These things are black market, designed by some tech firm in Japan. They emit a small pulse as normal but at a higher amp, which affects the human heart. When Josh frisked the bodyguards, he slipped one into each of their pockets, and then all I had to do was flick this switch, and all their hearts stopped simultaneously."

"So, to Trent, it looked like you just clicked your fingers and killed them with your mind or something?"

"Pretty much, yeah."

"You should've seen him," Josh shouts from the back. "It was beautiful!"

Frank smiles to himself as he looks ahead at the road. I don't think he's smiled once since he walked into my hospital room yesterday evening. I guess a lot's changed in those twenty-four hours...

We fall silent as we head into the center of the city, toward Trent's penthouse. The second part of the plan involves taking control of any physical assets on the premises, ensuring Trent's legacy is completely buried. It's not going to be easy. Aside from the few legitimate businesses that occupy the first couple of floors, the rest of the thirty-story building houses several illegal enterprises run by many of Trent's less-than-reputable employees. Getting to the top floor from the bottom will be close to impossible, so we need patience and discretion if we're to make it undetected.

Sadly, *I'm* involved.

We park across the street and look over. The entrance to the lobby has guards on either side of the door and a front desk just visible through the glass. I see three men around the desk, but there will likely be more inside.

Darkness has descended, and the rain has started to fall at a steady rate. High above us, clouds rumble in preparation for a storm.

"So, what's the plan?" asks Josh. "Basement? Service entrance? Disguise?"

"I was thinking front door," I say.

"You mean the well-guarded, very public, glass front door over there?" he counters, then sighs heavily. "What am I saying? Of course, you do..."

I shrug. "They'll already have received word about their boss's demise, if not from one of their own, then from the national news. They'll be disorganized and scared, which means they'll be easy prey."

Frank taps my shoulder and points down the street at two black vehicles approaching the building. "Who's this?"

The doors open on the first vehicle and four men step out. One of the guys who were traveling in the back looks like a prisoner. I've never seen him before. They escort him over to the entrance to Trent Towers and stand, waiting. After a moment, the doors on the second vehicle open. As before, four men step out.

"Shit," says Frank, pointing to one of the men who have climbed out of the back. "That's Duncan, one of Trent's two personal bodyguards."

I look over at him. He's a big guy, well built, and he certainly looks intimidating. Not someone I'd take for granted in a fight. I watch as he walks around the vehicle and opens the back door nearest the curb.

"Is that..." asks Josh, looking on.

"Sure looks like him," I confirm.

We watch as Duncan grabs Jimmy Manhattan by his arm and leads him to the front door. But before he gets the chance to open it, another man comes out to meet him. He's of similar build and height, and judging by his tense and nervous body language, I figure he's heard about his boss.

"That's Bennett," Frank informs us. "Duncan's partner in crime and Trent's other personal muscle."

"Those two guys are enormous," Josh observes.

"I did some research on them—both former cage fighters who got banned from the independent MMA circuit for excessive violence and persistent breaches of health and safety regulations. They went from working the doors to protecting Trent pretty quickly."

I study them both with a professional eye. I'm no slouch in a fight, but I know I can't take any chances with these two, should I ever confront them.

They talk for a moment, and I watch Duncan's body language change to match that of his colleague. Then they both drag Manhattan and the other prisoner into the building and out of sight.

"What do you wanna do, Boss?" asks Josh.

"We wait."

"For what?" Frank asks.

"Just playing a hunch. Give it half an hour and then we'll make our move."

20:38 EDT

. . .

I hate being right. Not all the time—especially when I'm arguing with Josh. But when I trust my gut about how bad I think a situation might get, I definitely don't like it when I'm dead-on.

As the rain pours down, the night sky periodically lights up with lightning. The loud wail of police sirens drifts across the city, gradually getting louder, like a crescendo of broken justice. After a few minutes, the entire Pittsburgh Police Department descends on the building. There must be over twenty cruisers, blue lights flashing, blocking the road and the entrance to the building. Cops pour out, covering the street outside the entrance, side arms in hand, taking up position behind the cover of their open car doors.

"Shit," I say.

"You figured they'd call in every corrupt cop they've got?" says Frank, more of a statement than a question.

I nod silently, formulating a plan in my head that would get me to the top floor without getting shot. Or at least, I'm trying to...

"We need to get rid of them if we're to stand any chance of getting inside there," says Josh.

"What are you thinking?" I ask.

"Well, those cops might be more bent than a boomerang factory, but they're still cops. If there's a big enough crime reported, they'll have to respond, surely?"

I shake my head. "No one would dare commit a crime that Trent didn't orchestrate himself in this town, and all those cops know it. No, we need something else."

We fall silent again. I lean against the window and look up at the building that towers over the street. We need to get to the top floor, and the only way in or out has the entire police department guarding it. If only we can—

"Sonofabitch..." I say, piecing together a new game plan in my head, annoyed at myself for not thinking of it sooner.

"What?" asks Frank skeptically.

I smile. "We need to think bigger."

21:00 EDT

I called Oscar Brown to make sure he was still in the city. Luckily, he was. He was surprised to hear from me again so soon after my last purchase but said he was happy to help.

Frank's driving. I'd told him to head back over to Oscar's place and asked Josh to pull together some of our newfound fortune, ready to spend. As we approach Oscar's warehouse, Josh appears behind me.

"I've moved one point five million into one of our accounts," he announces. "I'll move more if Oscar applies any insanity tax—which I'm sure he will. This idea of yours is fucking crazy, Adrian. Even for you."

"Just playing another hunch is all," I reply.

We screech to a halt in front of the warehouse entrance. I step out into the pouring rain and glance around. The other buildings are all quiet and look completely deserted. Only Oscar's has a light on in the main office, which floods out through the open door, where he's standing, leaning against the frame waiting for us.

"Back again?" he shouts over to us. "I could get used to this. You'll be putting my kids through college at this rate!"

"I hope I'm about to give you the means to buy your own damn college," I reply, smiling.

Josh and Frank appear next to me, and we all stop just outside Oscar's door.

"Guns all you got?" I ask.

He goes to reply but stops himself, regarding me with more curiosity than usual. He shifts almost nervously on the spot. "What makes you ask that?"

"Just the fact that all your warehouses in Allentown and here appear empty—but if they were, and you were the only show in town, you'd have moved into one front and center by the entrance, not tucked yourself away in the corner. Also, I say *appears* because there are fresh tire tracks in the mud by those two units, so there's definitely something inside them. I figure, seeing as you probably own this entire estate, you got more than guns in some of these other warehouses." I look behind me and gesture at them with my thumb. "I've got close to two million dollars to spend on what I hope you're hiding over there."

Oscar eyes each of us in turn, stroking his chin, as if in deep thought. He bursts out laughing.

"You ain't as dumb as you look!" he says. "Just like ol' Jimmy told me. Lemme just get my coat and I'll give you the tour."

As he disappears into the office, Frank nudges my arm. "What's going on? What do you think he's got over there?"

I smile. "Something much bigger than a few racks of guns."

Oscar reappears and leads us all across the complex to the first of the two hangar-sized warehouses. The rain's coming down hard, and more thunder rumbles in the dark clouds overhead. Time's running out if I want to get to Manhattan before what's left of Trent's organization decides it's simply easier to kill him than question him.

As we near the warehouse, I see there's no front office. It simply has two large hangar doors padlocked shut. He stops just short of the doors and spins around to face me with a serious look in his eyes.

"Now... a betting man would wager his annual salary that you fellas are fixing to do something real stupid," he says. "Am I right?"

"Stupid's a pretty broad term," I say. "I prefer to think of this as necessary insanity."

He grins and walks over to the doors. He unfastens the padlock and heaves both doors wide open. "Insanity's right..."

As the fluorescent lights flicker into life, illuminating the hangar interior, I hear Josh and Frank audibly gasp in shock. In front of us is a UH-60A Black Hawk helicopter, painted jet-black.

"Holy shit..." mutters Josh.

It looks in amazing condition, considering they've been out of active service in the military since '89. I walk inside the warehouse and slowly circle the helicopter.

"Somewhat of a collector's item, I admit," Oscar explains. "But she's in perfect working order. I've had a few inquiries about her over the years but never could bring myself to part with her."

"Well, I don't want to buy it," I say. "Just borrow it."

"Mind if I ask what for?"

Josh and Frank gather around too, eager to hear my plan.

"There's a tower block in the city that's surrounded by cops, and I need to get to the top floor. The way I figure it, it's easier to go in from the roof than it is from the ground, under the circumstances."

"Genius..." says Josh. "Except you can barely walk straight, let alone fly one of these things. What about you, Frank? Don't suppose you're a helicopter pilot, are you?"

He shakes his head.

"Josh, will you just relax? Ol' Oscar here's gonna fly it," I say, turning toward him. "Aren't you?"

"Well, I... I mean, I *can* fly it. Don't get me wrong..."

"Good. I've got a million dollars to rent your machine and half a million for your time and risk. Can you be ready to take off in fifteen minutes?"

Everyone exchanges looks of shock and concern but says nothing.

"I'll take that as a yes. C'mon, let's get ready."

I walk quickly back to the Winnebago, leaving the rest of them standing inside the hangar. The rain's getting worse by the minute, and as a flash of lightning illuminates the industrial estate, it looks like the storm that's threatened for days is finally unleashing its fury on Pittsburgh.

I can totally relate.

21:20 EDT

We're flying across the city, huddled in the back of the Black Hawk as Oscar expertly pilots us toward Trent's building. We're strapped into our seats. Josh and I traveled in the back of a chopper many times during our days in the military, but Frank looks a little under the weather.

"You okay?" I shout to him over the roar of the blades.

He simply shakes his head and continues his deep breathing.

I look over at Josh and smile. "I don't think he's a good flier."

We've left the Winnebago at Oscar's place and kitted ourselves out with every weapon we have. I've got my

Berettas at my back. Frank opted for a Mossberg 500 shot-gun, and Josh chose an M-16 assault rifle.

As we near our destination, I see the blue flashing lights below us, blocking off the entire street. We bank left and approach the building from the back. There's no hiding the fact that a huge helicopter is overhead, but there's no sense in making things too easy for them on the ground. As soon as we got near enough that we'd be heard over the storm, calls would've been made to every single piece of shit inside that building, making sure they're ready for us.

Definitely not the most discreet entrance I've ever made, but I'll take easy over quiet any day of the week.

The tower has a flat roof with a fire escape on it. Oscar hovers low so that we can jump out. Josh goes first, followed by Frank. I pat Oscar on the shoulder.

"I owe you one. Thanks," I yell.

"Bullshit!" he yells back. "You paid me a helluva lot of money for not much work. If anything, I owe *you*!"

"See you again, Oscar."

I jump down, landing on the roof with a thud. I draw both of my Berettas and take a deep breath, composing myself. Frank appears on my left. The double crunch of him cocking the Mossberg is loud in the rain.

"I'm ready," he says, nodding to me. "You've killed Trent. Now let's kill his legacy."

On my right, Josh stands next to me with his M-16 locked and loaded.

"You good?" I ask.

"I live for this shit, Boss!" he replies, barely able to contain his excitement.

We all stand side by side, our eyes fixed on the fire escape in front of us. We're soaked to the skin from the torrential rain that's pelting the ground around us. I take another deep breath. The numbness I've felt since killing Trent is finally letting up, allowing me to lose myself in the task at hand. Allowing me to start appreciating what we've accomplished. Taking down an entire criminal empire on our own is no mean feat, but we've done a good job so far.

"Are *you* ready?" asks Josh.

I turn to look at him, finally letting my Inner Satan off its leash. I feel the fire behind my eyes—the anger... the untamed fury... the pleasure. I simply smile back.

"Yeah... you're ready," he says.

We head for the door, full of purpose and ready for war. But deep down, we all know that getting in is the easy part. The challenge will be getting back out.

34

JIMMY MANHATTAN

It was a long and silent journey from Allentown, and the weather took a drastic turn for the worse along the way. As they finally came to a stop in front a tower block, thunder rumbled over the noise of the pouring rain outside.

Duncan got out of the car and walked around to the other side. He opened Jimmy Manhattan's door and dragged him out. Ahead of them, the other vehicle had pulled over, and the three men were dragging an injured Tarantina across the sidewalk.

Without a word, Duncan escorted him toward the main entrance. He was flanked on either side by what he assumed was Trent's private security. As they approached, the door flew open and a man came running toward them, visibly shaken.

"We got a problem," he said, ignoring Manhattan completely.

"Bennett, what's happened?" asked Duncan.

"It's the boss... he's dead," he replied.

His eyes went wide. "Mr. Trent? How?"

Manhattan chuckled, just loud enough that they could hear him. "I bet I can tell you how..."

Duncan turned to him. "You—shut the fuck up," he ordered before addressing Bennett. "Was it him?"

"Yeah, Adrian Hell and his partner attacked him at the Steelers game. I saw the news as it was happening. They had a big fight in the crowd. This Adrian guy was a maniac, man."

"Let's get up to the office and sort this from there. We gotta make some calls."

They all marched Manhattan and Tarantina into the building, across the lobby and straight to the elevator.

"No one who ain't invited comes through here without my say-so," said Duncan to the man sitting behind the front desk as they walked past.

They came out on the top floor and turned right, walking straight into a penthouse office.

"Sit there," he said to Manhattan, pointing to one of the leather sofas in front of the desk. Behind them, the three other men escorting Tarantina entered and shoved him down on the sofa opposite Manhattan. They grouped together beside the desk, in front of window looking out at the storm gradually raging across the city.

"So, what do we do?" asked Duncan.

"We prepare for him to come here," replied Bennett. "It's the only logical move he could make. He wanted to finish Trent off, right? Well, now that he's killed him, he'll come after what's left of his organization."

Duncan nodded, then turned to the men standing with them.

"You four, go and gather every man in the building. Tell them to arm themselves and call me if they see anything. Then get ten of your best and get them on this floor, guarding the elevator."

21:23 EDT

An hour or so passed without a word spoken to either Manhattan or Tarantina. Different men were in and out of the office, reporting to Duncan and Bennett.

Manhattan looked on with a bemused expression. It was refreshing to see people rushing around in blind panic at the prospect of Adrian Hell coming for blood and he not be one of them.

"You all right?" he asked Tarantina, who sat facing him, barely conscious.

"I'm good, Boss," he replied. "Just lost a lot of blood. Not feelin' too great, y'know?"

"This will all soon be over. Don't worry."

Duncan and Bennett walked over to them as the other men left to carry out their tasks. They stood side by side, arms folded, glaring down at them.

"So, you're the guy who took out Johnny King and staked his claim in Allentown, huh?" asked Duncan. "Mr. Trent was gonna make an example out of you, so I figure that job now falls to us."

"On the contrary," said Manhattan, unfazed. "I believe Wilson Trent was going to extend the olive branch and embrace a mutually beneficial partnership between both our organizations. Something I now believe would be in your best interest to honor."

"How you figure that?" asked Bennett.

"Because I have no doubt in my mind that Adrian Hell is on his way here with the sole intention of killing everyone in this building. But with my help, that could be avoided."

"I think we can handle him," said Duncan. "We've got nearly cop in the goddamn city stationed out front."

"You don't *handle* someone like him. You could have a squadron of Marines down there, and it wouldn't make a blind bit of different. No, you need *my* help if you wish to see tomorrow. Or you can go ahead and kill me, ensuring the complete and total destruction of Trent's empire. Your call, gentlemen."

Manhattan relaxed on the sofa and crossed his legs. He caught Tarantina's questioning eye long enough to let him know he was confident he'd done enough to guarantee their survival.

The two bodyguards looked at each other, their bodies tense. They knew Manhattan was right and didn't want to admit it.

"Okay, what do you have in mind?" asked Duncan after a minute.

Manhattan stood and walked around the sofa, gazing around the room. He was almost carefree, acting the part beautifully.

"To clarify something—yes, I ordered Mr. King be killed, but it was Adrian Hell who pulled the trigger. Mr. Hell and I have somewhat of a history together, and going into business on my own, I'd rather stick with the devil I know, so to speak. He agreed to take the contract I offered him to eliminate Johnny King—a move anyone in my position would've done, from a business perspective—in exchange for a future favor. He carried out the contract and found out King worked for Trent. He called me to tell me that Trent is likely to seek retribution and would be coming for me. I presumed he would forcibly summon me to him first, which he did."

"How is any of this helping us?" asked Bennett, crossing his arms impatiently.

"After doing some research," Manhattan continued, ignoring the interruption, "it came to my attention that Adrian and Trent also had a history. So, I let things play out, figuring the favor he would call in from me would likely be related to attacking Trent. From experience, I would never bet against Adrian Hell, and I was right. And now, as I predicted, I've wound up exactly where I thought I would, in a position to have this very conversation."

"Get to the point, or I'll shoot you," said Duncan.

"I suggest you willingly install me as your new employer. Give me control of this business, instantly merging it with my own, giving me power over the entire state. Once Adrian arrives, I'll convince him to walk away and leave things to me *before* he starts shooting *our* people. Given our recent dealings, I believe he will see it as an opportunity having me in charge—an unlikely, yet useful ally who can do him a bigger favor than originally thought. Once he's convinced there's no threat from me, I'll bury the sonofabitch. I've been setting him up from the beginning to have my revenge. So far, everything's going exactly as I've planned."

"Can you guarantee that you can stop him?" asked Bennett, unable to hide his growing concerns.

Manhattan looked at them both in the eye, then turned to Tarantina and regarded his wounded lieutenant for a moment before answering.

"Yes."

The bodyguards looked at each other and shrugged.

"What do you need from us, *Boss*?" asked Duncan.

Manhattan smiled, happy with his own progress. But his small celebration was short-lived as the sound of a helicopter overhead grew gradually louder.

"Ah, speak of the devil..." he said.

35

ADRIAN HELL

21:27 EDT

As the door swings open, Josh steps inside and expertly checks the angles. His gun is aimed forward, the barrel following his line of sight.

"Clear," he says after a moment.

Frank follows him, swinging his shotgun around with a technique he's probably learned more from watching movies than he has from any actual combat experience. I move in last, both Berettas drawn and thirsty for blood.

Immediately inside the door is a metal staircase. I lean over the handrail and look down. It appears to lead to a maintenance area a couple of flights below us. We head down the stairs but pause after just one flight. We hear a lot of commotion from underneath us.

"The helicopter maybe wasn't the stealthiest approach," observes Josh. His trademark sarcasm is like a shield on his arm as he enters battle.

"I'm done being discreet," I reply matter-of-factly.

Frank turns to me. "When did you *start*?"

Josh laughs. "Oh, the new boy shoots and he scores! You just got served, Boss!"

"You're both aware I currently have two guns and a real short temper, right?" I say.

They both fall silent again, re-focusing on infiltrating the top floor. I do enjoy our banter, especially during these types of situations. It's far easier to get through a tough spot if you act on instinct and relax into the moment.

We reach the bottom of the staircase and approach the fire exit, which must lead us out onto the floor. Once again, Josh takes point and quietly pushes the door open, letting in a crack of light from the corridor beyond it.

"Looks clear," whispers Josh. "I can see a closed door, unguarded, off to the left. I've no idea if it's Trent's office, or if that's at the opposite end."

I nod. "All the action will be near the elevators and outside Trent's door, so that room there is something else. We'll do things properly and clear it before moving on."

I look at Frank, who seems more agitated as the seconds ticked by.

"You all right?" I ask him.

He looks down at his Mossberg, then at the floor, almost as if he feels ashamed. "I can't do this, Adrian."

I holster one of my guns and put my hand on his shoulder.

"I know, Frank. It's all right. We couldn't have gotten here if it weren't for you, but this quest for revenge is mine, not yours. You've only spent your years being pissed at me, and I'd like to think we've moved past that now. But I've fixated on Trent since the day I found my girls dead, and I need this."

"No," he says, shaking his head. "I've spent my years

blaming you, but my hatred has always been for Trent, same as you. But now that he's dead, this all feels like overkill to me."

"Maybe it is," I say with a shrug. "But I killed Trent with my own hands, and I felt nothing. After all this time, there was no closure, no sense of freedom or happiness. There was nothing. This is my way of making sure I can move on. It's not enough to kill him. I need to bury him so deep that it's like he never existed. And burning this place to the ground is the only way I can do that."

He nods, understanding if not agreeing. "Okay," he says after a moment. "I'm with you—let's finish this."

On cue, Josh pushes the door open slowly and sticks his head out, looking down the corridor.

"It doglegs slightly to the right," he says. "I've got no visibility of the far end, but neither would anyone who might be down there, so we're clear for now."

"Move out," I say.

We walk quietly out into the corridor and look around. Frank and Josh move into position on either side of the door nearest to us, and I stand in front of it. We listen for a moment, but I can't hear anything from inside. Time is a factor here, so I simply open it and walk in.

It's a large room that appears to have been used for storage. Cardboard boxes line the walls all around, and there are some metal shelving units positioned in the center of the room. What I didn't expect to find, however, is a young girl, possibly a teenager, gagged and tied to a chair in the middle of the room, to the left of the shelving. There are two men standing watch over her, their backs to the door.

I don't know what's going on here, but it's not right. She's just a kid... what would Trent want with her?

I need to stay quiet, so I can't shoot these assholes.

The men turn and stare at me, momentarily frozen in shock. Without hesitating, I charge at them, kicking the guy on the left in the balls as I approach. As he doubles over in pain, I kick him again in the face, like I'm kicking a field goal from the forty-yard line. He flies backward to the floor and I turn quickly, lashing out with my right hand and catching the remaining guy on the side of his face with one of my guns. I hit him on the temple and he drops like a stone.

I put my guns away and look at the girl, whose eyes have gone wide. I put a finger to my lips.

"Shhh... it's okay, kid," I say quietly. "I'm not here to hurt you, I promise. I'll get you out of here."

She nods slowly as I pull the gag from her mouth.

"Are you okay?" I ask.

She nods again without speaking.

I untie her hands and help her up. I point to the door where Josh and Frank are standing.

"These are my friends. Don't be afraid, okay?" We walk over and I turn to Frank. "Get her out of here to safety. Josh and I can handle this."

Without a word, Frank nods and holds out his shotgun to me.

"Give 'em Hell, Adrian."

"I didn't get my name by doing anything less."

"I'll head back to the roof and call Oscar, see if he can come and get us," he says.

"Thanks for everything, Frank," Josh says. "I'll see you when this is all over."

"Take care, the both of you." He turns to the girl. "You come with me, okay? I'm gonna get you outta here."

She takes his hand and they walk back to the fire exit. As they open the door, she turns and looks back at me.

"Thank you," she says quietly.

I smile and nod, unsure what else I can say to her. They head back up the stairs and out into the storm. Josh and I press ourselves against the wall and make our way around the dogleg, likely walking into a storm of our own. Except right now, I'm the thunder, the lightning, the wind, and the rain. I'm a walking tornado of devastation, and God help all those who don't run.

"Stay behind me," I say to Josh as I crunch the shotgun.

I step around and come to a small lobby with two elevators on the right. Beyond that is a large double door made from expensive wood, with the left-hand side open, revealing the room beyond.

The wall opposite the elevators has a large piece of art mounted on it, but from this angle, I can't make out much more than the edge of the frame. Plus, I'm far too distracted by the ten heavily armed men that are standing staring at me, like rabbits in the headlights, completely unprepared for my arrival. Either that, or they knew I was coming but for some reason thought I'd take the elevator...

I level the shotgun, tucking the stock underneath my right arm and holding the barrel steady with my left. In the split-second of confusion, I charge at them, firing off two rounds from the Mossberg. I aim just off-center of the group, to the left first, then the right. The spray of the shots hits them like two cones, causing maximum damage. The front row, consisting of four men, is taken out instantly, launching them backward into the rest of the group. Blood pours out of the gaping wounds in their chests and stomachs.

I let out a visceral scream as adrenaline surges through me. I know that in this reasonably narrow corridor, I have no cover, and all it'll take is one bullet to put me down. I can't afford to hesitate and think about what might happen here.

I chamber another round and fire, catching two more men who are unlucky enough to get to their feet first. I aim low, catching the one on the left just below the hip, right in the center of his thigh. The guy on the right had taken a step back, and the blast caught him on the knee, taking the bottom part of his leg clean off.

The four remaining men scramble to their feet and head for the sanctuary of the room behind them. But one man slips on the blood, and as he loses his footing, I hear a three-round burst of gunfire from behind me. The bullets hit his sternum, killing him instantly. Josh appears next to me, his M-16 primed for another assault.

"Didn't think I'd let you have all the fun, did you, you crazy bastard?" he says.

The door slams shut in front of us as the three men make it inside. I'm not sure what good they think that door's going to do, given they know I have a shotgun and Josh has an assault rifle. They must be desperate and not thinking straight.

We take up position on either side of the doorway.

"How many more inside? Do we know?" he asks.

I shake my head. "Didn't get a chance to see. But it doesn't matter. They're all dead."

He nods. "Got your back, Boss."

"I'll go low. You go high, yeah?"

He nods again and moves in front of the doors. I raise my boot and kick them both open with enough force to almost take them off their hinges. I step inside and drop to a crouch.

Oh, shit...

In front of me are the three men who survived the

massacre in the hallway, standing in a line in front of a desk, facing me. The room spreads out to the left and right; it looks empty, apart from two leather sofas in front of the desk and some pieces of art. All around, the windows run floor to ceiling, displaying the impressive landscape of the city below, as well as the equally impressive storm that's battering down on it.

On either side of the doors is one of the two men we saw in the street earlier. What were their names? Duncan and Bennett, was it? They're both tall and look even more physically impressive in person. They both have guns in their hands, and they're both aiming them at my head.

"Drop it, asshole," says Duncan, on the right.

"Fuck..." I mutter.

I shouldn't have been so reckless. The adrenaline was clouding my judgment, and not for the first time. I toss the shotgun to the floor. He reaches behind me, takes my Berettas, and throws them down as well.

"You too," Bennett says, looking at Josh. "Nothing funny, or I blow his fucking brains out."

Josh hesitates, not wanting to lower his weapon.

"Do as he says," I say to him. "He has me dead to rights."

He sighs heavily and steps through, tossing his gun to the floor next to mine and raising his hands.

Duncan presses his gun to the side of my head. "Make a move and I'll shoot you. Now take a seat on the sofa."

I take a deep breath, stand back up, and walk forward. As I do, the line of three men in front of the desk step to one side, revealing Jimmy Manhattan. He's sitting in what I presume used to be Wilson Trent's chair.

"Fuck..." hisses Josh.

Manhattan's arrogant smile shows he's already celebrating his victory over us. I can't say anything. I just feel numb at having hit a roadblock I never expected to come up against.

"Adrian, glad you could join us," he says. "Welcome to *my* empire."

My jaw muscles clench as I stare at him, my anger rising to boiling point. "You sneaky, rat bastard sonofabitch!"

He smiles at me, full of arrogance. "Did you honestly think I'd write off our history, forgive and forget, then strike up a partnership with you? I'll admit, your involvement has made things easier for me, but this outcome was inevitable. And now I have all the manpower and the resources to finally bury Adrian Hell. How does it feel? Being so beaten?"

"Actually," interrupts Josh, "you *don't* have the resources. I stole all of Trent's money, so you're in charge of a building you can't afford the rent for and a small gang of inbred steroid abusers whom you can't afford to pay. Well done!"

Manhattan nods to Bennett, who steps over to Josh and slams his pistol into the side of his head, right on the temple. Josh grunts as he falls to the floor, not quite unconscious but incapacitated for now.

"A minor technicality," says Manhattan without skipping a beat. "Which *you* will resolve for me. Hand over the money."

I shake my head. "Couldn't if I wanted to. Didn't understand half the shit he said to me when he told me how he'd done it, but I know the only way to trace the money is with him in front of a computer. Given you just knocked him out, you'll have to wait…"

"Defiant to the very—"

"I haven't finished," I interrupt. "I was just pausing for breath. Like I was saying, I couldn't if I wanted to… but I *don't* want to. What I want to do is kill everyone in this room.

And you're going last, so you can watch what I do to everyone else."

I look at Duncan. To his credit, he remains next to me with his gun still on my temple.

"You want to know what I did to your boss?" I ask him. "I beat him half to death with my bare hands and then made him bite the curb. I killed him by putting my boot through the back of his head. I heard the crunch as the top of his spine snapped and his jaw damn near fell off."

I feel the gun start to quiver slightly against my head. I don't know if it's down to anger, fear, or both. I don't care, either. It doesn't matter. The point is that he's emotional, and he's going to make a mistake. And when he does, I'll kill him.

"Nice speech," says Manhattan. "But I'm afraid it's unnecessary."

The door opens, and another fifteen well-armed men dash in. They form a wide semi-circle between the door and me.

Ignoring the gun, I do a slow three-sixty of the room, turning clockwise and looking around to buy myself some time while I figure out my next play. I have fifteen men between the door and me. Next is a mostly empty space with a goldfish bowl on a stand in front of the large windows. Then there's the desk with Manhattan behind it and three men in front of him. The other guy, brought in with Manhattan, is sitting on the sofa, bleeding from a bullet wound and looking faint. And finally, the far wall on the right is, again, mostly empty, save for some artwork on the walls and a display cabinet containing two identical samurai swords that are probably worth more than I can imagine.

I clench my jaw muscles tightly in silent frustration as my viable options for survival decrease by the minute.

"As you can see, Adrian," he continues, "any threat you make is futile. You're done. I've waited a long time to see you die, and I intend to enjoy every second of it."

With Josh down for the count still, Bennett walks over to the desk and places his gun down in front of Manhattan. "Can I have the pleasure of beating him to death for you?"

Manhattan couldn't smile any wider if he tried. "Be my guest," he replies, then turns to Duncan. "Both of you can have a little fun, if you'd like."

Out of the corner of my eye, I look at Duncan, whose emotions are slowly being replaced by a wicked, confident smile. I let out a heavy sigh and brace for the inevitable. And sure enough, before Duncan put his gun down, he whips it into the side of my head, forcing me to one knee while the throbbing subsides.

I know they're both trained fighters, and I know not to underestimate their abilities. But I also know that, quite simply, I'm better.

Bennett is in front of me, with Duncan to my right. I'm still down on one knee, holding the side of my head. Waiting...

Bennett comes at me first. He throws a kick with his left leg, executed perfectly—he swings it around in a wide arc, his leg stiff. He's thrown his hip over, putting every ounce of momentum behind the kick. He's aiming for the side of my head, and if it connects, that one blow will end things right here, right now.

But I knew it was coming. I've been watching him. Out of the two of them, he clearly thinks of himself as the more senior, which means he was going to want to go first. And I've been watching his stance.

After speaking to Manhattan, he turns and puts his right foot forward, with his back leg on the ball of his foot. I'm on one knee, which practically begs for a head kick. As it swings around, I jump up and hook my right arm around his leg, grabbing hold and absorbing some of the blow in my side.

But I met his leg, instead of waiting for it to come to me, so it hadn't quite gained full momentum and consequently doesn't have the stopping power it would have otherwise. With his left leg held out straight and a look of complete shock on his face, I step through and thrust my left foot through his right kneecap, snapping his leg in half. I let go of his left leg, and he collapses on the floor, writhing and screaming in agony.

One down...

I turn to Duncan, who is frozen in shock at how swift and brutal my defense is.

One to go.

We face each other and I wait for his move. His stance is loose and his guard is high. His years of training will have made him an effective fighter. Patience is the key to beating him. Let him come to me, then defend and counter.

His eyes never leave mine, and they're burning bright with rage. I know what story my eyes are telling. After years and years of fighting and killing, I know what my Inner Satan looks like. It sometimes even frightens me, so God knows what this guy's thinking right now.

He snaps a jab forward, falling short of the mark, then follows it with a huge straight right. Knowing the jab won't come near me, I position myself for the obvious follow-up.

I side-step to the left and bring my right arm up, bending it to guard the right side of my head and creating a lethal point with my elbow. I time it perfectly, and his punch connects with my bent elbow at full speed. Even as the rain batters the glass all around us and the thunder and lightning assault the skyline, I hear the crunch as the bones in his hand shatter under the impact. He screams, dropping his guard to hold his injured hand and taking a step back.

"You bastard!" he yells.

Ignoring him, I swing a loose, half-powered left hook that catches him on the unguarded right-hand side of his face. Instinctively, he raises his left arm up in a weak attempt at blocking, but in doing so, he exposes his ribs on the left. I drop my right shoulder, duck low, and unleash a right hook in his side, just below his armpit. The ribs there are like matchsticks, and it only takes one decent punch to shatter them.

Again, the sound of splintering bones echoes around the room, which has quickly fallen silent in shock. Duncan crashes to the floor. I stand, breathing heavily but otherwise completely unaffected by their joint effort to kill me. I turn to look at Manhattan, whose arrogant smile has faded, replaced by an all-too-familiar look of resentment and frustration. I say nothing. I simply stare at him, my face devoid of all emotion.

Manhattan takes Bennett's gun from his desk and aims it at me. "You think that means anything? You think you still stand any chance of making it out of here alive? You're surrounded by nineteen guns. Even the mighty Adrian Hell can't survive this!"

I smile slowly. His face turns from anger to uncertainty almost instantly. "You don't get it, do you?" I say rhetorically. "Even though I agreed to work for you and took the opportunity to have you owe me one, it's not completely unexpected that you'd stab me in the back the first chance you got, given our history. End of the day, I only came to this city to kill Trent, and I did. I came here afterward to burn his legacy to the ground, for no other reason than I was angry and it was something to do to let off some steam. I've been building up to this day for almost a decade, and now that I've done what I set out to do, I honestly don't care if I get out of here in one piece or not. I'm done. I'm tired. I want to stop. People like me don't retire with their pensions, Jimmy. People like me kill for a living, and when we go, we go out in a blaze of glory. But let me tell you this: if tonight is my last night, I'm making damn sure there's nothing left of Wilson Trent. And that includes what remains of his business. You've taken over? Fine—just means you get to die before I do."

He lowers his gun, regarding me for a moment as silence descends. All around, the armed men look uneasy. Far below us, I figure the corrupt cops are standing by, waiting for their orders. Next to me, Josh has taken a seat on the sofa opposite Manhattan's injured man. He looks at me and smiles weakly. He would've heard my speech, but knowing we're still surrounded, he'll know there's nothing to argue about or discuss.

"I'll say it again," I continue. "If tonight's my night, I promise you that you're dying first."

Manhattan glances around the room. The clacking noise of eighteen guns being aimed directly at me fills my ears. He raises his again, his finger squeezing lightly against the trigger.

"For a year and a half, you've been a pain in my ass, Adrian," he says. "I had to play nice with you to get this far. It's made me sick, but it was the only way. When the opportunity arose, I knew I had to play it just right to gradually involve you and set you up for this very moment. And it worked perfectly. Apart from Paulie over there getting shot, it couldn't have gone any better. Now... good-bye, Adrian."

I watch as his finger tightens even more on the trigger. I look over at Josh quickly, exchanging a moment in which I silently apologize and he silently tells me to forget about it. Then I simply close my eyes and wait to hear the brief sound of bullets before an eternal darkness washes over me.

36

ADRIAN HELL

Huh. Still no gunfire.

What's going on? It's been at least twenty seconds... what are they waiting for?

Wait... what's that? It sounds like... is that a helicopter?

I open my eyes and see Jimmy Manhattan standing in front of me, still pointing his gun at me but looking distracted, like he's listening for something.

That's definitely a helicopter. Even over this storm, I hear the blades whirring away, getting closer with each second that ticks by.

I look around at Josh, who's clearly heard it too. He's moved to the edge of his seat and is straining to listen over the noise of the rain barraging against the glass and the thunder and lightning rampaging across the sky outside.

I glance at the eighteen men who are surrounding me. They haven't moved an inch, but they're all exchanging uncertain glances with each other as they presumably wait for Manhattan to give the order to open fire.

As I turn back around to look at Manhattan, a UH-60A Black Hawk helicopter banks to its right and swings into view outside, almost level with where I'm standing. Manhattan turns to see it. The men surrounding me do the same.

I see a bright flash and instinctively drop to the ground as gunfire suddenly erupts, shattering the glass and cutting through the group of men like a hot knife through butter. I'm lying face-down with my arms covering my head. I glance behind me to make sure Josh has found some cover too. I can't see him, so I'm guessing he has.

I roll away to my left, past the desk, and toward the empty space in the office. I look up at the helicopter hovering outside with murderous intent. A flash of lightning illuminates the night sky, and I glimpse Frank Stanton hanging out of the side of the chopper, holding an assault rifle.

I laugh out loud. Sonofabitch!

Josh appears next to me, sliding to a stop and planting himself flat against the floor.

"What the hell's going on?" he yells.

"It's Frank!" I reply over the noise. "That crazy bastard's leaning out the back of Oscar's helicopter with an M-16!"

I roll over on my back and lift my head to look toward the door. Of the eighteen men Manhattan had protecting him, I count fourteen of them down and out already. There's an insane amount of blood covering the walls, like someone has dipped a huge brush in red paint and flicked the bristles all around. The four who remain alive are trying to find some cover and return fire.

Out of the corner of my eye, I notice Manhattan's man,

Paulie, hit the floor in between the sofas. I can't tell if he's seeking cover or has taken another bullet.

"Get out of here," I shout to Josh. "Pick your spot and run for the door. Get Trent's money together in one of our accounts and lie low. I'll contact you when this is over."

He shakes his head. "No way, Boss!" he yells back. "We leave here together, or not at all!"

We're lying to the side of the desk, which is still the only effective cover in the room, despite having splintered beyond recognition from the onslaught of bullets. Manhattan's on the floor on the other side, frantically scrambling across the room, off to the right and away from the gunfire.

"I'm finishing this before I go anywhere," I say, pointing to Manhattan.

"I'll save the *I-told-you-so* for if we get out of here!" Josh says.

"Can't wait..."

I raise a hand over the desk, trying to catch Frank's attention and get him to quit shooting. After a few moments of me waving, he must've either seen me or run out of bullets, as he stops firing. I slowly get to my feet, squinting as the wind and rain blasts through the broken glass from outside and stings my face. I look out at Frank, whom I can see is now sitting down in the back of the helicopter, smiling. He gives me a salute, which I return. He then leans forward and taps Oscar on his shoulder, signaling it's over. The helicopter pulls away and disappears above us, out of sight.

The sound of the storm fades in as my hearing returns to normal. I survey the room, looking around for anyone left alive. It seems Frank managed to take out all the men...

BANG!

What the...

I spin around, stepping back into a fighting stance on

instinct, despite being aware that a punch is futile in a gunfight. Josh is down on one knee, holding one of my Berettas. He's aiming past me and away to the right corner. I follow his gaze and see the last man sliding down the wall to the floor, leaving a dark red stain behind him.

"Thanks," I say, turning back to him.

"Don't mention it," he replies. "Now will you go and kill Manhattan already!"

I walk away to the right, toward the display case with the samurai swords on their stand. The glass has shattered, like every window has. The strong wind is whipping the rain into the room, making the floor wet and slippery. Broken shards crunch underfoot as I stride purposefully toward Manhattan, who's sitting with his back to the other side of the display case stand.

"Jimmy!" I shout. "Get your ass out here!"

Manhattan stands and steps out into view. He doesn't have a weapon, and his suit has ripped in several places from the glass.

"You're done," I say to him. "And I'm gonna do what I should've done the first time we met..."

"I'm not letting you take everything away from me again!" he shouts. "I've worked too hard and been through too much to lose it all now!"

He grabs one of the swords and unsheathes it, revealing a shiny and sharp blade about three feet long. He grabs the hilt with both hands and charges at me.

Being unarmed against a weapon is never ideal, but I can usually manage in most situations. Although, I have to admit, I've never gone up against a sword before. The length of the blade means I can't get in too close without being stabbed or sliced, and there's little I can do from a distance with my fists. I have to maneuver myself close to him. I'm working on the assumption that Manhattan isn't a secret samurai master or anything. But he's lethal by nature, and I remember all too well his skills with a small blade. I'm not about to underestimate him.

I take a step toward him, and he swings the blade down at me, left to right. I lean back to avoid it and spin to my right, putting a little distance between us. As he loses his footing from the momentum of the swing, I take the opportunity to move toward the display case, taking the remaining sword. I draw it from its sheath and hold it in my right hand, familiarizing myself with its weight. It's a gorgeous weapon —the hilt is gold, adorned with blue and red crystals and formed at the end into the shape of a dragon's head.

Manhattan turns, raising his sword once more, poised for another attack. I hold mine out horizontally with one hand, lining the tip of it up with his chest.

"So, we're going to duel this out like two old-fashioned gentlemen?" I ask.

For a man who's in his mid-fifties, he's still pretty lively. He says nothing. He just screams with a visceral hatred and runs at me again. As he gets close, he lifts the sword high and slashes it down. I bring mine up to meet his, parrying the strike off to the left, leaving his left-hand side temporarily exposed. I step forward and thrust my right foot into his stomach, forcing him backward. He loses his footing on the wet floor again and falls on his ass.

"Fuck you, Adrian! You are my *nemesis*!" he snarls as he struggles to his feet.

"Really?" I say. "You're nothing to me. You're something I'd scrape off my boot and forget about."

I wait for his next attack. He's breathing heavily, and he's far too emotional to do anything remotely effective. This fight's already over.

He winces as he gets back to his feet. The effects from the kick to the stomach make his deep, heavy breaths look more painful. When he raises the sword again, even with two hands, he's noticeably struggling with the weight.

He takes one step and swings it up from his right hip across at me. I step back and left, so the blade moves away from me. As it does, I hit it with my sword, giving it added momentum that carries Manhattan away with it. He falls forward, his face bouncing off the floor and the sword flying from his hand. He slides a little on the wet floor, shards of glass cutting into his skin. He stops close to the edge, where one of many thick glass windows once stood between Wilson Trent and a thirty-story drop.

"Get up," I say, walking toward him. "Get on your feet and face me, you sad little shit."

He pushes himself up on all fours and looks back at me.

"You've destroyed everything, you sonofabitch!" he yells. "Everything!"

"Well, it serves you right for trying to make a living as a crime lord, when all you were ever good for was cleaning Pellaggio's shoes. You crossed me for the third time. That's two times more than anyone else ever has. And now it ends. Stand... the fuck... up!"

Slowly but surely, he gets to his feet again. He stands in front of me with his back mere inches away from the city below us, defiant to the end. The wind whips through the entire top floor of the building. With every window decimated and every inch of the floor covered in blood and glass, the cold rain blows in unhindered, stinging my face. I raise my sword, resting the blade on Manhattan's left shoulder.

"Any last words?"

"Yes," he replies with a sudden calmness that comes

with accepting the inevitability of his own demise. "See you in Hell."

I smile at him. "Be sure to save me a seat, you arrogant old prick."

In a flash, holding the sword in my right hand, I spin clockwise in a circle, whipping the blade around and cutting Manhattan's head clean off. As I complete my turn, before his decapitated body can slump to the floor, I lash out with my left foot and kick him out of the window and into the storm. I look down as his head rolls to a stop a few feet away in the corner of the room.

I look over at Josh, expecting a sarcastic comment, but he's just standing there with an apologetic look on his face. Next to him is Paulie, his torso covered in blood from the gunshot wound in his shoulder. In his good arm, he has one of my Berettas, and he's aiming it at Josh's head.

"Oh, for Christ's sake, Josh!" I say. "I turn my back for two minutes..."

"I was distracted watching you go all Highlander over there. I didn't see the sneaky little bastard coming up behind me," he replies, sounding almost embarrassed.

"Hey, assholes," interrupts Paulie. "I'm standing right here, and I've got the gun, so how about you both shut the fuck up, okay?"

I throw my sword to the floor. The clanging of the metal echoes around the room over the persistent noise of the wind and rain. Thunder rumbles outside as I stare at my gun in the hands of someone else and feel a renewed anger inside.

"Look, I don't know you," I say to him. "I've killed a lot of people in a short time, including two of the biggest criminal masterminds in the country. I'm tired. Just take this opportunity and piss off, will you? It's a one-time-only offer."

Josh drops to one knee and slams his elbow into Tarantina's stomach. He grunts and lets go of my gun, taken by surprise and not strong enough to do much about it. As he doubles over, Josh stands again, bringing his right knee up into his exposed face. Tarantina flies backward, landing spread-eagled on his back, unconscious.

"Thanks, Boss," he says.

"Don't mention it," I reply. "You about ready to get out of here?"

"I am, but there's one slight issue with that..."

"You mean all the cops outside?"

"Yeah, I imagine they're having a field day with that headless corpse that just landed on 'em!"

We both laugh and bump fists.

"That was just beautiful, Adrian. I didn't know you could handle a sword so well."

"Me neither," I admit with a shrug. "Saw it in a movie once and thought I'd try it."

Josh laughs. "Even your pop culture references end with a dead body!"

I smile and walk over to retrieve my Berettas, holstering them both at my back.

"Seriously, man, how are we getting out of here?" Josh asks.

"Maybe I can help you out with that?" says a voice from over by the door.

We both look up and see Frank standing there, smiling. I walk over and extend my hand, which he shakes firmly.

"You missed all the fun," I say. "Did you get the girl to safety?"

"Oscar flew us to the hospital," he explains. "I made sure she was safe and left her to check herself in—figured it'd prompt too many questions if I went in with her."

"Smart. I wonder who she was... and why Trent kidnapped her?"

He shakes his head and shrugs. "No idea. I didn't ask, and she didn't seem ready to talk to me, so I didn't push her. Just dropped her off, then flew back here to save your ass."

"Whatever. I had it all under control..."

"Sure, you did, Adrian."

The three of us laugh, then walk slowly back to the roof. The storm is still raging as we open the door. Lightning forks across the sky as the rain bounces head-high off the ground. The helicopter blades start up as we climb inside.

Oscar turns around in the pilot's seat. "You boys need a ride?" he asks, smiling.

"Thanks for the rescue," I say. "With this and the fact I just killed your biggest client, I reckon I owe you big time."

"Are you kidding me? You spent more money with me this week than Jimmy did in ten years. Fuck him!"

He turns back around. Moments later, we're flying over the city, away from the sea of blue and red lights on the streets below.

37

ADRIAN HELL

I'm sitting in the car outside Mount Lebanon Cemetery, gazing out of the window at the gates. The storm has passed, and while the gray clouds remain, the rain has finally stopped.

I've driven here this morning knowing that the last thing I have to do before I can close this chapter of my life completely is see my girls again. I'm reluctant if I'm being honest. I feel an enormous pang of guilt when I think that I wasn't here when they were laid to rest, and I should've been. But Josh convinced me it's the right thing to do.

He's next to me, drinking a coffee we bought on the way here. He leans forward and slides a CD into the player. We haven't said much to each other this morning. Just feels like one of those days where words don't quite cut it. Like the morning before a funeral.

I glance at the dashboard as I listen to the song playing quietly in the background—Stone Sour's *Through Glass*. I smile to myself. In another life, Josh could easily have been a DJ. His choice of music for the times in my life when my own words aren't enough is impeccable.

I take a deep breath and sigh heavily. "You mind waiting here?"

He shakes his head. "Take as long as you need, brother."

"Thanks, Josh."

He waves his hand away dismissively.

"I mean it," I continue. "Thank you. For everything you've ever done for me. For everything you've ever put up with from me. You've stood by me when you had no earthly reason to."

We bump fists and smile at each other.

"We've just stolen a quarter of a billion dollars, Adrian. Like I'm going to leave you *now*?" He smiles. "Now get out of here before I start crying, you soppy bastard."

I laugh and get out. I turn the collar of my jacket up against the wind and cross the street. I walk into the cemetery, and after a few minutes, I find the plot where Janine and Maria lie buried. Frank gave me the details last night, and as I approach, I see him standing by the grave with flowers in his hand.

"Hey," I say, stopping next to him.

"You found it okay, then?" he asks.

"Yeah, thanks. Never thought to bring any flowers."

"I'm sure they won't mind. You don't strike me as a flowers type of guy anyway."

I shrug. "Very true."

I dig my hands in my pockets as the wind picks up, swirling the fallen leaves around.

"Thanks for everything, Adrian," he says after a few moments of silence. "Seriously. These last few days... I've finally gotten my closure. I hope you've been able to get yours. I can't imagine what you've been through."

"I'm glad I could help," I say with a weak smile. "Y'know... when Trent died, I felt nothing. And that scared me a little bit. I just figured I was so completely dead inside that I was never going to find any peace. But then Manhattan died, and Trent's empire collapsed, and all of a sudden, there was nothing left. It was then that I started to feel something. A sense of achievement, almost. Like, this whole time, I've been on one long journey to get somewhere, and I've finally arrived. I guess that's my closure—knowing I'm not on a journey anymore. I can stop and just... be."

Frank nods and we fall silent once again. A few minutes pass before either of us speaks again.

"I'm gonna leave you to it," he says.

I nod. "What will you do now that Trent's gone?"

"Might find myself a real job. Get out of this hole I've been in."

"Well, before you go for any interviews, check your bank account. I've left you a little something."

"Adrian, I—"

"No arguments. I've just come into a quarter of a billion dollars. I can spare a few zeroes for my brother-in-law."

He smiles and we shake hands.

"Keep in touch, Adrian. And promise me you'll move on. I knew my little sister better than most, and there's no way she'd want you walking around miserable for the rest of your days. It's okay to look to the future."

"I'll do my best," I say.

Without another word, he pats me on my shoulder and walks off, leaving me alone with my family.

I look down at the gravestones and a tear rolls down my

cheek. This is the first time I've wept for my wife and daughter since the day they died. I drop to my knees, touching my hand to my lips before pressing it on the grass in front of me.

The tears flow more freely. The overwhelming tide of emotion that's been locked away for almost a decade finally runs free, and I allow myself to grieve.

"I'm sorry," I say quietly after a few minutes. "The first time you see me and I'm bawling my eyes out like a little girl..."

I smile through the last of the tears and wipe my face, looking around the deserted cemetery.

"This is a nice place, considering..." I say. "Frank did a good job. I'm sorry I wasn't around to sort it myself. I... I have no excuse. The choices I made led to you both being taken from me, and I'm sorry. It's taken me a long time, but I've finally made things right. Nothing can replace you, and I will never, ever stop loving the both of you, but the quest for vengeance that's consumed my entire life for so long—that's over. I feel at peace. I could never have forgiven myself if I thought you wouldn't have forgiven me first. But meeting Frank showed me how much I'd actually forgotten about you. I was so focused on avenging your death that I'd forgotten some of the best things about your life..."

My words trail off as memories flood into my mind. Locking eyes with Janine for the first time all those years ago in Egypt. Holding my baby girl in my arms just after my wife gave birth to her. Moving into our house and arguing over what color to paint the bedroom. I smile as I realize she wouldn't ever have blamed me for what happened, so maybe it's time I don't, either.

After a few minutes, I stand and dust myself down. I take

a deep breath and let out the last of the doubts, fears, and burdens with it.

"I love you," I say.

I turn and walk out of the cemetery. As I pass through the gates and stand on the sidewalk, I feel like a different man. A changed man. The killer—and the demon inside of him—is gone. All I have to do now is figure out what kind of man I'm going to be.

I cross the street and get back in the car.

"You okay?" asks Josh.

"Yeah," I reply as I start the engine. "I really am."

"Good to hear. So, where are we going?"

I pull away from the curb, turn the music up, and wind my window down.

"Josh... I have no idea."

THE END

Dear Reader,

Thank you for purchasing my book. I hope you enjoyed reading it as much as I enjoyed writing it!

If you did, it would mean a lot to me if you could spare thirty seconds to leave an honest review on your preferred online store. For independent authors like me, one review makes a world of difference.

If you want to get in touch, please visit my website, where you can contact me directly, either via e-mail or social media.

Until next time...

James P. Sumner

CLAIM YOUR FREE GIFT!

By subscribing to James P. Sumner's mailing list, you can get your hands on a free and exclusive reading companion, not available anywhere else.

It contains an extended preview of Book 1 in each thriller series from the author, as well as character bios, and official reading orders that will enhance your overall experience.

If you wish to claim your free gift, just visit the website below:

linktr.ee/jamespsumner

You will receive infrequent, spam-free emails from the author, containing exclusive news about his books. You can unsubscribe at any time.

Made in the USA
Coppell, TX
23 July 2023

19528188R00194